"This is a book written with skill and passion and . . . it will resonate with women who have never set foot inside a Mormon church." —*Washington Times*

"The end of the book . . . was perfection itself. *Wives and Sisters* is clearly one of the year's best books; riveting at times, painful at times, realistic always, and completely unforgettable. It not only makes you cry, it makes you think, which is my personal hallmark of an excellent read. Natalie R. Collins has emerged as one of the finest new authors I've ever had the pleasure of reading."

—*Rendezvous*

"Don't be surprised if you devour this book in one reading. Natalie Collins has captured the essence of a page-turner by giving us three-dimensional characters, plenty of action, and a healthy dose of controversy."

—*Midwest Book Review*

"Collins . . . draws readers in with her strong writing and compelling plot. *Wives and Sisters* stirs up emotions in the reader that will resonate long after he or she has closed the book." —*January Magazine*

"Heart-wrenching and suspenseful . . . *Wives and Sisters* is a gripping tale." —*River Walk Journal*

"This is not a book that can be put down. It's so compelling, so dramatic, with strong suspense and mystery elements, that I had to find out what would happen. . . . It's written with a frightening intensity. I had to check the locks before I could go to sleep after finishing."

—Perri O'Shaughnessy, *New York Times* bestselling author

"*Wives and Sisters* is a journey through heartbreak, tragedy, and self-discovery with a courageous woman who dares to think for herself."

—Tina Wainscott, author of *I'll Be Watching You*

"The most astonishing thing about Natalie Collins's *Wives and Sisters* is not that it tells such a dramatic tale of betrayal, fundamentalism, denial, and abuse, but that it all rings so true. She perfectly captures the mixture of love, pain, and frustration that accompany surviving trauma in a society where victims are often silenced."

—Martha Beck, author of *Leaving the Saints: How I Lost the Mormons and Found My Faith*

"A raw, emotional story . . . It puts a plain, unvarnished face on the secret workings of the human soul and the price of blind faith."   —TheCelebrityCafe.com

"Well-written, fast-paced, Natalie Collins's *Wives and Sisters* is suspense-filled satisfaction with a bone-chilling, thought-provoking similarity to recent events. . . . [It] tugs at the heart and pulls at the mind. Author Natalie R. Collins, with the skill of the masters, splashes truth, and warnings against dangers of concealing truth, onto the pages of this must-read thriller."

—WritersAndReadersNetwork.com

"The author brings authentic color and gripping detail to her book which underscore the very real mentality of protecting the Church at all costs."   —*Tucson Citizen*

"*Wives and Sisters* is an amazing achievement . . . Natalie R. Collins is an author that we shall be seeing great things from in the future."   —ReadersRoom.com

Also by
NATALIE R. COLLINS

Wives and Sisters

Behind Closed Doors

TIES
THAT
BIND

NATALIE R. COLLINS

St. Martin's Paperbacks

This is a work of fiction. All of the characters, organizations, and events portrayed in this novel are either products of the author's imagination or are used fictitiously.

TIES THAT BIND

Copyright © 2012 by Natalie R. Collins.

All rights reserved.

For information address St. Martin's Press, 175 Fifth Avenue, New York, NY 10010.

ISBN: 978-0-312-94199-4

Printed in the United States of America

St. Martin's Paperbacks edition / August 2012

St. Martin's Paperbacks are published by St. Martin's Press, 175 Fifth Avenue, New York, NY 10010.

10 9 8 7 6 5 4 3 2 1

"Dearly beloved, avenge not yourselves, but rather give place unto wrath: for it is written, Vengeance is mine; I will repay, saith the Lord."
—Romans 12:19 (King James Version)

"Behold what the scripture says—man shall not smite, neither shall he judge; for judgment is mine, saith the Lord, and vengeance is mine also, and I will repay."
—Moroni 8:20

PROLOGUE

Vengeance

No, the boy mouthed, his lips forming a perfect O. He was pretty. Boys shouldn't look like this, with china doll complexions, sky blue eyes, and pouty pink lips. It wasn't right. Not the way God intended. *Please no.*

He tried to speak the words aloud, but no sound came out. Other than a slight hiss, the statically charged air around them was silent. Silence was golden, and this golden boy would never speak again. Fitting. It was only fair. The words that had always come from his mouth had been fatal in nature. Knife-sharp and anger-driven swords of hate. They revealed his true nature.

The boy was never winning, kind, or charming, even though his looks implied such. He didn't help old women across the street, or concern himself with merit badges or Pinewood Derbies. The only good thing about him—his saving grace—was the way he looked. But it did not save him, not in the end. Of course, those looks served only as a façade: a lure, enticing foolish young teenage girls into thinking him lovely and witty and stirring fireworks in their stomachs. That same façade drew young men around him, as well, many of them boys who wanted to know the secret—who wanted to possess the magic potion that made him irresistible.

It gave him power.

And he abused it.

Vengeance had seen many like the boy before. There would be many to follow. This mission—one served with every facet of heart and soul, as though summoned to this work by the Church's highest leaders—was an eternal calling. Vengeance knew this.

Of course, the mission was unknown to anyone. It came straight from the top. The "head honcho," as it were. Not many could claim that.

And no one would ever know how the mission started. Or how it would end.

Even Vengeance could not see what was coming.

But as the life seeped out of the boy there was satisfaction to be found in the waxy pallor of the offender's face. Soon his beauty would fade. He would be alluring no more, and only those with the closest of ties would want to touch him.

The boy's eyes rolled back in his head, and he bucked slightly, convulsively, before all signs of life left his earthly body.

Vengeance knelt down and put a cheek near the boy's mouth, but there was no sign of breath or life. Birth and death, two absolutes, usually set apart by many years, were very similar. Violent. Leaving the body gasping for air. The boy had fought. He was strong, but Vengeance and God's plan were both stronger.

The boy's bowels and bladder emptied, and the foul

smell suited him. It was real. It was indicative of what he *really* was.

Now came the end-times. A chill ran up Vengeance's spine at the thought of eulogies, prayers, and stories that would praise the boy's useless life. "He loved the Gospel," they would say. "He knew this church was the only true church, and he tried to live his life accordingly."

This would be a loathsome lie, especially in the case of vermin like this one. He had known nothing good, nothing true. He had only known what made him feel good and had spent every hour chasing it.

No one had seen the truth of his character. No one but Vengeance.

The boy would have grown up to be a vain and selfish man, evil to the core, raising his own brood of bad seeds, sent to earth to torment the innocent.

Now his parents would know the truth. And it would hurt, a searing pain, burning in their stomachs. The aftermath would be like a forest fire, leaving them barren and blackened, and with little hope of eventual survival.

Vengeance shook with fiery passion, staring at the hands that carried forth the work of the Lord. It was not an easy job. These hands had seen death, caused death, worked miracles for him. God's world was not always placid and calm. In the underbelly there was extreme violence and wrath, necessary for the washing away of sins.

Blood must be spilled. The blood would renew. For time and all eternity, the quest would continue. Few would understand.

My Father in Heaven promised it, when He came to

me nightly, as I sequestered myself in prayer. I'd been promised this since I was a child. Promised that He would talk to me, if only I would open my heart and listen.

God spoke to Vengeance, sometimes whispering, sometimes screaming in His infinite anger. So the work continued.

Vengeance looked down upon the still, ashen body of the latest assignment. He would cry no tears for this heathen. Not even during the funeral, or during the necessary trips to leave the mementos that would clue the parents in to their sins. They would cry enough for everyone, anyway, and not realize what a huge waste of emotion it would be. No one would notice Vengeance did not join in their grief.

Jeremiah Malone had deserved an uglier death than he'd received. But the Lord was merciful, as was His servant.

The suffering was over. At least for the boy. For his parents, it was only beginning.

ONE

Home sweet home. Mark Malone walked through the side door that led from his garage into the kitchen of his serene house and let the cool, manufactured air wash across his face and body. His blond hair was neat, his body trim and athletic in his long golf shorts—just the right length to cover his sacred garments—and blue jersey-print polo Ashworth shirt.

Eighteen holes of golf on a hot August Saturday took the stuffing right out of a man. Still, it was necessary for his business to make these sacrifices. And he did enjoy the game, and even an occasional side bet, although that needed to stay between him and the Lord—and his biggest client and golf partner, a Catholic man who drank heartily and cursed vilely during every game. Next to that man, surely God didn't begrudge Mark a few small vices.

He worked hard at his insurance business every day and listened to people's problems every night, trying to resolve issues that local bishops could not. It was part of his calling as stake president: an overseer to the web of wards that constituted the Kanesville East Stake. Each bishop took care of several hundred families, and in turn, Malone took care of those bishops, which included intervening in problems they could not solve.

The Church of Jesus Christ of Latter-day Saints had a stranglehold on this landlocked state, and almost everyone who lived here was touched by it in some way, even if they were not regular, faithful, tithe-paying members.

That meant a lot of people, a lot of clients, a lot of problems.

His church calling constituted a difficult job—one that came with no earthly pay or training, but heavenly blessings. It often drained him more than he had believed possible. Sometimes he thought it was too much for any one man to bear. Just last night he had been faced with a young father addicted to Internet pornography—and it was destroying his marriage. The young wife's tears had stirred something inside Mark, and he'd admonished the man severely, counseling him to seek repentance with the Lord and to disconnect his Internet. Mark felt he'd handled the situation well.

When he'd received his calling he'd been flattered and thankful and, of course, secretly, overwhelmed at the prospect. Would he be up to the spiritual challenge? Was he in tune with his Savior enough to offer the right advice? Was God really inspired when He made his choice?

Mark Malone was not a man without sin. Yet surely God must forgive that sin, or he would never have been called. Everyone knew that Mormon callings were "inspired" and of the spirit. Knowing this, he had embraced his position. Unfortunately, his family had been, well, less than supportive. Especially Jeremiah. *Teenagers.* Having a father who was in such a position of responsibility within the church community seemed to be a burden to him. Mark's beautiful boy, who had once looked up at him with open, shining eyes and begged for a game of catch, now watched him with hooded lids and flashes of derision. All he "caught" was the hatred in the boy's glares.

As Mark thought of the resentful teen, his eyes flashed to the dormer window that overlooked the backyard and anger began to seep into his chest. The lawn was long and unattractive, and he was having his counselors in the stake presidency and their wives over tonight for a barbecue. The only job he had required of Jeremiah was to mow the lawn and trim and edge it, not very difficult for a strapping young man.

But it hadn't been done. Not one piece of grass had been touched.

One little thing. All he'd asked.

"Jeremiah!" he yelled, his voice strained and rigid with control. The anger was hot and tight inside him, wanting out, forcing the blood to pound through his veins. "Jeremiah, the lawn is still not mowed. What the heck have you been doing all day?"

No answering voice. Not even that of his wife, who had an entire barbecue to prepare. He knew where she was, of course. In her bed, sleeping away her horrible, horrible life. After all, she *only* had a beautiful three-thousand-square-foot home and a husband who was at the top of his church's career ladder, at least as far as one could go at a local level. She was not forced to go outside the home and work, like so many other Mormon mothers; her only job was to care for his house and his son, Jeremiah.

She had done neither very well. Mark felt the stirrings of guilt in his gut, the same things he felt whenever he considered Lydia's mental state. Had he somehow brought this on? Did he fail in this most important aspect of his life—being the solid cement that would hold together his eternal family?

There was a housekeeper/cook who provided meals that could be heated in the oven shortly before he got home. That woman also kept the house clean and the laundry up. The guilt moved aside and resentment filled his broad chest, mixing with the anger. It was a powerful combination.

Lydia had been writing her master's thesis in education when they had met at Brigham Young University. She'd been young and beautiful, her fiery auburn hair matching her spirit.

Now there was no fire. There was nothing but flat eyes and a flabby body and a vacant look that said he could be the mailman for all she cared. His eternal companion should have stayed young and vibrant and attractive and, most of all, still interested in him. And Lydia had given him only one son instead of a large family. Slowly, the person he'd married had slipped away and become just a semblance of the woman she'd been, emotionless except for resentment and a grief he couldn't identify or assuage.

"Jeremiah?" he yelled again. He opened a cupboard, took a glass from it, and walked over to the side-by-side refrigerator. He pushed the glass into the opening in the door, and ice, then water quickly chunked into his glass. He took a long sip and, carrying the glass, headed out of the kitchen and toward his son's room.

When they'd built the house, Lydia had insisted on a rambler, all one level, with the bedrooms close together. Although Jeremiah had been only eight at the time, she was already worried about his teenage years—him sneaking out, possibly getting hurt and never coming home. The Lydia-that-used-to-be hit Mark in the chest like a punch. Irrational and sometimes breathless with fears of which he would never even have conceived. Back then, that eccentricity had been part of her charm. Now it was her downfall.

He passed his study, the door just slightly ajar.

Of course. The reason the lawn was not mown and trimmed was in this room—the computer where Jeremiah spent hours doing who knows what. Mark and Lydia had put on trackers, content monitors, and parental controls, and yet somehow he knew his son had managed to get past them all. There was no proof Jeremiah was doing anything wrong. And every time Mark tried to see what his son *was* doing, he'd found him innocently chatting on a messenger program with some of his friends. But there were too many hours spent there, too much time unaccounted for. And a few times Jeremiah had cringed a bit and looked nervous when his father came into the room unexpectedly, but he could never find anything. Nothing incriminating, anyway. And the police never came to his door. The teachers at school did not complain. The only person who seemed genuinely concerned about Jeremiah's behavior was his father. Lydia had long since given up the ability to think rationally, the fears taking over her mind until she was incapable of doing the one thing she had always worried the most about: protecting her son from the world.

Maybe the only reason Mark Malone was so worried was because of the sheer loathing his son oozed in his direction.

Or maybe it was the knowledge that all males had vices. But everyone said to build trust. He had no proof. How could he take away Jeremiah's computer privileges when he had nothing concrete, nothing but a feeling that the boy had done something wrong? And yet the thought of the young father from the night before, and his crying wife, made President Malone's stomach churn. His whole life had been based on a feeling, his testimony of the truthfulness of the Mormon Church. He'd built everything he did around that, so maybe it was time to listen to the still small voice telling him something was up with Jeremiah.

Mark decided to surprise his son, and maybe finally catch him at something. He swiftly pushed open the door and headed into the room—

Then stilled. The water glass slipped from his hand and fell to the floor, hitting the hard pine and shattering into tiny pieces, much like his life was doing right now.

On the floor, in front of him, lay his beloved son, a blue silk tie coiled tightly around his neck, his face a matching blue, his body lifeless.

TWO

"Are you gonna eat that?"

"No, D-Ray, I bought it so that I could stare at it for a few minutes, and then hand it over to you," said Detective Sam Montgomery, irritation tingeing her voice.

"Just asking," Detective Ray Jones said, a mischievous grin on his dark-skinned, handsome face.

"Yeah, just asking, like you always do, just to annoy me." Sam grimaced, put the hamburger to her mouth, took a bite, and chewed. As always, it didn't taste as good as it looked. In fact, it tasted like dust, even topped with a generous amount of cheese and ketchup. After two more small bites, Sam gave up and put the burger on D-Ray's plate. She brushed a piece of her shoulder-length, carefully groomed blond hair back behind her shoulder. "You know, if you would just be patient, you would get the hamburger regardless."

"Yeah, but it's so much fun to do it this way," he said, pushing the bowl of soup he had ordered in her direction. "I'm all about the ritual, you know?"

"How about good old-fashioned manners? You eat your food, and I eat mine."

But it *was* their ritual. It made life bearable. Two bites of hamburger meant the past—and one memory in particular—didn't get to destroy Sam. Even if she literally choked them down.

Samantha "Sam" Rose Montgomery was the first woman detective in the history of Kanesville, Utah, a bedroom community nestled in the green foothills of northern Utah's Wasatch mountain range and located just twenty miles outside Salt Lake City. Like most of Utah, the town was surreptitiously controlled by the Church of Jesus Christ of Latter-day Saints.

Salt Lake City, despite its reputation as the headquarters of Mormonism, was actually one of the most liberal cities in the state. Of course, since "liberal" and "Mormon" were generally oxymorons, that wasn't saying much.

Being the first woman detective in Kanesville's history was quite a feat for 2011, Sam always thought. A feat for her and a sad narrative on the nature of sexism. Kanesville was a throwback to twenty years prior, and thus Detective Ray "D-Ray" Jones, an old school and neighborhood friend and onetime beau of her sister Amy, was Sam's only ally on the force. The rest, all men, treated her like they did every other woman in their life: superficially and with sexual prejudice.

Six months into this job Sam was already considering reapplying for a job in Salt Lake City, where she had gone to work right out of the police academy. She had left Kanesville all those years ago desperate to escape her suffocating hometown and the dark memories that clung there, like mist to the hills—and she had never looked back. Until now. She probably already would have gone back to Salt Lake, if it weren't for the fact that *he* still worked there—her ex–almost flame, best forgotten.

In Kanesville, "Equal Opportunity" meant that everybody had a chance to get to the urinal first. Since Sam didn't have the right equipment to use a urinal, she would never win that fight. Add to it all the troubling "suicides" of two teen girls that had recently shaken the entire small town in its foundation and it made for a tense stew of politics, religion, and sexism—where men played the roles of breadwinners and LDS priesthood holders and women served as their "helpmates."

"Look at it this way," D-Ray said, forcing Sam back into the moment. "I'm keeping you from having to discover that you just plain don't like food." A wide grin split his face.

"Yeah, but for once, I'd like the opportunity to discover that on my own."

D-Ray opened his mouth to retort but stopped suddenly when the radio Sam had hooked onto her belt squawked to life, making her jump. She removed it and put it to her ear, listening as the dispatcher sent uniforms to a possible suicide, victim *echo.* Sam felt the hair rise on her arms. Another one.

D-Ray dropped the soupspoon, letting it clatter dully on the wood table, pulled some bills out of his wallet, and dropped them on the table. Sam pulled money out of her pocket and did the same. They slid out of the table benches and headed swiftly to the door, listening to the dispatcher on the radio.

With Sam driving through the one-lane streets, they would reach the home of President Mark Malone in about three minutes, D-Ray holding tight to the seat as she rounded each corner with skill and—of course—excessive speed. The title of "President" referred to Malone's office as a stake president, guardian of a group of wards in his area. It didn't take much explanation around this area. If someone was introduced as "Bishop" or "President" you knew exactly what was meant. And these people were treated accordingly.

No matter what the Utah state officials might pretend, the LDS Church ran the state and everyone knew it. That made this call more important than most, at least to the other cops on the force.

Sam would treat it no differently than any other call. Everyone deserved the same respect, no matter their standing in the Church. Or what their clothes looked like. Or how many secrets were buried in their family's past.

THREE

Night or day, flashing police lights call out to people: a beacon that something has gone horribly awry. Four patrol cars sat in front of the Malone residence, two officers standing guard as neighbors began to gather outside their homes and in front of the house, some of them brave enough to wander up and ask what had happened to the president's family. These people called each other brother and sister. One big family. Undoubtedly, they thought they had the right to ask.

The officers were not inclined to share.

It was a hot August Saturday afternoon, and a light, sultry breeze served only to make the atmosphere even more uncomfortable and stultifying. The fires of Hell. It would make the death scene ahead that much harder to deal with. "Echo" meant "dead." Sam thought of President Malone's wife, who rarely left the house and had that vacant but terrified look in the edges of her eyes that screamed madness. Sam knew madness. It had been her uneasy acquaintance for years, in the form of her mother.

Did Lydia Malone finally give in to the demons and kill herself?

Sam and D-Ray whipped through the gathering crowd and into the home.

The incessant screaming from the back of the large, stately rambling house served as a beacon, calling them back to the scene of the tragedy and alerting Sam to Lydia's still-living presence.

Sam rounded the corner and headed down the hallway, following the keening of grief into a room where she saw the body of a teenage boy on the floor, paramedics doing CPR, as his father stood behind them, waving a small glass vial. Next to him stood the mother, screaming and wringing her hands, tears of anguish coating her face. She wore a frumpy housecoat, and mascara trailed down her cheeks.

A pang filled Sam's heart. She knew this look. Grief, shock, and something even more terrifying—a weird acceptance.

Next to the body was a dark blue satin tie, coiled in an S pattern. A snake, waiting to strike, and more than a little out of place. Especially considering the boy wore gym shorts and a DC T-shirt. Nothing else seemed terribly suspicious—unless you considered a dead teenage boy suspicious.

Sam Montgomery did.

The tie was definitely a red flag. Unfortunately, she had a feeling that it had been removed from the boy's throat, probably by her least favorite paramedic, Lind Harris, the inept man working on the body right now. He was also a deputy sheriff, and he should have known better. He *did* know better, but he considered himself above it all. A PP, as D-Ray liked to call them.

Priesthood Prick. Harsh, but true. Some Mormon males wielded their patriarchy like a lethal sword. And some held on to it for dear life, the only hope keeping them afloat in a crazy world.

"Please, you have to let me give him a blessing, please," President Malone pleaded, looking back and forth at anyone who would listen. He was dressed in a polo shirt and sharply pressed khaki shorts, his blond hair rumpled and messy, as though he had run his hands through it numerous times. His face was a contorted mask.

It seemed as though every paramedic/deputy in Smithland County had come to this scene, along with the four on-duty Kanesville officers, the fire chief and four of his EMTs, and two county crime scene techs. It made the room seem small, claustrophic, everybody jockeying for a space at the horror show in front of them.

Other than Lind Harris, and another deputy who knelt by the body, the emergency responders seemed frozen.

There was no talking or bustling around, like one often saw at a scene. The silence was almost reverent, except for the keening of Lydia Malone. Two of the EMTs tried to attend to her, but she brushed them off, turning away, refusing to move from the room.

Mark Malone leaned down and tried to push the paramedic closest to him aside, waving his bottle and pleading for them to let him use prayer and his conse-crated oil to bring life back into a body that would never, ever walk, talk, or play football again—let alone breathe.

Sam had seen more than one dead body, and Pres-ident Malone's son was definitely a goner. She also knew the "consecrated oil" was nothing more than olive oil that had been blessed by Mormon priesthood leaders. But like all desperate tricks, whether bathing in a "fountain of youth" or consuming an unproven and often deadly cure for cancer, the promise rested not in the bottle, liquid, or food itself but in the belief that God answered prayers and that sometimes nothing more than a miracle would work.

Jeremiah had probably been dead at least an hour, Sam guessed, from the color, the smell, and the position of the body. But the paramedics would try to resuscitate, both for the sake of the family and because they could charge for it. It was a cold, hard fact of life in the business.

"Let him bless the boy," she said quietly to the paramedics.

"But . . ."

She just shook her head, and, to her surprise, Lind nodded.

He didn't fight her, like he would have in just about any other case. It was probably out of deference to President Malone's position as the local stake president of the Mormon Church. She knew it had nothing at all to do with her.

The two paramedic/deputies rose to their feet, stepped back and the boy's father moved in. He knelt down, then looked around frantically. "I need . . . I need someone; I need someone with the priesthood. . . ."

Three of the Kanesville uniformed officers stepped forward, they all knelt and put their hands on the boy's head, and tears came to Sam's eyes as she listened to the father's frantic words, flung toward a celestial being that had been ignoring her for years.

"Father in Heaven, we come before You today to ask You to heal Jeremiah, and restore him to health. He's not dead. He can't be. You need to . . ." He faltered as the words eluded him. This was probably a priesthood blessing unlike any other President Malone had ever given. Not only was the rote phrasing off, but there was no doubt that "You need to" had never come out of his mouth before while speaking to God. Proper Mormon prayer must be phrased as a request, Sam thought, memories of her childhood swirling through her mind. God required a certain decorum, and telling Him how to do things did not fit the requirements.

"Father, I . . . Father." He began to sob uncontrollably, and one of the patrolmen took the small vial of consecrated oil out of President Malone's shaking hands and opened it, dabbing it on the boy's forehead and muttering a prayer laying all the power in God's hands.

How convenient, Sam thought. But no one else could do anything, so they might as well give the power—and maybe some of the blame—to God.

Jeremiah's mother stood in the background, tears streaming down her face. Her screams had been quieted by the prayers, but her anguish had not abated—and perhaps never would. A suicide could turn a sound mind sour. To a sick mind, it was like the most caustic acid.

From personal experience, Sam knew that Lydia Malone was not a mentally well person. What would happen to her now that her only son was dead? A disgraced death, no less.

Suicide. But something was off. Desperation, sadness, and despair always emanated from the body of a suicide. At least, that's what Sam had sensed whenever she'd come upon a suicide scene. But in a murder victim, the emotion was anger, red hot and toxic. And Jeremiah Malone was an angry corpse. Angry and bitter.

Sam shivered, and D-Ray started as her elbow bumped into his arm. He turned to look at her, but she pretended not to notice. Lind Harris gave her a look of complete disgust, now that there was nothing that could be done.

She would deal with him later.

Sam zeroed in on the face of Lydia Malone. Could she be involved? Another pang shot through Sam, and she tried to steel herself to be the cold, hard detective she needed to be.

The third teenage death in as many months. All from strangulation or hanging. Sam's eyes moved to the coiled blue silk tie, pushed aside as the paramedics first did CPR and then blessed the boy. Was it the cause of his death? That sure wouldn't add up to suicide. Unlike the room of the first teenage girl, this one had tall ceilings and no evidence of a chair or . . . She scanned the rest of the room. A large, powerful computer sat in the corner, resting on a beautiful dark wood desk. A screensaver—surfers in a powerful ocean swell—was all she could see. No evidence of premeditated death or depression.

Something was terribly wrong in Kanesville. Three months. Three dead teenagers.

Sam looked up to see a somber, gray-haired, portly man headed in her direction. Something *was* terribly wrong, and based on the direction Police Chief Mike Roberson was headed, it was going to be her job to try to figure out what.

The EMTs finally succeeded in convincing Lydia Malone to leave the room, but her sobs were loud as they moved her away.

"Well, Montgomery, this one's yours. It's priority, obviously." Roberson's face was solemn and distraught, and he looked around the room at the bustling chaos as though trying to figure out how so many people got into one room. Slowly, the unnecessary medical personnel filtered out. A bald, portly man in a white polo shirt and black khaki pants put his arm around President Malone and talked quietly to him.

While Sam did not know the man, she recognized the look and feel of the situation. Even the stake president had a spiritual leader, and this man was probably his ward's bishop; he probably sent his most difficult cases Malone's way. And today he had to comfort the man he served under.

Malone would not leave as they bagged the body. He stood and watched, hand to his mouth, tears streaming from his eyes. The other man stood stoically by his side, arm curved awkwardly—protectively—around his shoulders. They didn't speak as the crime scene techs finished scouring the body for clues, finding nothing out of place.

When they were done, Sam donned gloves, then stepped forward. She fought the urge to wince as she knelt down by the dead boy. She looked closely at the ligature marks, the chief standing right behind her, watching her every move.

"It's time to let them work, Mark," the stocky bishop said, and Malone seemed to fall into himself, no longer strong and powerful. He allowed himself to be led from the room, and Sam breathed a sigh of relief.

She continued examining the body, looking for any type of evidence, injuries, or foreign objects that would explain why the boy had died this way. There were marks on his throat, dark and vivid. Rigor had not set in yet, so he was still pliable but rapidly decomposing.

Sam picked up his left hand, examined it closely, and let it drop, moving to the right one. Neither showed signs of defensive marks, which didn't mean much. No clues screamed at her demanding justice. It would be easy to write this off as suicide, even though her every instinct told her it was something else. She'd never had a homicide of her own before. A few suicides, some accidental deaths—and the homeless man who froze on a cold winter night. Her rookie status hit her like a punch in the gut.

The smell seemed overpowering now that the room had emptied. Bile, blood, body fluids, and fecal matter left a stain that would never come out.

She finished, stood up, and nodded to the CSI tech who came over to the body. Sam's stomach roiled from the smell and the process, but she fought against showing any outer sign of turmoil. She had to be tough.

Sam and Chief Roberson watched solemnly as they encased the handsome young man in a black body bag. Jeremiah Malone took one of his last rides on a gurney, out of his childhood home and into the darkness of a morgue.

Once the body was removed, the crime scene techs returned and began casing the grid, looking for evidence. One was a petite girl with a bright smile and an encyclopedia of crime facts in her brain. Cori was her name, Sam thought. She wasn't smiling today.

The other tech was a tall, awkward brown-haired man named Austin, who was rumored to have Asperger's, so poor were his social skills. Both techs wore gloves, and

Cori picked up the tie, transferring it carefully to a sealed plastic bag.

Chief Roberson said, "About done here," and motioned Sam to follow him.

In the corridor of the beautiful Malone home, he told her what he expected of her.

"Solve this case, Montgomery, and solve it fast. If this boy committed suicide, you better come to that conclusion in one hell of a hurry. If you suspect it's something else, I don't want to hear a peep about it without facts. Either way, this one goes away quick. President Malone's an important man in this town."

"Are you trying to say the other two weren't important?" Sam shot back, immediately regretting her words.

"Do you really want to go there?"

"No, sir. I apologize."

The fact that the boy's death mattered so much more than the two teenage girls' rankled—though she realized it wasn't about Jeremiah, quarterback of the football team. This was about his father and what he represented.

"Watch your mouth, Montgomery, and get the job done."

Roberson turned and walked away, and Sam sighed as she headed for the EMTs who were tending to Lydia Malone.

Questioning an already unbalanced woman—whose son had just died a violent, premature death—would make this a very long, unpleasant Saturday.

FOUR

Modern drugs combined with religion were a godsend to many. To police officers, they were often a deterrent.

Sam was unable to interview either Lydia Malone—who was now off in la-la land thanks to a sedative—or Mark Malone, who was in "seclusion." She walked slowly through the house looking for anything out of the ordinary. And making sure that the techs employed by Smithland County didn't miss something she might need.

There was a picture of Joseph Smith in the main entryway, a picture of Jesus in the Mormon sitting room, and a copy of "The Family: A Proclamation to the World" along the main hallway, next to pictures of Jeremiah in various stages of youth. The "proclamation" was the same one hanging on the wall in Sam's childhood home and nearly every other Mormon home throughout the United States. It was the Church's credo about what made up a family: a man, a woman, and children. There were no two moms or two dads for

Mormons. Rules were rules, and black and white was black and white.

Sam wandered farther down the hallway and found Jeremiah's room, taking a quick look around. A jumbled mess of dirty clothes, CD cases, and empty pop cans were scattered through the room. The walls were decorated with skating posters, along with banners for the Utah Jazz and San Diego Chargers. "Go hard or go home," was written on a poster of an NFL athlete. A normal, messy, stinky, teenage-boy room; nothing jumped out. Without the family's permission, she couldn't conduct a complete search of his bedroom, and since the family was unavailable to her, she had no choice but to leave it alone for now.

She entered the den one last time, grimacing as the awful smell wafted up to her, then exited through the front door. The first thing she saw was Lind Harris. She took off after him almost before she'd realized what she was doing.

"You moved that tie. You took it off his neck," Sam spit out, not trying to hold back, hoping all the derision and disgust she felt for Lind Harris was apparent to him and anyone else within earshot. She was inches away from his face, having caught up with him just as he got into his police-issue Durango, complete with the Smithland County sheriff's insignia on the side.

"Get out of my face, Montgomery," Harris snarled back, his lip pulled up on one side. His face was ravaged with the marks of teenage acne, lips thin, chin almost nonexistent. He had a frosting of light blond hair that seemed to recede farther every time Sam saw him. She also saw, as she always did, that wild look of fear in his eyes. Like he had to carry a gun, just to be safe: one never knew when life would jump out and get you. Sam understood this feeling, but it did not bond her in the least to Lind Harris. "Having a little raging PMS today, huh? A little out of sorts?"

"Back off, Harris," D-Ray warned from behind her.

"Back off? Who is in whose face here, D-Ray, or did you miss that? She wants to act like a bitch, she better expect to get treated like one."

Sam shook off the hand she felt on her shoulder, never breaking contact with Lind Harris's weasel eyes. Finally, he looked away, shrugging and pulling his door in just a bit farther, trying to urge her to leave. She wasn't budging.

"You took the necktie off. You destroyed evidence in a scene that could be a murder. You are one step away from being busted down to watching prisoners take a dump in the jail, you know—"

"Shut the fuck up!" Harris yelled at her, sudden and violent, his eyes an angry blur, darting from her to the men she knew stood behind her, watching the two of them with extreme interest.

Lind's weak, almost-absent chin quivered as he fought for words to put Sam firmly in her place. At least the place where he thought she should be—not telling him how to do his job. But her anger threw him off. He didn't seem to know what to say.

"What's going on here?" came the voice of her chief, boisterous and loud, almost jovial—a deliberate attempt to break things up, and an unspoken message to take it private or shut it up. Closing ranks.

Sam turned and stomped away. Behind her she heard the door of Lind's Durango slam and the engine start.

"What's your problem with him, Sam?" D-Ray asked,

following her to their department-issued vehicle. "You want all the cops in Smithland County to hate you? Or just the sheriff's department?"

They got into their respective sides of the car—Sam driving, D-Ray in the passenger seat—and she stuck the key in the ignition, then turned to him before she started the car up. "Do you hate me?" she asked.

"Sometimes I don't like you very much."

"But do you hate me?"

"Of course not," he said, his voice gentle and melodic. "But what's your point?"

"You're a good cop and a good man. I don't want you to hate me. Him? He's isn't either one. I don't give a damn what he thinks."

Sam started up the car and left the Malone house—and chaotic scene—behind. They'd been there for more than three hours. CSI was still doing the last of the investigation and cleanup.

"Sam?" D-Ray said, his voice and tone a question. Fury still rocked through her veins, and she wished she could get out of this car right now and pound the pavement, running until her heart felt like it might burst and there was no room for any feeling except sheer exhaustion.

"He took the necktie off," she said.

"He probably did."

"So why am I only one who is pissed off about it?"

"He was doing CPR, Sam."

"The kid was dead, D-Ray. He knew it; you know it; everybody knows it. There was no reason to take the necktie off."

"He did it for the parents. Maybe to give them just a moment's more hope."

"Well, he just made our job hope*less*."

"No, he didn't. Maybe he messed it up a little, but he didn't make it hopeless. If the tie was around the kid's neck, it could have been one of three things: suicide, accident, or murder. Found by his side, the marks on his neck, it means one of three things. Can you tell me what they are?"

"Shut up, D-Ray."

She'd been dealing with assholes like Lind Harris from the day she started police academy at Weber State University. In fact, she had dealt with that particular asshole—who could never handle that she shot better, ran faster, and thought quicker then he ever could or would—since high school. Her marks earned her a place on the SLCPD, while he ended up as a Smithland County sheriff's deputy.

Then she came to Kanesville, an even more lowly rank. What the hell was she thinking?

She hated Lind Harris. She hated small-town cops. Too bad she was one now.

FIVE

It was 6:00 p.m. before they finally called it a day. Ravenously hungry, D-Ray talked Sam into stopping at the popular local café, Sill's, for dinner.

"So, what the hell is your problem with Lind, anyway?" D-Ray asked, tapping his fork on the table, drumming out a rhythmic beat Sam felt like she should recognize but didn't. They sat in a booth near the front, always ready to head out quickly if a call should come in. Bone-weary, Sam prayed for the radio and her phone to stay silent. She still needed to check on her parents, pretend to eat, pretend sleep wasn't restless and sparse.

"*So?*" D-Ray said again, his tone emphasizing the question.

"Why do you care?"

"Why are you a bitch?"

"Grow up, D-Ray. Welcome to adulthood. I don't have to answer to you, and when I'm being assertive it doesn't mean I'm being a bitch. When you're throwing your balls and your testosterone around, do I accuse you of being a jackass?"

"First of all, I do not throw my balls around. They are attached to my body, and I prefer them that way. Secondly, I've never thrown testosterone at anyone. And thirdly, of course you accuse me of being a jackass. On a regular basis."

"Well, only when you *are* being one."

"The world according to Sam Montgomery . . ."

"D-Ray, Lind Harris is a first-rate creep, and has been since junior high. He spent half of his time trying to cop a feel from girls who couldn't stand him, and the other half jacking off to yearbook pictures of girls who couldn't stand him."

"You talk like a guy."

"Comes from working with them all day, every day. Harris is the epitome of the nerdy creeper who becomes a cop purely as a power trip. You know they are out there. You see them every day."

"Yeah, Harris is a creep, but he's not a bad cop, from what I can see. And you're holding junior-high shit against him. I mean, come on, get real, Sam. Aren't we a little too old for that bitchy girl stuff?"

"If I grabbed your balls during a game of tag football, during a Mutual activity, wouldn't you be pissed?"

"At fourteen? Hell no. The reaction would have been exactly the opposite. And besides, you don't have balls."

Sam sighed deeply. "I give up. I don't like him. Never have, never will."

"You're such a girl."

"Make up your mind."

"Oh, I always knew you were a girl. I've known you

for a really long time. You just think you have something to prove."

The waitress. a petite, lithe redhead, young and nubile—barely out of high school—delivered their food. She looked familiar, Sam thought. She probably came from a family that Sam knew from some arena of Kanesville's small-town life.

She stared at the girl as she walked away, trying to place her, knowing the reality was she did not want to look at her food or take the requisite bite she always forced upon herself. The girl wasn't that familiar.

The greasy, starchy aroma assaulted Sam's nostrils and made her stomach roil.

Sam stared down at the mountainous hamburger D-Ray would be eating as soon as he figured enough time had passed for him to reach over and grab the food she'd ordered. Why was she here? She wasn't hungry. D-Ray was, of course. D-Ray was always hungry. In many ways.

Sam remembered back when her sister and D-Ray were an item, only behind closed doors of course, since Amy and Sam's father didn't approve of D-Ray's mixed background and his lack of a male role model.

She was little then, eight years younger than D-Ray and Amy and seven years younger than Callie. A tagalong. That's all she really remembered. D-Ray and Amy trying to ditch her and Callie covering for them.

Tall and solid, and dark-skinned year-round, D-Ray was a testament to his father's Tongan heritage. D-Rey's mother was a small, slight, blond woman with a bitter tongue and a smile like battery acid. Sam assumed that the mostly easygoing, laconic D-Ray took after his father, whom she had never met. D-Ray liked to say that his father, who had been brought over to Utah from the Tongan islands by the Mormons more than forty years before, had returned to his roots and was drinking mai tais and exchanging leis with local wahines somewhere in the Hawaiian Islands. That he was from Tonga made no difference to D-Ray. He didn't know much about his heritage, but everyone knew about Hawaii. He'd grabbed ahold of that like a drowning man grabs a life preserver. The truth was, he had no idea where his father was. D-Ray's teeth had been straightened by an orthodontist, his mother grumbling about how no son of hers was going to look like a common "native."

Now he smiled a lot. But there was bitterness and anger hidden within.

"Remember when you and Amy had a thing?"

"What?"

"You know, weren't you a couple?"

"We were kids."

"Yeah, but you liked each other."

"Like I said, we were kids."

D-Ray stopped talking, tightened his lips, and pulled Sam's plate toward him. He picked up the hamburger and took a huge bite. She knew this body language. He didn't intend to say more, but this went deeper. Maybe he still felt something for her sister, who'd disappeared years ago—literally. Sam hadn't heard from her in years. Her oldest sister, Susanna, wouldn't discuss Amy, and their father acted like there had never been two girls named Callie and Amelia.

Sometimes Sam wondered if she was imagining things. Or lived in an alternate universe.

"Just for once, I'd like someone to tell me the truth," she muttered.

"You can't handle the truth," D-Ray shot back—between bites—in his very worst Jack Nicholson impression.

Probably not.

Sam hated being one of those women who had "something to prove." But it didn't change the fact that she was, indeed, one of those women. It also didn't help that her blond hair was immaculate, complete with platinum and dark brown highlights touched up every six weeks, or that she never left the house without makeup, even to work out or just get the mail. Others thought she was vain and shallow. She knew she was using her appearance like ceremonial war paint—fighting off the demons.

Today's tragedy did not help her status.

D-Ray ate and Sam watched.

"Well, hello, Sammy," trilled a familiar voice.

Sam looked up, and her stomach lurched just a little. "Hello, Sister Miller," she answered dutifully as the blue-haired maven of her old ward—and neighborhood—tottered up to the table. The familiar pangs of humiliation roiled through Sam's already rebelling stomach. This woman knew all Sam's family's secrets. No skeleton in any Montgomery closet was hidden from Eliza Miller, whose husband had been ward bishop the year Sam's family imploded.

"Well, I swear you are just skin and bones! You need to put some meat on. Are you ill? How is that nice exciting job going? I hear you had a horrible case today, just horrible. Are you okay?" Sister Miller asked without pausing for breath, patting Sam's hand with her dry, wrinkled one.

Thankfully, Sam didn't have time to answer.

"Mom?" It was one of the Miller children—Carly or Karen or Christy; Sam could never keep them straight, especially now they were grown. "We really need to get you home so you can watch your show before bedtime."

"Bedtime," Sister Miller said with a sigh. "The indignity. I used to tell *her* when it was bedtime." She jabbed a bony finger at her daughter, who frowned, even while bouncing a baby on her hip. "Did you say hi to Sammy, Karen? You remember Sammy Montgomery. They lived just down the street from us. In fact, her parents still live in the same house."

"I remember," Karen said. She didn't say hello. She just glared for a moment, her face round and pudgy, her eyes tired, and wrinkles lining her face. She wore ill-fitting capris and a modest floral top, neither of which hid the "baby weight" she was undoubtedly still trying to get rid of. Her hair was slightly unkempt, not helped by the baby who kept yanking at it.

Karen gave Sam another angry look, then turned on her heel and headed to the door, her mother left sighing and shuffling after her.

I'm still the pariah, even after all these years.

Sam supposed she couldn't blame Karen for her disdain. In the back of Sam's mind she had a vague memory of holding the vain childhood-Karen's beloved curly brown locks over the toilet in the girls' bathroom at the wardhouse and threatening to flush—all sparked by a comment about Sam's unruly, uncombed short hair and faded hand-me-down dress.

But back then those sorts of comments had been commonplace. When Sam was six, her big sister Callie hung herself. In the wake of the tragedy that changed all of their lives forever, the mother who would have combed Sam's hair and made sure she fit in with the other girls became a shell, leaving Sam and her sisters to fend for themselves. The result was general chaos—and lots of teasing.

Sam watched Karen's broad backside as she walked out the door, and it made her smile. Then frown, as she realized how petty she was being. Karen hadn't aged well, but in her youth she had always been immaculate and pristine, as was befitting a bishop's daughter. Of course, two of the Miller girls had gotten pregnant in high school and ended up in adulthood a lot earlier than planned. Sam didn't remember if Karen was one of the two Miller girls who "married young," but it gave her a certain satisfaction in knowing that she looked better now—the tables had turned.

As a child, she'd spent years defending her family with her fists and her words. Grown-ups in the ward tended to "cut her slack," but the kids became her bitter enemies. Sam preferred the hatred. She could barely tolerate the pity that oozed from the pores of their parents.

People like Sister Miller, to whom she now waved a grateful good-bye.

She turned back to find D-Ray finishing the soup—since he had quickly downed the hamburger.

"I am not eating with you anymore," she said crossly.

"You wouldn't eat it anyway," he said, flashing his enigmatic grin, teeth white and straight.

SIX

"Hi, Momma," Sam said as she walked into the kitchen of her childhood home. Her mother only stared vacantly out the window next to the table, watching something fascinating—something so enthralling that she couldn't even be bothered to notice her youngest daughter standing next to her.

When would the hope die? The hope that she would respond, in some way, any way. Probably never, as long as that ragamuffin little girl still existed inside her.

"So, did you have a good day?" Sam asked. "Mine wasn't great. Had to go on a death call. Stake President Malone's son. Really sad case. He was only seventeen."

Her mother didn't move her eyes from the invisible panorama. Her lips were slightly parted, her eyes mostly unfocused.

"Please don't talk about things like that around your mother, Samantha," her father said, coming into the kitchen dressed in his "yardies," clothes he used to work outside, tending to his vegetable garden and fruit trees. He leaned down and kissed her mother on the cheek. There was no response. Not even a flinch.

"So, did you drop by for dinner? I'm afraid we haven't made anything. We're not very hungry tonight."

"No, Dad, just checking in. How's it going? How's Mom doing?"

Sam didn't want to tell him that watching Jeremiah Malone's mother descend into a dark madness propelled by grief—a pathway the woman had been traveling long before today—had brought to mind her own mother and her less-than-sound mental condition.

"Well, we went to see Dr. Call yesterday, didn't we, Ruthie? And he says her blood pressure is okay and her heart sounds good. He encouraged me to get her walking more, but you know what that's like. She doesn't much care for exercise, do you, Ruthie?"

Sam's father had used this pattern of speech for a long time, asking her mother questions as though any moment she was going to look him squarely in the eye and answer, "Yes, Gordon, I really don't like exercise."

But Ruthie Montgomery never did reply.

More than one doctor had suggested hospitalization and commitment. Sam's father refused. Instead, he pretended as though her mother had an extended case of laryngitis, as though she didn't require around-the-clock care and wear an adult diaper.

Sam's father looked gaunt and troubled. He had for as long as Sam could remember, but age and fatigue were setting in, his shoulders more rounded, his walk slower, his feet closer to the floor. As though any moment now he would just begin to shuffle his way out of this world. Would that change if her mother finally woke up and answered?

That was the real reason Sam was here tonight, late, after an exhausting day. Actually, "exhausting" did not do it justice. The weariness filled her bones, and she pulled out a kitchen chair and sat heavily.

"She doesn't hear us, Dad. She didn't hear your question, and she didn't hear my story about my day. I might as well have told her that I ate my cereal with Mountain Dew this morning."

"You don't know that, Sam. No one has ever proven she doesn't hear you."

She sighed and decided to ignore the obvious, just like he had been doing for years. "Do you want me to make you some dinner?"

"Oh no, we just ate. Like I said, we're not very hungry tonight."

Sam knew that "just ate" probably referred to some scrambled eggs that morning. Her father's thin frame attested to the fact that he was no longer capable of caring for her mother, let alone himself—although he had taken on thinking and speaking for her long ago. But he wouldn't give in. He wouldn't let go, perhaps for the same reasons she no longer existed. She was his link to the past. All they had left were the memories—and each other.

He wouldn't even leave her, except for brief periods once a week, when the sisters from the ward would come "visit" with Ruthie while Sam's father went to the Golden Age Senior Center. There he took classes on fly tying, computers, or dancing—all things he would never do or use.

"Would you like some chamomile tea, Sam?" He puttered around the kitchen, his old short-sleeved work shirt too big for his constantly shrinking frame. Sam watched as he poured water into two mugs, then heated them in the microwave. His hands were calm and steady and showed no signs of the palsy affecting many others of his generation. His full head of silver hair also made him look younger than he was, but his face was a dead giveaway. Lines and wrinkles and heaviness to the jowls spoke of a long and rough life. The only place he didn't have excess wrinkles was around his lips, because he rarely smiled. And why would he?

Sam tried to remember a time when her father had been happy, smiling and laughing, and was surprised to discover she had no such memory. She thought of him as gentle but definitely dour.

When the microwave beeped, he pulled the mugs out by the handles and set them on the counter. He opened a cupboard and peered inside but didn't appear to find what he was looking for. "I've been making chamomile tea for your mother every night. It calms her. Helps her get a good night's sleep, doesn't it, Ruthie? And there's no caffeine in it, you know. It's herb tea. Not against the Word of Wisdom. Now I know I just bought some when I went to the store two days ago. What happened to it?"

The LDS Church had a strict code against "hot drinks," including tea and coffee. Over the years, that had been interpreted to mean drinks containing caffeine. It certainly never covered hot chocolate, which was served at any Mormon function in the winter. Sam had long ago learned the interpretation depended on the person interpreting. For her father, that was always the prophets, and her father would never do anything that went against the teachings of the Mormon prophets. Since they had decided the evil in hot drinks was caffeine, or so he believed, he had been steadfast in his rule against it. Herbal tea was something totally different.

Sam rose and went to the cupboards, rummaging through them until she found the tea. "Let me do it, Dad. You sit with Mom. Tell me about your day."

Her father hesitated for a moment, as though to fight against her absconding with his self-appointed role, and then he gave in and sat down. Almost as heavily as Sam had just moments before. Probably with even more weight, despite his thin frame. He'd been carrying the burden of her catatonic mother for twenty years now.

"Well, let's see. I worked some on my pear trees. And the peaches are getting ready to come on. Those are going to make some mighty tasty pies."

Or would, if anyone here made pie. Or could even manage to peel a peach. Her father was no cook, so Sam knew the peaches would fall to the ground and rot or Dad would give them away to the neighbors. Same as last year.

Sam put one tea bag in each mug and carried them over to the table to steep. She set them both in front of her father, since her mother would only drink the tea with Sam's father's help—and even then most of it would run down Ruthie's chin and onto her clothing.

"No tea?"

"No thanks," Sam said.

He leaned over and sniffed the tea, closing his eyes briefly, letting the aroma and steam float up over his face, and then opening them again. "Did you hear about Gladys Knight?" her father asked her, as though sensing that her next words would be filled with ideas and options he did not want to hear. She'd said them before. He never listened.

"Gladys Knight the singer?" *Here we go again.*

"Yes, she joined the Church. Isn't that wonderful?"

"I think we've talked about that before, Dad." *Once a week for the past few years. Whenever you don't want to talk about what you know is going to come out of my mouth.*

"Oh," he answered, looking slightly confused. "Well, it's certainly good news for the Church, isn't it? Such a testament to the truthfulness of the Gospel."

Sam clenched her teeth to keep the acerbic reply that sat on the end of her tongue from escaping. The ringing of her cell phone saved her from having to answer.

"I need you at the seminary building at Smithland High School, Montgomery." The chief's voice was loud and stress frosted every word. "We've found something that ties the Malone kid to the others."

"It's not suicide," Sam said, almost to herself.

"Doesn't look like it," the chief answered.

"How did you find it?" Sam asked a nervous patrolman, twenty-one-year-old Eldon Watts, fresh off his church mission and just out of the academy. They both stared at a computer screen, barely able to take their eyes away from the scene in front of them. Watts moved from foot to foot, as though he were twelve years old and being questioned by the seminary principal. Of course, it probably hadn't been that long since Watts had taken church classes in this very building. Every good Mormon boy and girl took seminary, and Watts came from a family that had arrived in Utah in covered wagons, with Brigham Young as their guide.

Sam had ditched seminary class every day, so she wasn't all that familiar with what the seminary looked like inside, although she had a vague recollection. From her survey today, it looked like a mini Mormon chapel, both inside and out. Now *those* she was familiar with, since ditching out on church services had never been as easy as skipping seminary, which was held during school hours. It was called released time, in an effort to separate church and state. The attendance of seminary did not affect one's attendance at school, and thus Sam and her friends considered it their free period. As long as they didn't get caught.

As far as Sam knew, each public junior-high and high school in Utah had a seminary building in short walking distance from the school. Close enough that it was possible to get from the building to the next class without being tardy. She didn't know if someone donated the land whenever a school was built or how it was managed, but the buildings were owned by the Church of Jesus Christ of Latter-day Saints.

Someone in "released time" had had way too much free time, gauging from the PowerPoint presentation splayed across the computer screen.

"I actually found it," said a voice from behind them, and a tall man stepped forward from the back of the room, where he had been talking to Chief Roberson and D-Ray. It took Sam a moment to place him, his familiarity so strong to her. But it wasn't until he looked away, almost shyly, that she knew who it was. Paul Carson. Her high-school sweetheart and a man who— once upon a time—she even thought she might marry. Those days were gone.

"Hello, Sam. Good to see you again. I'm the seminary principal."

"Paul," she said with a smile, and she moved forward

to hug him. He stepped back just as she did, and there was an awkward moment until finally she stuck out her hand. He accepted the gesture and shook hers, then quickly pulled away, as though her touch was too much to bear.

"Wow, seminary principal. That's quite a . . . an interesting job," she said, trying to ease the awkwardness of the situation.

The man had changed a lot, very different from the teenage boy who used to feel her up in the backseat of his father's car, parked down a lonely road on a weekend night. Paul certainly didn't look like any seminary principal Sam had ever seen. He still had thick, wavy dark hair, a little too long for Mormon decorum. He had dark green eyes and a straight, square jaw. He was well built and muscled and wore running pants, sneakers, and a white T-shirt with "Nike" emblazoned across the front of it. He looked like an adult, but she could still see the vestiges of the boy he used to be: the boy who had teased her and made her stomach flutter whenever he smiled or trailed his fingers across her bare stomach. There was no flutter, now. Too much time and water under the bridge, so to speak.

"I haven't seen you since, oh, what was it, high-school graduation?"

"No, I think it was later that summer, at our Pineview Reservoir party," he answered, meeting her eyes again, for a moment, then looking away. "You know, when everyone got together for a last farewell before college, and missions, and . . ."

"Life."

"Yes, life. You look good, Sam. I heard you were back."

"Yes, I'm working on the local force now. I'm a detective."

"I know," Paul said, his voice soft and melodic, his half smile showing the dimple in his left cheek. "First woman detective in the history of the Kanesville PD."

"First woman cop, period."

D-Ray walked over and stood next to her. "Yo, Paul," he said, reaching out his right hand. "Good to see you again."

The three childhood friends stood in a semi-circle, no one sure what to say next. Finally, D-Ray cleared his throat, gave her a questioning look, and then spoke. "So, Principal, er, Brother Carson here is the one who found it," D-Ray said.

"Call me Paul, please. We've known each other too long for formalities. I apologize for my casual dress, but I was getting ready to go for a night run when I remembered that I'd left my notes here for a talk I have to give in sacrament meeting tomorrow. So I drove back over, and when I got to the front door, I noticed it was unlocked. I knew something was wrong, because I locked up myself on Friday. No one comes in on Saturday."

"Is there an alarm?" Sam asked.

"Yes, of course. But it had been disarmed. I figured it must be one of my teachers, so I went ahead inside. And when I got into my office, I found this." He pointed to the computer screen. Sam winced again as she viewed the macabre scene.

Over and over again, the pictures of the dead bodies of three teenagers played in a deathly slide show.

After each picture, in a font that was chilling and bloodred, scrolled the word **VENGEANCE**.

SEVEN

The Mormon seminary building hosted at least fifteen hundred kids every day, Monday through Friday. Enough fingerprints to send any computer system into a tailspin.

Sam watched as the CSI techs from Smithland County dusted the seminary building for prints. They would probably only find a few thousand and there would be few matches on those prints. If any did come up, they'd most likely be sealed juvenile records.

She'd already walked the grid with D-Ray, taking notes. There was a frustrating—unnerving—dearth of evidence. The place was spotless. And considering that it was generally filled with immature humans who stuck gum on the bottom of desks and didn't seem to know what a trash can was for . . .

"We have people come in and clean nightly," Paul Carson said.

"A paid service?"

"No, we have families who take turns. Mormon families."

Sam stopped writing and lowered her notebook, looking Paul in the eye and matching his gaze for the first time. "Mormon families who clean? For no money?"

"Yes," he said. He didn't squirm, just stared back into her eyes.

"And they do this *why*?"

"It's part of being a good Mormon. They clean the churches, too."

"I don't remember this," Sam said.

"Guess you haven't been active for a while," Paul said with a quick grin. "It's a cost-saving method used by the Church. They started it up a few years back. And it gives everyone a chance to give service."

"And saves them a whole hell of a lot of money," Sam said.

"Well, yes, but the money is better used in other places."

Sam wanted to spout out something rude and derisive but chose to contain herself. She was a professional, this was a crime scene, and it didn't matter who this man standing before her used to be. Right now, he was a source.

"So, was this building cleaned this evening?"

"Oh no. It was cleaned Friday after school. No one's been in here since . . . Well, at least as far as I know, no one has come in. Until . . . this." He waved his arm at the computer that was currently being dismantled by the techs. Paul had willingly agreed to allow it to be taken to the crime lab for extensive testing.

"Did you leave before the cleaning staff . . . uh, cleaners did?"

"No, I always stay while they clean. Sometimes I help. A lot of hands make it go quicker."

"So you locked up?"

"Yes."

"Do the people who clean have keys?"

"No. It's another reason I stay."

"Who does?"

"Me, my staff, and CES headquarters, of course."

"CES headquarters?"

"Church Educational System. HQ is in Salt Lake."

"How many staff members do you have? I'll need their names and contact information as well."

For the first time, Paul's face darkened. "Nobody on my staff did this, Sam."

"You don't know that, Paul," Sam said, trying to keep her voice gentle.

"I know my people. And I know—"

"Look, Paul, I'm just doing my job. I need to talk to these people, even if just to rule them out."

"So my word wouldn't be enough?"

"What kind of cop would I be if I took everyone's word?" Sam asked, fighting back frustration at his attempt to re-create a trust between them that hadn't existed for years.

"The kind who believed me."

Sam felt a presence and turned to see D-Ray watching the exchange with interest. She tightened her lips. "Names and contact information please," she told Paul tersely.

He moved his eyes to D-Ray, then back to her. After

a moment, he sighed and walked over to his desk, where he picked up a Rolodex.

Sam turned to D-Ray, who was still watching her closely.

"What?" she snapped.

"Nuthin' " he said, rolling his eyes, and then walked over to Paul. "So, Paul, watcha been up to besides teaching kids the words of wisdom?"

Sam just shook her head as she waited for the names of the seminary teachers. She hated the push and pull of small-town crime scenes, and this one was hitting way too close to home.

The three dead teenagers might as well be sitting in her childhood living room.

Suddenly needing to move, she turned impatiently to look at a bulletin board. And found herself staring into the cold, blue eyes of Gage Flint.

For a moment, Sam was completely speechless— even thoughtless. First Paul, now this—it was too much for one day. Every sentence that came to her lips seemed stupid or inappropriate. She felt the silence run on too long but couldn't seem to make herself behave normally.

Finally, the chief seemed to sense that the situation needed rescuing. He stepped forward and put his hand on Gage's shoulder.

"Sam, as you may know, this is Detective Gage Flint, Salt Lake City PD. He handled a case a while back involving some college kids and a suicide pact, and managed to put it to rest pretty quickly. I figure we can use his experience."

"But—"

"No buts. We're short staffed and he's between cases. Consider him on-loan and at your service."

At her service. The man who—just six short months ago—had destroyed her first shot at a big-city career.

"Something wrong, Montgomery?" Chief Roberson pursed his lips tightly after each sentence, as though worried the wrong words would come out of his mouth. Casually dressed in a too-tight polo shirt, faded Levi Dockers, and brown shoes that had seen better days, he didn't look commanding. In fact, he looked a little dumpy. There was a stain on the shirt where his belly protruded, and his usually chaotic hair was more haywire than normal. Sam imagined he'd been comfortable in his worn-out recliner when this call came in, watching reruns of *Little House on the Prairie, Matlock,* or something equally hypnotic and mundane.

The chief was rarely immaculate in the office, so his attire here was no surprise. His broad, ruddy face showed the wear and tear of years of police work, even though he had spent his entire career in a small town. In the thirty-five years Roberson had served on the force, Kanesville had seen kidnappings, murders, drug deals, sexual crimes.

And suicides.

When things were slow at the office, he liked to regale them with tales of Kanesville in the days of only one stoplight, but he rarely spoke of the serious crimes he had solved. Sam usually tried to keep busy to avoid his memory lane strolls. Sometimes, she wondered if he did it on purpose, just to keep everyone working.

In short, the man was one to be reckoned with. Gage

stood next to the chief, giving him several surreptitious glances. She knew Gage was summing him up. She almost wished he would make the wrong judgment call and underestimate Chief Roberson.

She could also tell from the way they stood next to each other that they had never met until tonight.

"Sam and I have worked together," Gage said, getting right to the point. "We were on an undercover case last year."

"Oh, well, that's good. Then you're familiar with each other, and can quickly put together a top-notch team to stop this . . . whatever it is. I expect you'll cooperate fully with Detective Flint, right, Montgomery?"

A gleam in his eye told her he was perfectly well aware that she knew Gage and that this might be a volatile situation. She remembered the chief talking about his academy friend who was the "big honcho" in Salt Lake and felt her stomach begin to churn. Was this how she got the job in her hometown? Had Gage never really been gone from her life?

Maybe the whole Clarkston fiasco been common knowledge for everyone in Kanesville, including her boss. Maybe she'd been hired out of pity. So where did Gage Flint measure in?

Sam felt the sudden narrowing of her throat, the urge to cry abruptly, surprisingly strong. The one reaction that could bring her down. She swallowed back the tears. Maybe she owed Gage more than she knew. And that was a bitter bite of acid.

She hated that *he* was the trigger.

"I need to run down a few things with Flint, and then he's all yours," Roberson said. He motioned at Gage to follow him over to the computer, and Sam turned away and swallowed hard. She was pretty sure that it couldn't get any worse. A difficult case—three cases—the man she loved in high school, and the man who had made her feel like no other but thrown her to the wolves when things got hot.

Great.

She closed her eyes and remembered the beginning. The day she met Gage Flint—those flashing eyes whose electricity she felt the moment she shook his hand. A thrill of excitement had rolled through her body as she realized that her placement undercover meant constant contact with this man.

But then the case . . . it had been the beginning— and the end.

She remembered standing for the first time in the big warehouse/kitchen supply store belonging to the Clarkstons, undercover on the biggest case of her young career. She kept her eyes on the floor, meek, submissive. The man who stood in front of her, carrying a clipboard and eyeing her up and down, was mollified by her subjection, even though she was wearing jeans and a loose T-shirt. The girl who stood next to her, Mary Ann, wore a long dress, work boots, and had her hair in a thick braid twisting down her back. She kept her eyes down as well. Sam was a quick study and had learned from Mary Ann what was needed to survive in the Clarkston clan.

The group was closed, secretive, and tightly woven, and infiltrating them was not going to be easy. Sam had become friends with shy, ungainly Mary Ann, who was known to be the daughter of one of the highest leaders of the Clarkston order. Befriending the sad, lonely, mousy girl was easy. It hurt Sam to see how truly alone Mary Ann really was, but she had a job to do.

They'd met at the Salt Lake City Public Library, because it had been set up that way. Mary Ann didn't know.

Sam had bemoaned her lack of a life and her lack of a job, and before she knew it Mary Ann had brought her into the very entryway of the Clarkston clan—their main business, a kitchen supply store. Getting further than that had proved difficult.

The Clarkston "organization," as those in the know referred to it, maintained a remarkably low profile in Utah, despite the fact that they were building a huge financial empire.

Getting close to understanding just how much money the Clarkstons had had taken police detectives months, and they still only had a ballpark figure. They knew that the holdings were worth at least $200 million.

But you wouldn't know that driving by the shacks and shanties where the Clarkston wives lived, scattered throughout North Salt Lake and Salt Lake City.

Tracing the clan's holdings was difficult, given the Clarkstons' penchant for placing businesses and real estate holdings under corporate titles and other names. This device managed to shield them from direct scrutiny.

The easiest way in, as far as the investigating detectives had seen it, was through Mary Ann. And an entry level position at the kitchen supply store that also served as the church's headquarters and place where they held their Sunday meetings.

The undercover job not only introduced Sam to the

intriguing Gage Flint, but for once she thought she was going to be able to be the savior. She might actually be able to save someone, to change someone's life.

This time, she might make a difference.

After Roberson finished up with Gage, he sent him over to Sam and turned to one of the techs dismantling the computer. Gage met her eyes without restraint, and she fought to maintain her composure, forcing a look of ice over her face.

Don't react . . . don't react. . . .

"So, we meet again."

"I don't need your help." The words tumbled out of her mouth before she could stop them.

"That's not very friendly, Sam. I think your chief wants us to work together in the spirit of police brotherhood." His eyes glinted with humor, making her even more uptight. Anger burned in her stomach. It matched the electricity she felt, which pissed her off. On her first big case she had wanted to prove something and the electricity sparking between her and Gage was an additional bonus. Or so she'd thought.

"Look, I have work to do, and I really don't need your help. I appreciate the offer, but we're fine."

"I think I'll just stick around and see what's what." He smiled at her. "Since the chief invited me, it might be bad manners to just leave."

She looked over at the chief, who was listening to the tech with interest, seemingly unaware of Gage and Sam's confrontation. She turned back to the tall, muscular man and talked herself into a form of composure.

"I have no doubt that this was not an invitation, and did not just happen by accident," she said, her voice almost a whisper. "You forced your way in here. Or used your connections to get here. The only question I have is why? Why are you here?"

"I'm here to help," he said calmly.

"I don't need your help," she said again, through clenched teeth. "Go back to Salt Lake. Any ideas you have are of no interest to me."

"Sam, are you ever going to get past the Clarkston case?"

She crossed her arms and glared at him. She could feel her lips tighten, and her scalp tingled as she watched his eyes narrow.

"What? Why are you looking at me that way?" he asked.

"Get past the Clarkston case?"

"Yes, that's what I said."

"Get past the fact that a young girl was about to be married to her fucking uncle, literally, and was scared out of her mind?"

"It happens every day. We couldn't stop it. Her only hope was for us to bring the entire family down, and free her that way. And you know it."

"No, no I don't, because later that night she ended up dead, didn't she?"

Sam knew her voice carried across the office, and she self-consciously looked around before motioning him closer.

He stepped closer, but there was fire in his eyes. His broad chest moved rapidly, and she saw he had his hands in fists. He took another step closer, then spoke: "She died, because you let her think she might be able to get away. You gave her hope. Your job was not to help her escape. It was to bring down that family. And you failed."

His words cut into her like she was nothing more than warm butter and he was holding a spoon.

"I could have saved her."

"You got her killed."

Sam turned and walked away from him, fighting back tears, because neither one of them would ever know the truth. Could she have saved Mary Ann? If it hadn't been for Sam, would the timid girl just have gone along with her family's horrendous plans and married a man—her uncle—who didn't want her? Unhappy, molested, but alive—was that a better life?

Sam would never know. And neither would Mary Ann.

Then Sam turned and walked over to D-Ray and Paul, the lesser of two evils. Paul was the past and sad memories, but Gage was still with her. It pissed her off that she couldn't forget him. Even worse, she wanted to hate him and knew she didn't.

EIGHT

Sam pulled up into the driveway of her town house, located in the middle of Kanesville, a short walking distance from just about everything, including the police station. Of course, she never walked anywhere. She either sped in her car or ran on foot.

The tree-lined road to her home was dotted with older houses on each side, abodes that had been there since long before her birth. Her own town house was newer and stood out like a sore thumb among the small redbrick and white cottage-type houses that made up old Kanesville. She both liked and hated the location. Much like her life.

She'd known all along these weren't suicides. The fact that someone had taken pictures of the dead bodies proved it. Add to that Gage's reappearance in her life—if only her work life—and she wanted to scream. Now what? And why?

The night air was stifling and hot, still nearly eighty degrees, but she hadn't turned the air conditioner on for the short drive from the school to her house—she had a chill that would not go away.

The pictures of those three teenagers danced through her head, and she closed her eyes tightly, then opened them, hoping the images would be gone. It didn't work; the slide show seemed permanently engraved.

She left the department vehicle parked in the driveway, enough to the side that she could get her own personal vehicle out of the one-car garage, should she need it. She slammed the door shut and hit the keypad to lock it, then headed for her front door. She hadn't expected to be this late, so there was no burning porch light to guide the way. A shiver ran up her spine. She pulled her small flashlight off her duty belt and shined it at the door.

Juggling her keys through her fingers, she cursed silently as the hair on her arms stood upright. She finally found the right key and inserted it into the lock. A shuffling through the grass closed in on her rapidly. She fought back a scream. Pushing open the door, she accidentally dropped her flashlight. The unmistakable squeaking sound of feet moved softly but quickly through wet grass. The automatic sprinklers came on every night at 10:00 p.m. What might have been the silent approach of a predator was instead given away by the moist lawn.

She dropped her keys on the ground, reached into her duty belt, and drew her gun.

Whipping around, she screamed, "Freeze, or I'll blow your balls off!"

A sudden harsh bark and growl told her that she had been frightened by the neighbor's cocker spaniel, a particularly loathsome creature who was apparently nocturnal and did not like people. Including Sam. Undoubtedly he had been leaving a doggie present on her lawn, despite the fact that she had made numerous trips across the street to talk with his owners about him running loose and pooping in every yard but his own.

She watched as he turned his head away from her, snout high, probably affronted by her verbal assault on his doggie genitals, and trotted back across the road.

Her heart slowed down as she flipped on the inside light and spotted her flashlight back behind a long-empty clay pot. Sam reached down to grab it, her hand touching something warm and small. She squealed and pulled her hand back. Standing to reach inside the house, she flipped on the porch light, scanned the perimeter for intruders one more time, then looked back down at the place her flashlight had fallen. Next to it was a small, dead rodent.

Sam shivered, realizing she had touched it. And it had been warm. *Not dead long.* She looked across the street at the cocker spaniel's house, eyes narrowing in suspicion. But dogs didn't bring warm, dead presents. She'd heard cats did, but she had no cat.

Shaking off the feeling this was not an accident, she carefully picked up her flashlight, avoiding the mouse, and entered her lukewarm town house. She shut the door behind her, engaging the dead bolt. Cleaning up the mouse would have to wait until D-Ray dropped by. A girl had her standards. She plucked her keys off the ceramic tile entryway and flipped on the hallway light.

There was little doubt that her first major case on the Kanesville force was creeping her out. She was damned glad she didn't have to explain to the cranky old lady across the street why she had shot the family pet—as horrible as he was.

She headed to her room, removing all her police paraphernalia and placing it in her bedside table drawer as she always did. Then she quickly shed her clothes for shorts and a tank top.

Her air-conditioning seemed to have two settings: warm and warmer. She hadn't got around to calling a heating/AC company to fix it yet, so the house was toasty. Just what you didn't want on a hot Utah summer night. Sam walked into her kitchen and pulled the chain on the ceiling fan above the dining room table, hoping to get a little circulation going in the stagnant air.

She opened the fridge and looked inside, pulling out one of her protein drinks. One of the few things she could stomach, that didn't make her feel like she had to go throw up, because . . . Because why?

Because you think you're too fat. You have body dysmorphia, like Michael Jackson did. Good thing you can't afford plastic surgery. You don't see yourself like you really are. Skin and bones.

"Shut up, Callie," she said to the voice in her head. She'd long since resigned herself to speaking with her dead sister—maybe it was the only reason Sam had stayed sane all these years. Or maybe she wasn't sane. *Don't go there.*

As she was taking a long sip of the chocolate protein shake, the doorbell rang. She jumped, spilling chocolate down her white tank top.

It was late. Too late for visitors.

Heart pounding, thinking of Gage, Sam hurried to her front door, trying unsuccessfully to wipe off the chocolate stain. When she reached the door, she peered through the peephole.

Paul Carson.

Sam considered ignoring him for a minute, but curiosity got the best of her. She opened the door.

"Paul."

"Hi, Sammy," he said. His familiarity grated on her for reasons she didn't really understand.

"Why are you here, Paul?"

"I know it's late, but it's usually customary to ask someone how they are or say hello when you haven't seen them for a while."

"I just saw you half an hour ago."

"Well, before that it had been a long time. At least ten years."

It was late, Sam was tired, and Paul was a virtual stranger to her. She wasn't in the mood to play nice. "How did you know where I live?"

"Ward directory. I live just around the corner."

"Oh, the joys of a small town. You can be living just blocks away from someone you knew years ago and have no idea. I guess that's what happens when someone stops going to church." Sam swallowed as she threw out that small tidbit of information. Then the fact that she was on the ward directory hit her. "Why am I on the ward directory? I asked for no contact years ago. I had my name removed."

"Maybe God isn't ready to let go of you yet."

"What the fuck is this, a bad episode of *Touched by an Angel*?"

Paul winced at her harsh language, and Sam felt a mixture of shame, guilt, and victory that she could still shock him, raise emotions in him.

"You've certainly changed," he said with a grimace.

"Not really. You just didn't look very close. I want my name taken off that directory. I don't exactly need people showing up at my house at all hours of the night."

"Talk to your bishop."

"I don't have a bishop, Paul. I just explained that. I had my name removed years ago. I shouldn't be on anyone's directory."

"Well, they call it a neighborhood directory nowadays."

"Yeah, well, how did they get my information?"

"Probably your family."

Sam sighed, knowing he was right. "I should have gone to law school and then sued the Mormon Church for harassment. Why is it such a big deal to let me go?"

"Why is it such a big deal to *be* let go?"

"Because I don't believe any of it."

"A lot of it is good, Sam."

"A lot of it is not, Paul. And you still never answered me. Why are you here?"

He avoided her question yet again, his eyes focusing on the dark chocolate stain on her tank top. Sam became aware that she was wearing nothing under the tank and the spill was right over her left nipple. She watched Paul flush a bright red color and then turn away.

She fought the urge to cover herself and instead stood brazenly with her hands on her hips. "Guess you've noticed I spilled. I need to go change."

He didn't take the hint and met her eyes again. "I can see that."

Sam could tell he wasn't going to leave until he got

out whatever he wanted to tell her, so she invited him in, told him to sit on the couch, and hurried into her room to put on a bra and a T-shirt.

"All right, Paul," she said when she got back into the living room. He sat comfortably, leaning back on the sofa, looking as though he belonged there. She fought back the irritation and the desire to tell him to get out. But she didn't intend to make it comfortable for him. Sam chose not to sit but to stand, hands on her hips. "Why are you here?"

"Because what happened tonight, what I saw, was so horrible. And all I could think of was you. And you trying to deal with it. And I felt like . . . I don't know. I felt like I needed to be there for you."

"That's nice, Paul, but it's been a long time since we knew each other at all. This is my job. This is what I do. Don't worry about me. I'll be just fine."

"Well, I just needed to see. Wanted to check on you."

He had aged well, with a strong jaw and mostly un-lined, still-handsome face. As a teenager, his smile had always stopped her cold and made her stomach flutter. Sam guessed more than one teenage girl had a crush on this seminary teacher. Back in high school, he'd been irresistible to her.

That was a long time ago. Now, despite his good looks and apparent availability, she saw him only as a harbinger of bad memories.

"I'm fine. Thanks for checking. But I'm really tired."

"Okay, I'm sorry." He stood up and walked over to the door. "I'm glad you're okay. It's really good to see you again."

"Nice to see you, too." She didn't know what else to say.

"Take care, Sam."

He started to walk away, and she remembered the mouse. But something made her hold back. She'd leave it for D-Ray. Sam stood in the open door and watched as he reached his light-colored four-door sedan. He turned back, waved, then got into his car and drove off.

She shut her door and locked it, wondering why he had come. What point was there in going back?

It was all unfinished business, but that chapter was over for her. Unfinished or not. He'd moved on, in a big way, and so had she.

Which didn't explain why he had shown up at her door late at night. Or why she had let him in.

NINE

Sunday morning dawned cloudy and cooler than the past week, sort of like someone had turned the stovetop down from a rolling boil to simmer. Sam forced herself out of her comfortable bed and into her running clothes, silently cursing this obsession that kept her from being lazy on just one morning—Sunday, the day of rest!—and instead impelled her out of her slightly warm town house and into the street and soaring temperatures, pounding her feet on the pavement.

Heat roiled up off the blacktop and curled around her legs as she ran past sleepy houses and slumbering trees. She felt as tired as the world looked around her, but sleep was impossible. Last night's discovery of the macabre slide show had played over and over in her dreams, and even with the sounds of Sara Bareilles in her ears, "Gravity" blasting loudly through her earphones, it just wouldn't go away. She made her way up Fernwood Road, trying to dislodge the mental images of three lives ended way too soon, one after another.

She ran just a little harder, breathing deeper, sweat pooling between her breasts and across her brow, wishing the entire scenario would fall out of her head and melt away into the searing pavement.

Of course, that didn't work. "You loved me 'cause I'm fragile, when I thought that I was strong." The song reminded her of Gage. *Love? Who's talking about love?* Another memory to haunt her.

Sam shook her head sharply, taking a left turn into the Kanesville City Cemetery. Located in the center of the town, on the north end, it had long been a focal point for her, even when she was living in Salt Lake City. Houses used to be farther away from the eternal resting place, the gullies and meadows behind it a common playground when she was a child. But as with the rest of the town, progress had encroached on the cemetery, and houses now rimmed its perimeter, the living going about their daily business among Kanesville's ancestors.

It was a familiar pathway, the same one she always traveled. She paced herself and ran the outer perimeter of the grounds, not looking at the headstones and markers that littered the green grass. Pretending that she was at the track of the local high school or maybe running the New York City Marathon.

Anywhere but here.

Tawny Lynn Griffin. Madison Williams. And now Jeremiah Malone. Three teenagers attending the local high school. All little more than children. All dead. Tawny's death was immediately pegged a suicide. She was found hanging from a backyard tree, two of her father's best church ties knotted together to form a makeshift noose. Her parents had been gone for the evening, out at a Mormon Church social. They returned home to the loss of their only child, a popular cheerleader with a reputation for being a mean girl. She left a note. All it said was a hastily scrawled "Sorry." A small stepladder had been kicked over and lay askew beneath her dangling feet. Details of the brief note were never released to the press, more out of concern for the privacy and grieving of the family than anything else.

More than one chubby, lonely teenage girl or pimply, geeky rejected boy had admitted to not feeling a great loss upon Tawny's death.

Still, no sign anyone would kill her. That was an extreme reaction that seemed unjustified. But then Madison, Tawny's good friend and fellow cheerleader and not-so-nice girl, was found hanging from a statue of town founder Robert Kane, in the center of the Kanesville City Park. Again, no sign of anything but a very public suicide. A stepstool was knocked over beneath her dangling legs, explaining how she got high enough to tie a rope—not a tie this time—around the head of the Robert Kane's horse. While the first girl had left a one-word scrawl, a longer note was found in Madison's pocket, explaining she was tired of having to try so hard. She wanted peace. She wanted to sleep. She wanted to atone. That last word, "atone," had hit Sam wrong. Yes, they learned these things as children, but teenagers didn't talk like that.

And now Jeremiah. One big difference was no note. Instead, there was a slide show, delivered to the Mormon seminary where all three teenagers had been instructed in matters relating to their religion.

Murder. Serial killer. Those words escalated, darting through Sam's brain, and she tried to shut them down. She didn't want this to get worse, but it was already pretty transparent. Any second-rate detective could come to the murder conclusion and investigate it. And she was no second-rate detective. She refused to be. This couldn't be a suicide pact, unless the three had planned this out with the first girl leaving a one-word note, the second leaving a longer note, and Jeremiah Malone leaving a graphic slide show.

Of course, that wasn't possible. Because the slide included pictures of Jeremiah, dead.

Sam supposed he could have been acting it out, but she'd seen the body and there was little doubt in her mind that he was dead when the picture was taken. Newly dead.

Either they had a killer or this was one hell of a suicide pact. The appearance of the slide show meant there had to be someone else, a fourth teenager. Someone who had placed it in the seminary and someone who was, themselves, in grave danger from their own hands. And the fact remained that whoever put the slide show on the seminary computer had used a key and knew the alarm code.

Who had access to the seminary building?

Paul Carson and all the teachers—three instructors and the people who had cleaned the building last. All scheduled to be interviewed this afternoon. She had little doubt all would have a solid alibi.

If it looked like a duck and walked like a duck . . . How did that duck get inside the seminary building to leave the slide show?

Sam's gut told her these were murders.

On her fourth time around the outer road, she finally slowed, decreasing her pace from a fast sprint to a jog, then a walk. She paced over to a spot filled with larger statues and monuments, tributes to loved ones placed there by those left behind. Sam walked purposefully toward a smaller, light gray headstone, careful to avoid stepping on flat granite markers.

Once there, she paced back and forth, putting her hands on her hips, elbows out, trying to regulate her breathing, looking anywhere but at the headstone in front of her. Ignoring the reason she was here. Ignoring the reason she always came.

Callie was buried next to some of Kanesville's founding families. The graves of Bloods, Bones, and Steels could be seen all around. Strong, gritty, metallic, and earthy names. Pioneer stock. "Montgomery" seemed so out of place here—so off.

As did the dates of birth and death. Despite the heat, the day was overcast and dark, and a shadow slid across the stone as Sam bent down to touch her sister's resting place.

"All right, I'm here. I'm listening. What are you trying to tell me?"

There was no answer.

Sam ran home fast and hard, trying to remove thoughts of work by making damn good and sure her lungs could barely function. It wasn't working. She might pass out, but she knew she'd wake up to the same scenario running through her head.

And if she wasn't thinking about them, she would think about Mary Ann Clarkston, who was in Sam's thoughts almost as much as Callie. Sam just hoped that Mary Ann didn't start talking to her, too, or she might have to check herself into the loony bin. Maybe she and her mother could get a twofer deal.

Knock it off, Sam. You know you aren't crazy. And you know you did all you could for Mary Ann.

Sam stopped on her front lawn, hands on her knees, panting, trying to get some air back into her lungs. She had a wicked cramp in her side, and her calves ached in rhythm with her lungs. And still, thoughts of Mary Ann roamed through her head. Having Gage show up at the seminary building didn't help with that.

Sam had been working at the supply store with Mary Ann for three months and didn't seem to be making any ground. And tensions were high; as lead on the case, Gage needed to be able to show results. The Feds were already murmuring about stepping in. Something needed to break. Then one day, Mary Ann came into work, crying. She wouldn't tell Sam what was wrong, at first. But finally the twenty-year-old admitted that her father had convinced one of his brothers to take her on as a wife. She was getting too old to live with her parents. She wasn't desired as a bride, since she had a cleft palate that split her upper lip all the way to the tip of her nose and misaligned teeth that stuck out at weird angles. It destroyed an otherwise delicate, almost beautiful face.

That day Mary Ann's face, always free of makeup, was streaked with tears and a despair that was almost palpable. When Sam asked her what was wrong, she looked around hurriedly and then whispered that she was to be married off on Saturday.

Not married, but "married off." The words hit Sam

hard, like a punch in the gut, as she considered their implications. She tried not to react. "How come you didn't invite me?" Sam asked, innocence in her tone, hurt ringing through it. "I would love to see you get married. I thought we were friends. You didn't even tell me!"

"Our family does things differently," Mary Ann said, her voice little more than a whisper.

Then the manager of the store, Owen Clarkston, sidled up behind them. Sam had been aware of him the whole time and knew he'd been paying attention to them and the conversation. He'd been a major part of her plan. He'd been giving her lascivious glances the entire time she'd been working here, mostly when he thought she wasn't watching. What he didn't realize was that it was her job to watch every move everybody in the building made. So she saw him and made little accommodations to ensure his interest continued, even though it made her physically ill to have him perusing her body with his lizard eyes.

"You should have someone with you, Mary Ann," he said. "I'm sure they won't mind if Sam comes. I'll talk to my father."

"Why wouldn't they let someone be there?" Sam had asked innocently, as though she had no idea who the Clarkstons were and what a marriage in this clan signified.

Mary Ann glanced quickly over at Owen, then back down at her feet. She knew better than to say anything, but Owen had made this overture, and Sam didn't miss the desperation on Mary Ann's face. She really wanted Sam to be there with her, although she knew her desire alone would never make it happen.

"They will if I say so," Owen said, puffing up his chest a little.

Jackpot, Sam thought.

"Great. Glad you have such important friends, Mary Ann. What should I wear? What time should I be there? Actually, uh, where should I be?"

Mary Ann turned and ran off, headed for the restroom.

"Jitters," Owen said. "She'll be fine. She's not the first bride to get nervous. But getting married to one of God's holy priesthood bearers is the only way into the Celestial Kingdom. She knows that."

He gave Sam another once-over and then touched her chin. It took all she had not to haul off and punch him in the nose.

"Why don't you take your cute little self in there and see if she's okay. And tell her to hurry out, because we got customers."

Sam smiled, trying not to gag as it felt like worms were crawling up and down her throat. She turned and walked to the bathroom. She couldn't let this man see her distaste. She had a job to do.

"What's the matter, Mary Ann? Why aren't you happy?" Sam asked when she discovered the girl sobbing in the restroom. Of course, Sam understood a lot more than she had let on. Her every instinct told her to sneak this poor girl out of the store right then and there—get her the hell away from these evil people who believed God was talking to them and only them.

"I don't want to marry him. He's my . . . He's my . . . I don't want it. I don't want to be here."

"Then don't," Sam said. "You are a woman and you

have rights. This is not the eighteen hundreds. You don't have to marry anyone you don't want to."

"You don't understand. You don't know my family."

"What do you mean?"

"I can't talk about it."

"Look, I can help you. I can help you get out, if you want out," Sam said, knowing the words were a mistake even as she said them. She had to stay in her cover and play the part. But this girl was desperate. She needed help. She needed to escape.

"How?" Mary Ann whispered. "How can you get me out of this? It's my destiny."

"I can find you a safe place. You're just going to have to trust me on this one."

Sam didn't miss the dawning of hope in the girl's eyes just as there was a sharp rap on the bathroom door.

"Hey, what are you two doing in there?" Owen yelled.

"Coming, coming," Mary Ann called, wiping her eyes.

"We'll talk later," Sam told her.

But they never did.

That night Gage pulled Sam off the case. And Mary Ann disappeared. Her body was found three months later, out in the desert on property owned by the Clarkstons. They claimed she had run away. The body had been too decomposed to identify a cause of death.

Sam's lungs finally stopped fighting for air, the ache in her side eased, and her calves only throbbed slightly. She couldn't run from her ghosts. She wasn't sure why she kept trying.

Because you're damned stubborn and you always have been? Gage is here to help. Let him.

Sam shook her head. *I don't need his help, Callie. I know the look you have on your face, I can see it like you were here by my side just yesterday, and I'm telling you, I can figure this out. I can keep more kids from dying.*

The answer was a whispering breeze through the tops of the trees. For once, Callie wasn't talking. Recalcitrant, even in Sam's mind Callie was still the teenager she had been when she died. She never cooperated.

"I need some answers."

"Don't we all."

Sam whirled around to see Gage standing three feet away, a cup of coffee in each hand.

"Speak of the devil," she muttered.

"You wound me. I come in peace. Bringing gifts, no less." He held the coffee cups out, and Sam couldn't help but sniff the air. Good coffee was one of her weaknesses, a total departure from the way she was raised. While good, believing Mormons didn't drink coffee, Sam Montgomery drank it by the pot. Perhaps another way of sticking it to her past.

And Gage remembered that weakness.

Sam glared at the ruggedly handsome man standing before her. He wore faded Levi 501s, button fly— always button fly for him— *Stop. Get your mind out of the gutter.*

He had on a tan Roosters Polygamy Pale Ale T-shirt that pronounced: "I tried Polygamy in Utah." Over the top of the T-shirt was a large, short-sleeved black shirt with an understated white print. From where she stood it looked like a Kokopelli design. Since Gage was known to take off for days in the southern Utah desert alone, it suited him. He also wore an NBA Jazz basketball cap over his dark, crisply shorn hair. Under the cap, his dark eyebrows furrowed and his blue eyes seemed to spark electricity. Nothing about his attire really went together, and yet on him was all in perfect synchronicity. The black shirt was large and open and untucked, and she knew that on his right hip, camouflaged by the shirt, he had a Smith & Wesson model 357PD in .41 Magnum—a revolver that didn't jam like an automatic, which made it simpler and more reliable. His preferred "off-duty" gun. The department made him carry a Glock. But on his own time, he made his own choices—ones that made him both dangerous and, to her, incredibly alluring. The rough-and-tumble instability of her youth led Sam to want to always be protected. She never went anywhere without a weapon. She knew Gage was the same.

Even in his casual attire he held an appeal and charisma she could not understand. She did not want him to be attractive to her, or to anyone else for that matter. She wanted him to be ugly and stubby and . . . bald. Bald would be good.

How about it, Callie? Can you help me out here? Ask God to send Gage a little bald curse?

"You're thinking bad thoughts about me, aren't you?" Gage said drolly, folding his arms across his chest, which of course emphasized his muscular build. He had never been much of a talker—Sam had always assumed that his stint in the Army had taken care of any outgoing tendencies he might have once had. He didn't speak much about those days, but they were in his eyes, the lines on his face. And yet, history aside, his subtle sense of humor was always there, constantly simmering beneath the surface.

"I am not," she protested, but it lacked enthusiasm. *Who am I trying to kid? Even bald, the man would be hot.* "Why are you here?"

"To talk about the case, of course."

"It's Sunday. I'm off-duty."

"A cop is never really off-duty. Especially a detective."

"Gage, why are you doing this? Why don't you go back to your little haven in Salt Lake, and leave me with my case. I—*we* don't need your help."

"You say that, but you aren't even giving me a chance to offer my expertise."

"I know. You're always right, and everyone else is wrong, and you call the shots. And pull people off cases when they are making headway. That kind of expertise is one I can do without, thank you very much."

"I don't call all the shots, but when I'm in charge I have to make the decisions. When it's life or death it's my ass on the line if something goes wrong. I don't intend to let anyone die under my watch."

"Well, it isn't your watch this time. It's not your case. You made sure I failed miserably in Salt Lake, and if you've come here to do it again, it's not going to work."

"Sam . . ."

"No, no 'Sam.' No saying my name or sweet talk, or buttering me up by looking at me like that. This is my case, and I will only say it one more time. I do not need your help."

"Why is it I don't believe that?"

"Believe what, that it's my case?"

"No, that you're only going to say it one more time. Because I'm not going anywhere."

"Well, maybe you aren't, but I am. Good-bye, Gage."

She turned and ran up the steps to her front door, pulling the key out of her fanny pack. She turned to see he stood watching her but didn't follow.

Why did you turn, idiot?

"I have coffee," he called as she slipped the key in the lock.

"No thanks. Too hot for coffee today."

She went into her house and shut the door, leaning back against it, palms down, as though to keep out evil demons. Or one sexy detective.

He might be here to stay, but she damn sure didn't have to make it easy for him.

When she pulled away from the door and looked out the peephole, she saw he was gone.

Good.

She waited for relief to wash over her, but instead she found herself aching, in the very core of what made her tick. He'd left a hole that she was afraid would never be filled by anyone else. And she'd be damned if it would ever be filled again, especially by him.

So why did she feel so lost?

TEN

Later that day, Sam dropped in on her parents—she always spent Sunday afternoons watching her father treat her mother like a living, breathing doll.

"Hi, Dad. How was church?"

"Oh, we didn't go today," her father answered as he stared across the kitchen table into her eyes. He broke the gaze and turned to the woman sitting at his side. "Ruthie just wasn't feeling up for it, were you, dear?"

"Oh, well, I'm sorry you had to miss. Maybe next Sunday I can come over and sit with Mom while you go to your meetings. At least to Priesthood." The truth was, Sam's father hadn't left the house to attend church meetings for years. Not since her mother lost her mind. But it was a game Sam and her father had been playing for quite a long time, and she didn't know how to break the cycle. Or maybe she was just afraid that any break would be a permanent one, irreparable, like a crack that quickly fissured up and outward on a windshield until it was nothing but shattered glass. While the church sisters would come visit during the week, they wouldn't miss their own weekly meetings and thus affect their eternal salvation. She didn't really understand why her father wouldn't go back to the Church he held so dear. She had offered to sit with her mother on Sundays time and time again. Why wouldn't he go, unless he held more against God than he would ever willingly admit?

"Oh, I'm betting Ruthie will be more up for it next week. She just had a rough night last night, didn't you, Ruthie?"

An abrupt twist of her head almost sent Sam crashing from her chair to the floor.

"Mom? Dad, did you see that? She just shook her head. She just . . ."

"What do you mean, Sammy?"

"She moved. She shook her—"

"Oh, Sammy, she moves all the time. I've been telling you kids that for years. You just don't listen. You just don't hear what I hear."

"She talks?"

"In ways. You just have to learn to listen. That's all."

Sam continued to stare at her mother, eyebrows furrowed as she perused the lined face of the woman who now seemed so oblivious to anything around her. Had Sam imagined the reaction, the sharp twist of her mother's head in response to Sam's father's comment about a rough night?

What about last night had her mother so agitated? Was she really agitated?

"Dad, you said she communicates. I have to admit I've never seen it. But that seemed like a real response to me."

"Sam, of course she responds. She eats; she sleeps. I put food in her mouth and she chews. She's still there, and you kids know it. It just takes more work to get through to her. That's the problem with your generation, no patience. Well, I have patience."

Sam sighed. "Yes, Dad, you do. Unending patience." She reached across the table and put her hand over his old, weathered one. "You have the patience of a saint."

Her father just chuckled and pulled his hand away. "Don't be condescending, Sammy. It doesn't suit you and it irritates me. Now I need to get your mother ready for bed."

"It's seven o'clock," Sam said.

"I told you, she had a rough night, and now she needs her rest. Come on, Ruthie, time for bed."

He stood up and walked to her chair, putting his hands on her elbows and guiding her upward out of the chair. She cooperated, shuffling away from the table with Sam's father following behind.

"Good-bye, Sammy. Come again soon," her father said over his shoulder.

She had been dismissed. What a strange relationship her parents shared, and yet it always seemed like everyone else was a complete outsider. Nobody else believed her mother was "still there." Not Sam. Not Susanna. Certainly not the neighbors or ward members. They'd given up on that long ago. And yet her father never, ever gave up hope.

What would it be like to be that optimistic? That patient? Sam stood up and walked to the back door, letting herself out into the large yard where she had played as a child. The tree was still there. She'd begged her father to cut it down, remove it from their lives, but he'd refused. The tree was not at fault. Of course it wasn't, and yet . . .

She wondered if she could do it herself. What would happen if she revved up a motor-driven saw and decimated the tree that had changed their lives so drastically?

What would her father do?

The tree was larger now, with more branches and leaves, reaching skyward. Large, bumpy roots cratered the ground around her, as well. This tree had a life of its own, perhaps the one it had taken from her sister.

Sam turned away and fought the urge to run, prickles of fear running down her spine as she tensed, watching for the branches of the tree to reach out and grab her, pull her in, and destroy her, like they had Callie.

She gave in to her fear and ran like a child, around the side of the house and to the front driveway, stopping short at the last square of pavement next to where she had parked her car. There, etched in the aging concrete, were the familiar names and handprints she had seen many times before.

"Susanna, Amelia, Callie, Samantha." Next to each name was the print, Sam's so small it seemed impossible she had ever been that young, that fragile. She bent down and placed her hand palm down onto the print, her long fingers engulfing it and obscuring it from view, although she could still feel the grooves and ridges beneath her fingers.

Missed me, missed me, now you gotta kiss me. Red rover, red rover, send Sammy right over. We're waiting.

Sam shook off the childish voice in her head. *Who was waiting?* It had been so long ago, so many years, and so much agony. This was a wound that time would not heal, unlike the claims of so many proverbs. Instead, every year seemed to make the pain worse, the ache stronger. How could her family grieve, mourn, and then walk away with her mother perpetually frozen and gone? They had lost two members of the family that day.

Both Sam's mother and Callie, gone forever. Looking back over the house, along the roofline, Sam could see the long branches of the tree as they reached up, like spindly, spidery arms, poking upward and waving gently in the summer breeze, as if they were taunting her.

I'm still here, and I'm still growing.

A shiver racked through her spine, and goose bumps rose on her arms. The warm, sultry August evening seemed to darken.

It's a tree, Sam. Just a tree.

She turned to her car again, and the uncanny sense that someone was watching her, something real and live, and evil, washed over her along with another wave of chills.

"Quit creeping yourself out, Sam," she admonished herself, and jumped into her car, starting it up and zooming away.

She laughed wildly as she drove down the street. It was still light, the summer sky not even giving a hint of the darker blue that would lead to night. How could she be so afraid of a tree?

After Sam got home, she found herself restless, so she decided to numb her mind with work. She sat and stared at the computer screen, the copy of the DVD in her hard drive, playing the slide show of the three dead teens, over and over. The CSI techs at the Smithland sheriff's office had made the copy for her and kept the original. The pictures were not beautiful. Death was most often violent and messy. Bodily fluids, bile, contorted body shapes, smells that seemed to emanate even from the pictures. And whoever took them had seen that. There could be little doubt the pictures were real.

Sam was looking for clues. What clues she didn't know; so far, all she had managed to do was sicken herself.

She stopped the frame on each teenager, looking closely for something, anything, that might lead her in the right direction.

Sam wore only a pair of men's boxer shorts and a thin white tank top, with spaghetti straps that kept falling down over her thin shoulders. She would push them up again and again, and they would just keep falling. If she would just take the time to tighten them, it wouldn't happen. But she didn't want to bother.

The desk was an old hand-me-down from her younger self. She'd taken it from her room at her parents' house. It had moved with her, first to Salt Lake City and then back to Kanesville. It was the one thing she clung to, because she could remember her mother standing beside her as she labored over learning to write her letters. "No, Sammy, that's an *E*. Remember the *F* only has two horizontal lines."

One of the few good memories. The desk often made her melancholy and yet tied her to something she needed desperately to have a connection with.

Tonight, with work on her mind, she was paying little attention to the desk—or the past.

There were no words in the presentation, no names, no clues, nothing that said, *Look here,* aside from the bloodred **VENGEANCE** that followed each slide.

The cordless phone on the desk rang, and she picked it up from the base. The caller ID notified her it was an "unknown" caller, but she always answered her phone. She didn't know who she was waiting to hear from. Maybe Callie? Maybe her mother? More than once a hapless telemarketer had hung up on Sam, undoubtedly hating their job after she let them have it.

She answered absently, "Montgomery."

"I think you have a serial killer on your hands, Sam." The voice was Gage's and the anger that immediately surged over her came from the past, but she fought to tamp it down, not let it roil around in her stomach and heart. She'd fought off thinking about him every day since she'd left Salt Lake.

And now he was right here in the middle of her case.

"Really?" she answered, more than a trace of sarcasm lacing her words.

"Don't be smart. It doesn't suit. And you wasted a perfectly good cup of coffee."

His word usage betrayed his background, which was a little bit of Georgia farm boy mixed in with suburban Utah Mormon. He'd spent time as an Army Ranger, stationed for a while in Fort Benning, Georgia, and from time to time the years there sautéed his words with southern spice, as though he were a born-and-bred southerner. But he shared her roots. Utah Mormon pioneer stock.

"It suits just fine, Gage. And I'm not stupid."

"I know you aren't, Samantha," he said, his voice a harsh, sexy drawl. "I'm sorry if you think I'm trying to take over your case. I'm not. But I know enough about this kind of stuff to help you. All you have to do is let me."

"I don't want to."

"Well, you don't really have a choice."

"So why act like you are here for me, huh, Gage? Why pretend? Anyways, right now, it's Sunday night, and I don't have to work with you until tomorrow morning.

"So right now I'll say good night. See you tomorrow."

Sam clicked the off button on the phone and then slammed it into the base for good measure.

She'd never been good at men or relationships. She did okay with the sex part. Something about her skinny body, gangly arms and legs, and smooth, pale Nordic complexion seemed to appeal to men.

But bonding, mating, forging long-term contacts— those things were all foreign to her. Did someone teach these things to girls? All the girls who ended up with nice, successful, handsome husbands seemed to know how to do it. They must have had mothers who taught them to wear lipstick and comb their hair and giggle when a man said something he thought was witty— even if it wasn't. The one boy she had thought loved her—Paul—had walked away without a backward glance, leaving to serve a mission for the Church while she was still aching from a loss she couldn't come close to understanding.

Her mother had been one step away from being a

corpse. Sam grew up learning how to fight and defend, passionate and ardent but not at all refined. Maybe that was why she was good at the sex thing.

She'd had her share of lovers, but none she'd allowed to get emotionally close or put down roots anywhere near her. Sex was easy. She'd learned the pain and dangers of love early on in life.

And then there was Gage, a man she had found herself inextricably drawn to on a difficult case. He affected her in ways she couldn't explain yet had never been her lover or even her friend. He hadn't been a one-night stand or a friend with benefits. Instead, there was just that incredible pull—gravity. They'd never consummated a relationship that bordered on cinder hot. Maybe that was why he could still crawl under her skin and set her nerve endings on fire.

The bond they'd formed during those very dark days had been irretrievably broken when he'd shown her just how disparate they really were, telling their chief that she was too close to the case and more of a detriment than a help. Stood up in front of their boss and claimed her unfit to remain in the undercover position.

He'd betrayed her.

Sam closed her eyes and let herself drift back to a time when the fireworks between her and Gage were of a different sort. She wanted to fight it, but his return to her life had triggered too many feelings and emotions. Maybe if she just let herself remember, it would get out of her system quicker. *He* would get out of her system.

Her mind wandered back to the night he first cooked for her, in his house in Farmington.

"Oh, you're good," Sam had said, watching as he expertly sautéed mushrooms in a pan, never missing a beat as he checked on the steaming asparagus. Outside, steaks were grilling, and he kept leaving to check on them, finally coming in with two perfectly done medium-rare fillets. He dished out the plates, scooping out the mushrooms over the top of the steaks and adding a steaming heap of asparagus, which he topped with a pat of butter.

"Oh yeah, you're good," Sam said again, cutting into a steak that practically fell apart with her fork.

"Sammy?" He drew in close, picking up his wineglass, and she picked up hers. Their arms intertwined, and they both took a sip.

"I am only good at two things. Killing people and making love." He gave her a wicked grin, and she felt her stomach flutter and moisture pool in places she didn't know could react to a sexually charged statement like the one he had just uttered. Although she wasn't quite sure how to take the "killing" statement. She knew he'd been in the Army and, after his enlistment ended, he came to work for the Salt Lake City Police Department. She wasn't sure why he had decided not to reenlist for another tour of active duty, except she suspected his "good at killing" statement probably had something to do with that. She wanted to know more. She wanted to dig deeper. Instinct told her to wait.

"That's not true," she said softly. "You're an excellent cook. This is the best steak I've ever eaten."

"All part of the lovemaking."

The phone rang again, knocking Sam out of her reverie. She shook her head briskly as though she could dislodge the daydream, memories past. She didn't *need* him. She didn't *want* him. She picked it up, clicking the on button.

Harsh, jagged breathing.

"Hello?" Sam said into the phone, staring hypnotically at the electrically lit square face of her caller ID unit. "Hello?" This time her voice was quiet, a ragged whisper. "Mom, is that you?"

The caller ID lit up brightly with her parents' phone number.

ELEVEN

Whitney Marcusen abruptly found herself wide awake, sitting upright in her bed, slapping at the spiders whose prickly, sticky little feet had been marching across her skin. Beads of sweat poured from her forehead, and moisture pooled between her breasts and under her arms.

She could still feel the light pinpricks and see the spiders that had crawled from Jeremiah's sightless eyes and over his body to attack her as she lay frozen underneath him, their bodies still conjoined in post-coital limbo. She'd wanted to scream, "I'm not dead. I'm not dead!" but no words would come from her mouth. But as the fog of sleep left her, the spiders faded away into the cobwebs left from the dream. Her body moved, tears poured down her face, and grief and despair—her constant companions for the past few days—took their place.

Jeremiah. A sob escaped from her throat and she clapped a clammy hand to her mouth, trying to keep the noises inside, to keep her mother and father from hearing. They would want to comfort her. They would think this was ordinary grief, the kind a high-school girl felt for her first crush.

The wave of nausea that roiled up from her stomach told the real story.

The noises she could keep inside. The vomit she could not. She ran to the bathroom connected to her bedroom and heaved up all of dinner—not much really. Her appetite was sparse before, and now, with Jeremiah gone, it was nonexistent.

After the nausea passed, she moved to the sink and turned on the cold water, cupping her hand under the faucet and bringing the water to her mouth. She swished it around, then spit it out, and reached for her toothbrush, wanting to rid herself of the foul taste.

In the mirror she saw someone she didn't recognize—a young brunette girl with a pixielike pretty face and big, warm brown eyes. Her exterior didn't show what was going on inside: what was growing inside.

A sharp rap at the door made her jump.

"Whitney, are you okay?"

"Yes, Mom. I just . . . I had to go to the bathroom. I'm just washing my hands, and then I remembered I hadn't brushed my teeth."

"Do you need anything?"

"No, Mom. I'm just going to do this, then go back to bed. Sorry I woke you."

"All right, hon."

Whitney heard the hesitation in her mother's voice, knew she wanted to say more but was treading carefully.

Finally Whitney heard: "Good night. I love you." Her

mother's footsteps shuffled away, and a bit of tension left Whitney's body.

"Night. Love you."

"Love you." Jeremiah had said those words to her, at least four times. Every time he had pushed his way inside her body and made those strange grunting noises and cooed foreign phrases to her. Things like, "Feels good, huh, babe?" and, "Let me show you what a real man feels like." Like she would know any different? He was her first. She was thinking he would be her last.

But she was only seventeen. Seventeen, and knocked up, and the father was dead. He couldn't be her last. She couldn't be pregnant. He couldn't have killed himself.

Whitney turned away from the sink and clasped her hand to her mouth again, trying to keep more sobs of despair inside her. Maybe, if she filled up with enough despair, the baby would have no room and have to leave and Whitney could pretend it had never happened.

She could pretend that she'd never violated all the tenets of her religion and had premarital sex. That the boy she had loved so easily, and fallen for so hard, was now dead.

She dropped down to the floor, her bottom pushed up against the bathroom cupboard, the hard wood biting into her back, and fought back the tears.

Sex had been nothing like Jeremiah promised. But she wanted him, wanted the status of being seen on his arm. Wanted the prom date he had dangled in front of her. Wanted to be popular and so unlike that other one—the new girl. The one who had turned on Jeremiah. The one who had called him out. The one they all hated.

The worst part was that Whitney was pretty sure

that Jeremiah had not killed himself. Oh no. She was pretty sure he'd been murdered.

And she was more than a little worried she was next. That would certainly solve the problem of telling her family she was pregnant.

TWELVE

Sam stuffed her feet in some flip-flops, grabbed her gun off the dresser where it always sat, ready for action, and ran out the front door, headed for her car.

She reached the detached garage and almost entered the code for the automatic garage door opener when she realized that she was holding the keys to her department vehicle. She turned and ran for it instead, clicking it open with the remote and throwing herself into the driver's seat, quickly starting the car up, and heading to her parents' house. It was only six blocks away, but it felt like six hundred miles.

Who had called her? She knew it was her mother, because Sam's father would have had a conversation with her. If he'd been awake, which he never was at midnight. The only person who would have made that call and not spoken was her mother. Was she coming out of her catatonic state? Worse, if it wasn't her calling, who was it? The same maniac who was killing teenagers?

Sam reached her parents' house, pulled into the driveway haphazardly, and propelled herself out of the car, barely stopping to pull the keys from the ignition. She snatched her gun off the right passenger seat, where she had put it hastily when she turned the car on.

Gun in right hand, keys in left, she reached the front door and shakily went to enter the house key she still had—then realized that she *didn't* have it, because she had only grabbed her work keys. But instinct kicked in, and she turned the knob, and of course the door opened. Her father hadn't locked the doors to their house for years.

He was still waiting for Callie to come home.

Or for someone evil and menacing to come in and destroy her family again—this time for good.

Sam's heart beat so loudly she felt as though it would draw every criminal in Smithland County to her. A melodic, angry beat screaming, *Come and get me! I am terrified! Ba-dum-bum!*

She entered silently, trying to control her breathing, and she kept the gun slightly in front of her, ready should she have to fire.

She inched her way down the hallway, using the crouch and spring methods to make sure that the living room, small kitchen, and bathroom were clear. She carried on down the hall to her parents' room and fear melted her heart, turning her blood to sludge as she slowly creaked open the door.

All of the old lessons came back to her then. She had made so many mistakes. She hadn't called for backup, lesson number one. You have to call for backup. No one knew where she was. She had fled her house without using reason or thought process, so sure that either

her mother was trying to talk to her or someone was trying to kill her.

Nonetheless, even knowing how many rules she had broken, she proceeded. If this was nothing, she didn't want to share her private embarrassment and agony. She'd done that enough growing up. Too many people felt pity for her. It made her want to beat them up.

Sam flipped on the light, to see that her father was sound asleep, mouth slightly open, snoring loudly. He lay on his back, as he always did, wearing only his thin temple garments. The sheets and comforter covered him to his waist. The sacred marks over each breast rose and fell as he breathed in deeply, sound asleep, having slept through crying babies, suicidal children, and a catatonic wife. He was just so tired that nothing could rouse him at night.

Where Sam's mother normally slept, however, there was only the indented impression of a head on the pillow, and mussed sheets and blankets.

Ruthie Montgomery was gone.

Sam finally called for backup. Despite her strong sense of privacy, she'd been right. Something was wrong here.

What the hell is wrong with you, Sam?

Was it Callie speaking to her or herself offering up derision on a plate, like it was a palatable assortment of cheese and crackers?

The sound of sirens reassured her. This was her world, and she was comfortable in it. Then she looked down at her attire and winced as she realized she wore boxer shorts, a thin tank top, and flip-flops. Not exactly fitting for her position.

The patrolmen on night duty had arrived quickly.

Both gave her a second glance, then looked quickly away, and turned to their duties. They began to scour the house while Sam tried to rouse her father. He finally sat up, groggy and disoriented and very cranky. At least as cranky as he got.

"Oh, for hell's sake, Sam. Why didn't you just wake me up? I would have told you where to find her."

Never mind that Sam had tried, unsuccessfully, to rouse him for quite a while. And she believed there was a killer on the loose in Kanesville. And she had received a phone call from her parents' house—a phone call her father denied making. *Just disregard all that, Dad, and pretend nothing is wrong, like usual.* She knew he was telling the truth about being asleep and not making the phone call. He always fell asleep during the 9:00 news on Channel 13, after he set the sleep timer on his bedroom television. And he never moved again until morning.

"Why didn't you just ask me where's she been?"

"Hey, where have you been? You know you are going to get caught, Amy. You have to stop this."

"Oh, please. No one knows I was gone. Who cares? Just let it go."

The words in her head stopped Sam cold. It wasn't just Callie's voice, this time, but also Amy's. Sam tried to remember more, but nothing came to her. Her father's words, so similar, had triggered it. Was it a memory? She shook it off.

"Wait a minute, what do you mean you know where to find her? She's done this before?"

Sam's father sighed harshly and asked for his robe, covering up quickly and glaring at the patrolmen who had invaded his bedroom. He looked at Sam, his eyebrows a low, menacing warning sign, one she had known to heed as a child. But she wasn't a child anymore, and this was serious.

"Dad? She's done this before?"

He sighed, and all the fire went out of him. Sam had been a little surprised to see it there in the first place, because it had been so many years since he'd been anything but weary and resigned.

He jerked his head in the direction of the backyard, and she followed behind as he led her out the back door and into the large, tree-filled space behind the house. The two patrolmen followed closely behind.

And then she saw the immobile white shape at the base of the largest tree, the peach tree where Callie had died. Lying among the tangled, bumpy roots that had forced their way out of the ground, facedown, almost in supplication, was her mother.

THIRTEEN

Paul sat on the couch, staring forward at a black television screen. To the outside world, he probably looked like a man entranced by a basketball game, intense television program or movie. In his line of work, maybe even an LDS inspirational video. Except there was no residual glare from the television screen. No power switched on. He stared at the black. Waiting. Waiting for something that would never happen.

In this room, everything looked normal. He looked normal. As long as his visitors didn't stray from this room, no one would ever wonder about him. No one would ever say, "I don't think he ever got over the accident."

No one ever got past this room.

Paul supposed that he was always going to be waiting for her to be there when he came home. To look up at him as he walked through the door and say, "Hi, honey, how was your day?" Trite, he knew. But he missed her. He would settle for trite.

He was responsible for her death, but in some ways so was Sam. She didn't realize it, of course. She had walked away without a backward glance.

Liar. You walked away. Took the coward's way out, and went on a mission, knowing full well you had left her . . . . Well.

He didn't want to go there again. Not tonight. It was the reason he was a seminary teacher. It was the reason he did all the things he did. He was atoning. He'd known that for a long time.

It was easy to imagine the God he loved forgiving others. Him? Not so much.

He missed her. And he missed Sam. And he missed the children he had barely had a chance to know.

Sam. Just the thought of her made the guilt roil through his stomach. Sam had been the reason. For all of it.

The worst of it was, his wife had never even known how much he loved her. She died thinking he carried a torch for someone else. Did he? If he did, why did he miss his wife so much? Every. Single. Day.

How do you continue to live normally when the worst comes to visit? How do you walk and breathe and act as though nothing is wrong when the devil comes calling at your door and hands you the death card? Even worse, when you know you are responsible, how do you manage to put one foot in front of the other the next day? And the next. And the next . . .

Paul had been taught all his life that as long as one lived the principles of the Gospel—i.e., going to church, paying a full tithe, attending the temple regularly, living the law of chastity—his reward would be great.

Paul's problem was that reward seemed hopelessly empty now. Now he was all alone, filled with despair, missing the woman he had killed and housing unhealthy emotions toward the woman he had abandoned.

When he sat with his colleagues at testimonials and meetings, he listened to them talk about the last days, the second coming of Christ, the Celestial Kingdom. And he wanted to scream. He wanted to yell, "This would be a good time. Now would be good!" Because this life was completely and utterly empty.

How I am supposed to walk on, every day, empty, unfulfilled, until that time comes? I am only human. I have needs. And they are stirring again. She makes me feel things I shouldn't feel.

He was aware of a cramping in his hands and looked down to see he had his fists clinched tightly into balls, his fingers white. Sharp pains arced through the digits as he spread them out, opening up and closing the fist, regaining the feeling he had lost. If only the loss of real life could be solved as easily as the loss of circulation in his hand. Just open it up, move it a bit, and everything comes back to where it was before.

Before. Sam. She belonged to before. Before he had met his beloved wife. And the feelings Sam brought up in him were primal, and wrong.

What would happen if he acted on these strange, primal feelings? Would he lose his place in Heaven? Would he be destined for a life on the Terrestial plane, the lowest of God's three kingdoms?

Would it be worth it?

Did you really just ask yourself that question?

If he were to hurry it up, worried about his eternal salvation as well as his burning loneliness and desire for a woman who was against everything he believed in, he wouldn't get that reward. Suicide was against God's laws.

He would just have to wait, living as an empty shell, until he could rejoin his wife and children in the Celestial Kingdom. Never again touching a woman. Never again feeling skin against skin. Never touching Sam's quivering upper lip.

His heart pounded in his chest as he dropped his head into his hands and considered his dilemma. Sam had become his problem. His obstacle in the pathway leading to his Savior's kingdom.

What was he supposed to do? Continue to get up every day and shower, shave, and get dressed. Go to work. Teach teenage children the principles of the Mormon Gospel and when they asked him questions answer like he knew the secrets of God's kingdom.

He was a lonely, flawed man, responsible for his wife's death and desirous of activities treacherous to his eternal salvation.

Or so the teachings said.

Do I believe this doctrine? It's all I've ever known. Sometimes I wonder. Sometimes I wonder how it could be this way. And I know my questioning of my faith, alone, is a great travesty. I don't know how to change this.

What he did know was he loved his wife. He had treasured her.

And he'd killed her.

FOURTEEN

Ruthie Montgomery, never terribly compliant, was in no hurry to move. It took quite a while for them to get her to leave the base of the tree, and one of the patrolmen insisted they should call the paramedics, even though Sam's father insisted that Ruthie's lack of response was a normal state.

"Dad, maybe she should be checked out in the hospital."

"Sammy, this is ridiculous; she comes out here several times a week. I keep telling you kids she is still *in there,* and no one listens. Well, this is just an example."

"Then maybe this is a good sign, Dad, and if we get her help, maybe she'll really come back to us. Isn't that what you want?"

He stood, silent and staring, his face only half-lit by the bright spotlight he had turned on to light the backyard. The rest of his profile hid in mistrust and anger, and maybe a little bit of fear. He'd been living this way for so long, if things were to change, what would happen to him? Sam wondered if he would even be able to cope with it.

"Dad, please. Let's get her checked out. She called my house tonight. Called it. Found the phone number, somewhere, and called. That's progress."

Her father stayed silent. Sam felt tears well up in her eyes, and she closed them tightly, not willing to cry in front of these patrolmen she outranked. It was hard enough to be the only woman on the squad, but any sign of weakness would be the crack through which the derision and disdain would enter. Bad enough she stood before them barely clothed.

"Sammy," her father said, his voice gentle. "That will cost money, and that's something we don't have a lot of. Medicare only pays so much. There is always something left over for me. And I don't have it." Her mother's condition had forced Sam's father's early retirement from his civilian job at Hill Air Force Base, and she knew that finances were a constant concern. The Church had stepped in to help many times, especially when she was growing up and still dependent on her parents for her basic needs. Hand-me-downs. Church welfare. The bishop's storehouse. A large lump formed in Sam's throat and she wanted to scream, to yell, to fight, to do anything to remove it. She didn't want anyone's pity, but she saw it clearly on the faces of the two patrolmen.

She shook her head angrily and glared at the one she knew as Traydar. So called because he had a sense for when someone would be speeding up Kanesville's main east–west road and he made a lot of revenue for the town. His name was Trey Olsen.

He looked away hastily, unsure why he was the victim of this particular glare, not knowing Sam was just protecting herself, her family, her reputation.

She steeled herself for her father's reaction, and the resulting pity and sympathy she would feel from the two patrolmen who had been forced into this highly personal drama.

"Dad, I'll pay for it. Whatever is left, send the bill to me, but please. Please let's get her checked out."

"Sam . . ."

"Dad. This has gone on long enough. Please, do this for me. If they say there is nothing they can do, then I will never ask again. Just do this one thing. Please. For me."

This time the tears welled up in her father's eyes, and she saw the years of frustration, fear, and, even worse, desperation painted across his face. But she knew that now was the time to stand firm. She was an adult now, a police officer, trained to deal with crisis and conflict. No more little Sam, the one who lost her way when Callie died.

"Dad, it's time to get help. It's time to admit you can't do this anymore. It's time. It's just . . . It's just time."

Sam knew she was repeating herself, but she couldn't think of any other way to phrase it.

"Fine," her father said, reaching up quickly to wipe away a stray tear that had begun to course down his weathered cheek. "Fine, just call the paramedics. And when you get the bill, you just remember that I said no, this was not necessary. And it's not going to help. It's time you grew to love your mother for what she is, instead of trying to fix her."

He turned and walked away, his shoulders hunched,

his back curved, his pace shuffling and almost bear-like. He had become old in the past few years, older than his seventy-five years even.

Grief aged people. Sam should know. Today, she felt like she was 102.

"Call the bus," she said to Olsen. Then she knelt down and stroked her mother's arm, even though there was no response from the prone woman. "It's going to be okay, Momma. I know it doesn't feel like it, but I promise, it's going to be fine."

There was no response. No reaction. Just like it had been for so many years, except now Sam felt a quickening of her heart. Something was different here. The phone call. And her mother had moved her head, abruptly and roughly. Ruthie Montgomery had reacted. Sam had seen it.

Could they find Ruthie again, lost as she was in the maelstrom of grief and loss? Sam was damn sure going to try.

FIFTEEN

Late August, nearly every day dawned hot and dry in northern Utah. Usually, the sunshine picked up Sam's mood, but not after the events of the evening before.

It was lunchtime, and as usual, D-Ray was holding court.

"Gage is a pansy-ass name," D-Ray said to Sam, speaking around the McDonald's fries he was shoveling into his mouth.

The "pansy ass" D-Ray referred to had been sitting outside Sam's house this morning, leaning against her department car. Again. Holding two coffee cups from the local Starbucks.

"Don't you ever give up?" she'd asked tersely.

"No. It's why I am so good at what I do."

"Fine. I'll take the coffee." Sam reached out and accepted the cup, then asked him to move out of her way.

"Sam, when are you going to talk to me?"

"How about at two? In the conference room at the station. We'll have a powwow. Sound good?" She didn't wait for an answer. She got into her car, he stepped away from it, and she drove off.

And now she was ready to beat someone to death.

As she sat with D-Ray in the unmarked cruiser in the McDonald's parking lot, he seemed a likely target. Sam sipped at a Diet Coke while D-Ray polished off more food than a human being should ever consume in one meal. She was tired and cranky. The previous night's events had set her mind to racing, especially after she and her father had left the hospital. Her mother had been admitted into the psych ward of McKay-Dee Hospital for testing.

Sam's father had spoken little as they drove together to the hospital behind the ambulance. He gave only yes or no answers when the medical staff asked him questions, and the look on his face was one of resentment and anger.

Then Sam had driven him back home. He sat silent and brooding in the seat next to her, staring out the window into the darkness. His own form of a catatonic stupor. He wouldn't let her come in, and slammed the door as he exited her car, shuffling toward his dark house, which only hours earlier had been filled with people and light as they searched for Sam's mother.

Sam had removed the only reason her father had for living. Whether or not it should be that way was not the point. As she watched him, she wondered if she had made a big mistake. A single light came on as he entered the house, then went out just as quickly. Was this really about her? Did she really need to force this issue?

D-Ray's repetitive chewing brought her back to the present and began to eat at her last solid nerve. She turned to glare at him. "You are going to die before you hit fifty," she told him crossly. "Your arteries will be so clogged with fat that your blood cells won't be able to get through. You probably have fat running through your body instead of blood."

"You on the rag?" D-Ray asked, a look of complete innocence on his face, even though he knew how offensive the comment was.

She gave him a look that could stop a perp cold. It didn't even faze D-Ray. He knew her too well.

"Does your momma know you eat with that mouth?" she said.

D-Ray's face darkened, and he chewed away with more gusto, turning away from her. It was a low blow, but he deserved it. The "rag" comment was too far.

"Sorry about making fun of Gage's pansy-ass name," he said, without looking at her.

"Sorry about bringing up your momma," she shot back. She'd immediately regretted telling D-Ray that Gage had shown up at her house on Sunday and then again this morning. The words hadn't been out of her mouth more than two seconds when she realized what she had said—and wished she could take them back. This was a man's world, and she needed to remember the rules. Sharing information like the fact that an old love had shown up uninvited, on the day she was tired, vulnerable, overwhelmed, and nervous about solving this difficult case, could only lead to chaos, derision, and sexist remarks. Even from D-Ray.

"Don't talk about my momma, Sam." He glowered at her, waiting for the fight to move into the ring.

They could go on like this all day. Sam had got up with a dark cloud over her head. Might as well have D-Ray join her. Only thing that would shake off this particular crankfest would be a murder or something equally adrenaline filled.

"I've become the person I never wanted to be," she admitted aloud. "Wishing something awful would happen so I can just work the case and not worry about anything else."

"Sam?"

"Yeah, D-Ray?"

"If you don't talk about my momma, I won't talk about yours."

Sam felt the anger stirring in the pit of her stomach. They hadn't discussed it, but she knew he was aware of the events of the night before. Everyone in the office knew. But D-Ray wouldn't push. He would wait for her to open up. To say something first. And she wasn't talking. She turned to him to give him an angry retort, just as the car radio squawked to life.

"Thank God. I was going to have to shoot you," she murmured as she took the call.

They rode in silence to the scene of a family dispute. Nothing like a good domestic to clear the air, make you forget that your mother was a mental vegetable and your partner's mother a closet alcoholic.

"So, what do you have for me?" Chief Roberson asked as he lounged in the door of her cubicle, his solid shoulder butted up against the flimsy wall, making Sam worry that any minute the divider would fall.

He wore a cheap suit coat, a too-tight white shirt, and a necktie that looked like a bad Father's Day present. Probably the same brand she had given her own father, year after year. Roberson's slacks were neatly pressed but ill fitting, and his hair was about sixteen strands shy of a bad comb-over. They could expect that in the next few months, she knew. Maybe sooner, if they didn't solve this case.

"I've arranged for the conference room at two p.m.," Sam told him. "We'll go over everything then, if that's okay. I just have a few phone calls to make."

"Two it is. Did you tell Flint?"

"Yes, Chief, I did," she said, working hard to keep her voice pleasant. "We have to have the whole *team* there."

Sam picked up the phone, gritting her teeth as the chief walked away. The team. She punched in the number of the crime lab, only to learn there was no new evidence. No prints or foreign materials. Next, she called the medical examiner, who had not yet started on Jeremiah Malone's autopsy. Sam requested copies of the other two victims' autopsies and was promised they would be e-mailed to her by late afternoon. She pressed him to get to Jeremiah's quickly.

"Two other suicides, an accidental shooting, and a murder-suicide this week, Sam. Sorry, I'm back-logged," said the ME, weariness lacing his voice. "I took this job because Smithland County was such a nice community. Can't figure out why there's so much death."

The next call was to Paul Carson's cell, checking on the list of cleaning people she had asked him to provide. It went to voice mail, and she left a brief message.

After Sam hung up, she looked at her watch and saw it was 1:55 p.m. Just enough time to get set up in the conference room and be composed and ready for action when the rest arrived.

She walked down the hallway to the conference

room, only to find that Gage was already waiting, two cups of coffee in front of him.

"This appealing to my caffeine addiction has got to stop," she said.

"How do you know this is for you?" he asked her, a half grin emphasizing the large dimple on his right cheek.

"Oh, sorry. I just assumed, because every time you show up you're trying to ply me with—"

"I was kidding. It is for you." Gage pushed the coffee cup toward her.

She took it, then purposely walked to the far side of the square table and sat down. "Coffee isn't my only vice, you know," she said, then regretted it.

"I was hoping."

She prayed she wasn't blushing, and was grateful to see the chief and D-Ray saunter in together, discussing the latest results of some sporting event. When everyone was seated, the chief spoke.

"Okay, first of all, Sam, is there anything new on the case?"

"No, unfortunately. I called the ME, and he hasn't gotten to the autopsy of Jeremiah Malone. Something about a few other deaths in the county."

The chief sighed loudly.

"There is no new information from the crime lab, and the computer from the seminary building is proving useless. Whoever made the slide show did it at the seminary building, or is one hell of a computer hacker. I'm still waiting for the list of people who had access to the computer. I'll stay on top of Carson to get that. And I have some appointments set up with Jeremiah's friends."

"That's it?" Roberson said, a scowl on his ruddy face. His furry eyebrows—which seemed to have more hair than his head—knitted together as he spoke.

"Yes, unfortunately, that's all."

"The media is all over this, Sam, and you know how they are. Everything is getting twisted, and it looks like we aren't doing our job."

"They are still officially suicides," she reminded him.

"Officially. But somebody is rumbling. Three suicides? That's a lot."

"Three too many," Sam said wryly.

"Yeah, yeah, you know what I mean. Three suicides, in three months. That reporter from Channel Five, you know, the . . . er, aggressive one? She's been calling for me since eight a.m. Wants an on-camera interview. Has a few questions."

Sam knew the reporter he was referring to, and she flinched a bit as she considered his words. Pamela Nixon *was* a bitch, really. Aggressive, loudmouthed, pushy, underhanded. She would do whatever it took to get the story. Just like thousands of other female reporters across the United States. Of course, here in Utah, Pamela's job was made that much harder by the male domination of police forces and public offices and, of course, the belief in Mormon male priesthood authority.

It just made Pamela Nixon bitchier. She'd told Sam, once, that it didn't matter what she said or did, if she asked the wrong question or pushed the wrong male suit, she was going to get labeled as a bitch. Might as well live up to it and own the title.

That was back when Sam was still working for the Salt Lake City Police Department—before she decided to take her upbringing head-on and move back to her childhood town. *Dumb idea, Sam. You're smarter than that. If you are going to be a coward, you just should have stayed where you were. Because I told you, something is rotten here. Rotten.*

Callie's voice rang through her head, and Sam frowned, trying to shake it off. It was rarely this strong, not during the day.

"You really aren't clinging to the theory that these are suicides, are you?" Gage asked Sam pointedly.

"Do we have proof that they aren't?" she countered.

"A lot of damn coincidences if they are," he answered.

"Kids make suicide pacts all the time. You read about it on the news," D-Ray interjected. "It's not that rare."

"No, it's not. But we need to make sure that's what we are dealing with," the chief said. "Keep on it, all of you. I want this resolved. If these kids had a suicide pact, dammit, I want you to find it."

And bury it right alongside their bodies.

No one wanted to think that their community held a secret that led to teen suicides. But a murderer would be even worse. A serial murderer who couldn't be stopped because they were too busy looking at suicides.

Even though you all know that's not what's happening.

"Chief? I think you're a damned smart man," Sam said, "And I think you know, just like I know, that these aren't suicides or some suicide pact. Gage is right. It's too well thought out. Too organized. Too methodical. Pictures of each body taken postmortem."

"Suicide would be better," he said tersely. She didn't take offense. She knew what he meant.

"Push the ME on the autopsy. They need to get their shit in order and get it done. Push some buttons, Sam. This is Kanesville, for hell's sake. These son-of-a-bitching things do not happen here."

"I will," she assured him, slightly worried about the bright red shade of his face. He was not a thin man or in good shape, and a coronary might not be that far off. The more upset he was, the more he cursed. She knew that every Sunday Chief Roberson put on his Sunday best and sat up in front of his ward, serving as a first counselor in the bishopric. His language was undoubtedly cleaner at his church meetings, but it was a funny thing about cops and soldiers. It didn't matter where you were or what religion you espoused . . . everything you saw and dealt with had to have an outlet. And one of those outlets was cursing. Sometimes it was alcohol. And sometimes it was even worse. Whenever you touched the dark side, you never came back whole. And something always tagged along.

Sam knew. She'd been the one to find Callie hanging from the biggest peach tree in the family's backyard. Sam's mind had since blocked out most of it.

But something always tagged along.

SIXTEEN

The meeting dispersed with Sam sending D-Ray off to interview the high-school football coach. D-Ray and the chief resumed their discussion on sports as they left the conference room. Gage followed closely behind Sam, so close he would run into her if she stopped suddenly.

"So, boss, what's my assignment?" he asked, more than a hint of needling in his voice.

"You could go through the Dumpsters behind the seminary building and look for evidence," she suggested, an innocent look on her face. He knew, as she did, that the job of sorting garbage had already been handled by two uniforms and, as usual, nothing had come up.

"I'll just come with you," he said.

Panic filled her stomach. She thought fast. "Actually, I do have a job for you. I'm going to interview Devin Templeton, Jeremiah's best friend. I also need to meet with Brother Eldon Green, his ward youth leader.

You can do that. I never do really well with the men, since I don't have the, uh, priesthood."

Gage grinned at her, making her stomach churn with frustration. He knew she did not want to be alone with him. She gave him Brother Green's number and sent him on his way, relief flowing through her system as they drove off in different directions.

Sam drove through the streets of Kanesville slower than usual, taking time to peruse the town's newer portion of high-end suburban homes. She eyed the fancy brick-and-stucco houses and wondered what evils lurked inside the beautiful exteriors.

The city was an interesting mix of new and old, with a history dating back to pioneer times, although the town fathers had recently allowed two very old buildings—a pioneer cabin and the original city hall—to be destroyed to make way for parking lots. The Kanesville tabernacle had hosted one of the oldest structures in the town, but the Church dictated that parking was more important than a building.

Sam didn't understand this dichotomy of progress and history. She remembered hearing about the Mormon pioneers in church classes almost every Sunday. The martyrs, the deaths, and the horrible travesties the pioneers endured as they crossed the plains, wanting only to be able to worship God's true Gospel. That lesson was underscored with trips to the actual places her ancestors lived, worked, and worshiped.

Soon, those stories would be nothing more than *stories*. How would the younger generation take these tales with no physical reminder that the people in them had actually lived?

Would the annual "Pioneer Trek"—where the Church

attempted to re-create the actual conditions without killing off the teenagers—be enough?

These kids were raised on Facebook, cell phones, and instant proof. Would the Church slowly start to die away?

Sam slowed as she reached 4799 Green Street, a large, stately cream and redbrick two-story that could have housed two to six families, as far as she could tell.

Undoubtedly, the boy she was here to see went on the Pioneer Trek every year; and probably smuggled in his iPhone, taking pictures along the way, documenting his journey, uploading them to a social networking site seconds after they were taken.

"So, did your friend Jeremiah act like he was depressed? Did he ever talk about taking his own life?" Sam asked the morose, broad-chested, handsome teen sitting in the easy chair across from her. His name was Devin Templeton, but he went by "Slick," for reasons she could not quite fathom. He did not look slick right now. Maybe a little nervous, belligerent, and sporting an arrogant façade, but underneath was a skeleton of pure fear. Why?

They sat in his living room, with his mother hovering not too far away in the kitchen, making kitchen noises, while trying, Sam knew, to listen to every word. The father sat in the other chair across from Sam, silent, arms folded, lips pursed.

Patriarchy. Had to love it. Until it got in the way of doing your job.

"He wasn't depressed," Slick said, finally answering her question. "He was the toughest guy I knew. Always up for fun, and always up for a par— I mean up to go out and have a good time." He shot a nervous glance at his father, then looked back at her.

"So no indicators that he was having problems at home, or at school? Nothing that might make him so depressed that he wanted to kill himself?" Sam tried to keep her tone gentle, but the boy's attitude was not helping. There was grief there. She could see it, underneath the layers of fear, apprehension, and anger. But it was almost buried, which was not common in teens. She'd grown to learn that pretty much whatever they were feeling at the time was splayed out for everyone to see in living color. Not here. He was hiding something.

"He wasn't depressed." Slick's words were stubborn, recalcitrant, fired at her like pellets from a BB gun—intended to sting but not seriously injure.

"No girlfriend problems, or maybe problems with his grades?"

"I told you, no! He was fine. Just fine."

"Devin," his father chided, anger furrowing his brow. "That is not respectful. You apologize."

"Sorry," Devin said. Slick was gone. Banished to the nether regions by a father's influence and priesthood authority.

"Look, I understand this is hard. You've lost a good friend." Sam leaned forward and caught Devin's eyes. "I'm sorry I have to question you like this. But we are trying to find out what happened to Jeremiah. And you knew him best. You were his best bud, right?"

Devin looked away and tightened his lips, closing and opening his eyes a few times, to blink away tears. "He was my best friend," he said, without looking at her. "He didn't kill himself. He wouldn't."

"So you think something else happened? Maybe an accidental death?"

He pursed his lips tighter and didn't speak.

"Look, this is really hard for him," Eric Templeton said, rising from his chair next to his son's. He wore a short-sleeved shirt that showed his garment line, khaki dress pants, and the frazzled look of a father in over his head. He was nearly bald, with a rather large nose, and his face was dotted with the remnants of freckles that would have made him hard to take seriously. He looked kind and rather effeminate and nothing like his son. "He just lost his best friend. I know you're trying to do what's right, but I have to think of my son, and I don't think he has any information that will help you."

Sam didn't agree. She also knew that if the father had not been sitting there, she could have gotten more out of the boy. But Eric Templeton wasn't going anywhere. He made that clear from the very beginning.

"I'm not just trying to do what's right, Mr. Templeton," Sam said. "I'm trying to find out what happened to a seventeen-year-old boy who is now lying on a slab at the morgue."

Sam heard a gasp from the mother in the kitchen and instantly regretted her words, but she would never take them back. Sometimes it was necessary to tread roughly on the graves of the dead in order to get them to rise.

Eric Templeton's lips tightened, and he stood. Devin's eyes widened and a tear escaped, trailing down his cheek, leaving a path of moisture and regret. He swiped at it angrily with a fisted hand.

"I think you are out of line here, Detective Montgomery," Mr. Templeton said. He didn't raise his voice, but Sam knew this was his "tough" stance. "He doesn't know anything. He's grieving. This needs to end now."

"It may end now for you," Sam said softly. "But there are two parents who have no idea what happened to their son. They woke up one day, a normal day, and their whole world imploded. They need to know what happened. They need to be able to put this to rest, in order to move on."

And then Devin "Slick" Templeton surprised her.

"And so do I," he said, his voice a mere whisper. "Dad, I need to do this on my own."

Eric Templeton left the room reluctantly, but not before leaning down and whispering in his son's ear. Devin shook his head sharply, and his father's face tightened, a grimace of worry. He left the room and headed into the kitchen area, where Sarah Templeton was moving pots and pans around, apparently cooking—or pretending to be busy.

"What did he say to you?" Sam asked, her voice low and conversational.

"He wanted to give me a blessing," Devin said, a grimace of disgust crossing his face. "It's his answer for everything."

"My dad's the same way," Sam said.

"You're Mormon?" Devin asked, surprise crossing his face, and his eyes shifted to her sleeveless ribbed tank. She'd removed her jacket shortly after they started the interview. One sure way to tell a Mormon from a non-Mormon, at least in Sam's age bracket, was the evidence of garments.

"Born and raised. Not really practicing," Sam admitted calmly.

Devin cocked his head, a dimple in his cheek appearing as he gave her a breathtaking smile. His eyes were a dark, solid blue, and Sam figured he made many a young girl's heart flutter. But she wasn't impressed. She'd heard about his reputation—and Jeremiah Malone's—as a hard partier and ladies' man. As D-Ray so crassly put it, the boy liked to "dip his wick."

"Why?" he asked. "Why don't you go to church anymore?"

"It's a long story. You wouldn't be interested."

"So you're an apostate?" he asked, his face suddenly arrogant, his demeanor cocky.

"No, I'd say I'm a detective," Sam answered coolly. Her attempt at putting him at ease had failed. He had, instead, decided she was less worthy and thus did not deserve his respect.

"Yeah," Devin said, his look darkening. "But I don't think I have much to say to you."

"I thought you wanted to know what happened to your friend," Sam said.

"I do. But I don't think you'll figure it out."

"Why's that?"

"You just won't. You can't."

"Because I'm not a guy? Because I don't have the priesthood?" Sam guessed.

"I didn't say that." Devin sat back and crossed his arms. All his earlier charm of the moment before was gone. He was back to being morose, a step away from childlike grief, teetering on the edge of adulthood and yet not ready to dive into the pit.

Life, the impish devil, was going to push him right in. He just didn't know it yet.

"Then why?"

"Because you can't understand it. I don't understand it."

"What don't you understand, Devin?"

"How the whole world could turn upside down. Things were normal, the usual, everything going on like it always had, and then one day it just switched. And they started dying." His voice lowered as he spoke, and he looked around nervously.

"What do you mean by things just switched?"

"Look, you aren't *that* old. You know how high school is. You have to remember. There are groups and everybody has a place."

Sam grimaced a bit at the "*that* old" comment but let it slide. She knew he had a direction, and she wanted to guide him there with as little interference as possible.

"I remember."

"Well, I've known most of these kids all my life. And they all know where they fit. The jocks hang with the jocks, the band geeks with the band geeks, the hot girls with the other hot girls. . . ." He looked up at her and flushed a bit, smiling at her, trying to look über-cool. "I bet you were a hot girl."

Sam's eyes widened. She still hadn't recovered from the "*that* old" comment. Now she was a "hot girl"?

"Uh, well, you'd be surprised."

"You were a cheerleader, right?"

"No, I ran track."

"Oh." He looked a little disappointed. And Sam fought back the urge to shake her head a bit, trying to rid herself of the image of this boy imagining her in a cheerleading uniform.

"Anyway, I know how it goes. Everybody has a place. Things are easy to understand." She smiled disarmingly at him while inside she winced. She didn't like this type of police work, but it was opening him up and she was going to stick with it.

"Yeah, well, then this new girl came to school. Bethany. Moved here from Germany, or somewhere. Mom's in the military. And she's not Mormon, but she's hot, and she fit in with the other girls. Until she got into a fight with Whit. And it's because Whit was jealous. She caught Jeremiah kissing Bethany after a game one night. Jer wouldn't have anything to do with Whit after that, because she was being such a bi—uh, well, a . . ."

"Go on, Devin."

"Well, so after Jer dumped Whit, she told everyone the truth about Bethany. She was a slut in Germany, and had sex a lot, and Whit said she even got pregnant and had an abortion. Bethany told her all about it when they had a sleepover one night."

Ah, girls. Teenage boys would just beat the shit out of each other and then shake hands and move on. With girls, it was a lifetime of turning your back and waiting for the knife to be inserted.

"Sounds like typical teenage stuff, Devin."

"Yeah, but then Tawny died. And then Madison."

Sam shook her head slightly, still not getting the connection. "Well, those both appeared to be suicides, and I'm not sure what either had to do with Jeremiah or . . ."

"Those girls? They're Whit's friends. Two of her best friends."

Sam tried to lead Devin a little more. "So you think Bethany had something to do with it?"

"You do the math."

"What about Bethany and Jeremiah?"

"He dumped her. She was a slut, just like Whit said." He flushed again but looked defiant this time.

"Why didn't you talk to the authorities after the girls died? Tell them you suspected something?" Sam felt a burning in her stomach as she considered the other two deaths, which had been largely handled by Kanesville uniforms and Smithland County deputies.

"You're the first cop who ever bothered to ask whether or not I think they killed themselves. I never thought they did. None of us did."

"But no one said anything?"

He just shook his head.

"And you think Bethany is somehow involved."

He raised his eyebrows and then looked away, the cocky look fading as his father reentered the room. "You about done here? Devin has homework, and I think he's been through enough trauma."

"I think I'm done for now," Sam said, rising from the couch. "Thanks for the help, Devin. Oh, one more thing."

"Yeah, what?"

"Do Bethany and Whit have last names?"

"Bethany Evans and Whitney Marcusen."

Sam felt the blood drain from her face.

SEVENTEEN

Sam's oldest sister, Susanna, had married young, right out of high school. Her beau, Roger Marcusen, was a returned Mormon missionary from an upstanding Kanesville family. Still, her father had been dead set against the marriage, which Susanna defiantly told the family would take place the Saturday after high school graduation.

Her mother, of course, had no opinion at all. She had long since stopped functioning as a human and become little more than a living, breathing home accessory.

Susanna had been filling the role of matriarch in the Montgomery family since the day Callie had been found hanging from the peach tree in the backyard. Sam was distraught at the loss of her mother figure.

"But who will comb my hair, Sissy?" Sam had cried, tears welling in her eyes as Susanna packed up her things the day before she prepared to move into an apartment with her new husband.

"Amy will help you," Susanna said, wiping at her

own tears. She leaned down and pulled Sam close to her. "Look, baby, I have to go. I have to have my own life, and this is the only way. You understand, right?"

Sam had not understood at all. But Susanna had left and Amy had never combed Sam's hair, then had disappeared from their lives. Sam had lived the rest of her childhood in a rough-and-tumble scrape of altercations with neighborhood children, lectures from the Mormon sisters about cleanliness and bathing, wearing dresses, doing your hair up and ladylike behavior, and a desire to right the wrongs of the world.

In a way, Susanna's departure, so wrong in Sam's mind, was the beginning of her law enforcement career.

Now she stood in Sus's living room, wondering how to tell her that she feared her own daughter, Whitney, was somehow entangled in what looked more and more like a series of murders.

"Well, this is a surprise," Susanna said, wiping her hands on a dish towel she had carried in from the kitchen. "I can't remember the last time you stopped by to visit. What's the occasion?"

There was a slightly bitter cast to Sus's tone, and her features were pinched, the wrinkles on her forehead and around her eyes prominent. Underneath her dark brown orbs were deep shadows of unmet dreams and wasted potential. She hadn't bothered with her hair in years, usually just pulling it back into a ponytail, the gray showing through the streaks of brown. Susanna had taken after their mother, who also was a natural brunette, while Sam had been gifted with the light blond, thin, and fine hair from her father's side of the family. They did not look like sisters.

After she married, Susanna had quickly become pregnant, and two of those children were already grown, one a returned Mormon missionary now attending Brigham Young University, the other serving his time in the Ukraine, tracting for potential members of the Church of Jesus Christ of Latter-day Saints and sending desperate letters home to his family, begging to be allowed to return without finishing out his time.

Susanna was torn between wanting her son to "return with honor" and wanting to rush to the airport and bring him home herself, keeping him safe from the terrible ills of a world that was violent and war torn.

Roger Marcusen was strictly on the "return with honor" side. He'd served his own foreign mission, to Brazil, returning home with stories of honor and the powerful nature of the Gospel, and he wasn't about to let one of his boys besmirch that tradition. Besides, he said, "missions make boys grow up."

Sam wasn't so sure. She'd seen the missionaries drive through a neighborhood at top speed, barely missing small children or pedestrians. They were still teenage boys, full of testosterone and hell-bent on having fun. Grow up at nineteen? Why? Why was this so important? Wasn't nineteen when teenage boys were still acting like morons, drinking too much, and chasing girls who were easy and cheap, and not thinking about tomorrow and eternity?

Not here.

Sam knew all this information about her nephew not because she was her sister's confidante, but because she spent many hours in her father's kitchen, where he shared the news of her sister with her and "Ruthie," offering up family secrets like the chamomile tea that helped him sleep through one more lonely night, his mentally vacant wife by his side.

Sam's father had been desperate for companionship for years. No one else seemed to see it but her, and so she had learned a lot of family secrets, growing up fast, knowing more about her sisters than they would ever have wanted her to know. But Susanna was really the only one left to see. Callie was long dead. Amy had left the state. And the ward members were busy trying to help her father cope with her mother—his personal desires not at the top of their list.

So he talked to Sam and Ruthie. And Sam found out that the upstanding Roger had turned out to be a serial adulterer. And the reason Amelia moved out of state was because she'd been one of the women he'd had an affair with.

Sam was never quite sure why her father gave her all this information. He handed it to her on a plate, like dessert. Was it because she was the only one who listened? Or the only one who actually heard what he said?

"What's this about, Sam? You look like the cat that swallowed the canary?" Susanna said, a question in her voice. She sounded almost fearful.

"I don't think that's how I look. I don't feel smug right now."

"You know what I mean. What's up? This obviously isn't a social visit. You never just drop by."

"I haven't had a good reason to stop by," Sam said, feeling anger and betrayal burn in her stomach, and she hated herself for acting like the child she had been. She'd been so angry when Sus left. Would she ever get past this feeling of abandonment?

"Just visiting family isn't enough reason?"

"Look, is Whit here?"

"No, she's at cheer practice. Why are you asking about Whit?"

One would think stopping by her sister's house wouldn't bring so many questions, but this was Sam's life and it had never been normal.

"I need to talk to her about Jeremiah Malone's death."

Sus's face blanched and she swayed a little. "Why do you want to talk to Whit about that? What does she have to do with him? They just dated a few times. But she's still bothered by his death. She isn't sleeping well. Why do you need to bring it all out again?"

"Bring it out again? He just died, Sus. They haven't even buried him yet. This isn't going to ease up for quite a while."

"Well, I just don't know what you think Whit could possibly have to do with it."

"I just need to talk to her, Sissy," Sam said softly, using her childhood name for Susanna. "She knew each of the kids. Was really good friends with them, in fact."

Susanna blanched. "That doesn't make her involved."

"Sissy, what is wrong with you? Aren't you worried about her? I mean, if this is a suicide pact, aren't you worried that Whitney could be next—"

"Suicide pact! Are you kidding me? Did you really just say that to me? My daughter would never kill herself! Suicide pact?" Susanna was yelling so loud Sam took a step back, watching in dismay as her sister fell apart before her eyes.

"What kind of crap is this?" Susanna raved. "What

are you trying to say, that my child would do such a thing, such a terrible, terrible thing—"

"Whoa, Sissy, calm down," Sam said, stepping forward and putting a hand on her sister's shoulder. "You are out of control here. What's up? What's wrong?"

"I just can't believe that you—"

"Sissy, these are Whit's friends and, apparently, her most recent boyfriend. And they are dead. I have to do this. It's my job, but I'm concerned, believe me. And right now, I'm more concerned about you than anything else. You are falling apart. What the hell is going on?"

Susanna collapsed inwardly, her shoulders slumping, the fire leaving her eyes as quickly as it had entered. She shook her head, over and over, but didn't speak. Didn't seem to be able to speak.

Tears began to fall from her eyes, and she moved toward a chair and fell into it.

"Please, talk to me," Sam said gently, moving closer. "What's wrong?"

"This is not the life I thought I'd have," her sister whispered, wiping at the tears streaming down her face. "Roger Junior has been kicked out of BYU for violating the honor code. Pornography. Can you believe it? Jace hates his mission, and wants to come home. He feels like he's in jail, and I guess he is, because Roger won't let him come home early. Trapped in a foreign country with no one around to love him or help him. And Whit . . . Something's wrong with Whit. She's always been popular, sometimes saying or doing things I didn't like, but that's her, and who she ran with. Maybe a little wild, but I always watched her, always grounded her, always made sure she was behaving. But now . . . ."

"What?"

"I think she's pregnant," Susanna whispered, as though the words wouldn't be real if she kept the volume low enough. "A mother knows. And she hasn't had her period for several months. She is sick all the time, and she's nervous and anxious . . . ."

"Good God."

Susanna flinched at her sister's curse and then put her hand to her forehead.

"But, wasn't she dating Jeremiah Malone?"

"Yes. Yes, she was. And now he's dead, and won't be able to marry her. The whole world will know. And I'm not old enough to be a grandmother. And God knows that Roger is absolutely no help whenever life isn't picture perfect. He just disappears and . . . never mind."

Susanna's face portrayed unimaginable anguish, the sorrow lines deep across her forehead. A straying husband. A pregnant teenage daughter. Sam could not understand how her sister and so many others like her could keep going back to church, time and after time, trying to reason away the cruelties of life as "God's will."

God wanted everyone to suffer?

And the mental image of Sam's teenage niece pregnant was too much to comprehend. Whit was vain and sometimes cruel, more worried about clothes, looking cute, and boys than anything else. Sam liked her but couldn't help but wince when she was around her, knowing Whit was the kind of girl who would have teased Sam mercilessly when she'd been a motherless waif trying to find her way through life without guidance.

"Have you told her you know?"

"No, we haven't talked about it. I need to, but with everything that has happened in the past few months . . . ."

"Uh, Sis, this is one of those things that really can't be ignored."

"I know that," Susanna said, giving her a disgusted look. "And why are you acting all concerned anyway? You never come by, never call. You moved back to town months ago, and this is the first time you've been here since you returned. Why act so concerned now? You couldn't care less about me and my family."

"I've always cared, Sissy. I just had a hard time dealing with you leaving us. I felt betrayed, and your family was my competition. I'm sorry. I know this all goes back so long ago, and it's really juvenile, but it is what it is."

Susanna started to cry again. "I know. I know, Sam; I'm sorry. I'm such a mess today. I'm so worried. So worried about all of my kids. Worried about you. Worried about Mom and Dad. When does it ever get easier? When?"

"I don't know. I'm not sure it does. But I'm going to have to talk to Whit, Sissy. I'm sorry, but it's my job."

"I know," Susanna whispered. "I'm just afraid of what you might find out."

Sam sat in the bleachers of the Smithland High School gymnasium. She watched as Whit went through the motions of the cheers listlessly, the fourteen-member squad now down two members. The two dead girls had both been on the team, and they had been the closest of friends. Before, it had seemed like a sad set of tragedies. Now, it seemed like impending doom was ready to settle in. Would another of these girls be next? Would it be Whitney?

With her long reddish-brown hair, pert nose, full lips, and perfectly shaped body, petite Whitney had always had the attention of all the boys, and more than one girl's hatred. It didn't bother Whitney. Sam knew her niece was a little spoiled and pampered. But she didn't look that way right now. Today she looked tired, and scared.

The girls ended the practice and chattered aimlessly as they gathered up their pompoms and scattered clothes and stuffed them into their cheer bags. Sam rose from where she sat in the bleachers and headed down the wooden stairs, listening as a dull *plonk* sounded with each footfall.

This was the same high school Sam had attended, and it still smelled the same, looked the same. Brought back those same mixed emotions. Sam fought them away like pesky flies. This was her job, not some melodramatic movie.

Whitney watched her come, sitting on the gym floor, holding her pompoms. She didn't move, just watched as Sam drew closer. The other girls noticed her then, and the chatter stopped, and they began to back up a bit, perhaps sensing Sam was a different creature. Not one of them, a preppy, popular cheerleader.

"Hi, Whitney, hi, girls," Sam said.

"Hi, Aunt Sam," Whitney said, her voice still and surprisingly calm, though she looked as if the world were about to explode around her.

Most of the other cheerleaders gathered up their bags and skittered away, a few giving vague hellos. Others stood and watched, wondering what this was about, perhaps sensing trouble. Or something to gossip about later.

"We need to talk, Whit," Sam said gently.

"Yes, yes, we do," Whitney answered, again her voice calm, her face shattered.

"Is now a good time?"

"Let me just go put my things in my locker, okay?" Whitney said, and stood up shakily.

Sam reached out to steady her and she flinched and pulled away.

"I'll just wait here," Sam said, and watched as Whitney wobbled away. The other cheerleaders followed, sneaking glimpses back at Sam and then whispering to each other.

They all seemed to know who she was and what position she held. Her gun was covered by her light jacket and she hadn't pulled her shield out, but still, they all knew and they were all leery of her. Since when did good Mormon high-school students disrespect the police?

Especially cheerleaders?

Sam sat down on one of the hard benches and waited for Whitney to come. After about five minutes, Sam stood up and went into the locker room. It was empty. No chattering cheerleaders. No one. Including Whitney.

But there was a note on the floor, written on the same lined paper Sam had used years before when she was a student at this school. Written in red lipstick, the paper had only one word on it.

"Bethany."

EIGHTEEN

Sam went back to the police station after being ditched by Whitney. She'd tried calling Susanna but got no response.

"Learn anything?" she asked D-Ray as she walked past his cubicle and into her own.

"The football coach thinks they had a shot at a state title with Jeremiah as quarterback, but now there's no way," D-Ray said, rolling back on his chair to the edge of his cubicle and shooting a small foam basketball into a net he had attached to the wall. "Score. Two points. The crowd roars."

Sam rolled her eyes. "Let me rephrase the question. Did he have any information about Jeremiah Malone, and whether or not he was suicidal, or had a lot of enemies?"

"Nope. He's just crying in his Cheerios because the team is going to suck now. And apparently he has a phobia about dead bodies, because he is not looking forward to going to the funeral or viewing. He asked me if it would be open casket."

"Huh?"

"Yeah, what do I seem like, a mortician? Anyway, I'm headed home. Time for dinner and a movie with my girl. Unless Your Highness has anything else for me to do."

Sam shot him a look that would shrivel a plant. He just laughed.

"Night, Sam."

She sat down at her desk and looked through the pink message slips the secretary had left on her desk. The lady whose pet cat had been killed wondered if there had been any headway in the case. The local video store wanted to know if Sam had followed up on the graffiti they had found sprayed on the side of their building. Apparently, someone in the community regarded R-rated movies as "Smut and porn." Nothing about the suicides. One note from Pamela Nixon. That one made Sam wince.

She heard someone approach her cubicle and turned to see Gage standing there. "Well, according to Brother Green, Jeremiah was a fine young man. Did you know BYU was looking to sign him as a freshman? A freshman! Imagine that."

Sam couldn't help but chuckle. "Did you really think he was going to open up to you?"

"Then why did you send me?"

"Covering all the bases. He could have had some helpful information. You know that."

"Yeah, well, he didn't." Gage watched her for a moment, and she met his stare without backing down.

"So, you going to work all night, or can we get some dinner?"

"Gage—"

"Just a working dinner. I have some questions for you."

Sam sighed. "Not tonight. I have things to take care of."

"All work and no play make Sam a dull girl," he said, grinning at her.

She didn't return the smile. She might have to work with him, but she wasn't about to let her defenses down and have real conversations with him. She needed to concentrate on what she was doing here and not worry about a man who didn't believe in her skill as a police officer.

So she would play nice in the office. It was either that or kill him, and that didn't seem like a viable option.

"You look like you would rather shoot me than have dinner with me." An uncannily accurate assessment, Sam thought.

"I don't shoot for no reason. Just don't give me one."

Gage laughed. "It's just dinner, Sam. No strings attached. Nothing to be afraid of."

A challenge. He knew how to get to her, even now. And she could see the merriment in his eyes as he tried to paste an innocent look on his face.

His eyes crinkled in the corners, and his teeth flashed white against a permanent tan. He was a man who spent nearly every free minute outdoors, and the dark angles of his face showed it. Nothing fake or too smooth about him. Sam felt a familiar warmth pooling in her stomach and remembered what it had been like to purely like this man—his humor, his rough readiness and rock-solid core.

And she remembered his awe and what she had thought was respect the first time he saw her shoot at the firing range.

"Damn, Sam," he'd said. "You hit that target dead center."

"I'm a good shot."

"You aren't a good shot. You're a great shot."

"Thanks."

"Of course, it's a little different when you are shooting a target and when there's a live human being in front of you."

"What are you saying, Gage?"

"I'm just saying that you are a good shot. And I hope to hell you never have to find out what it means to kill another human being. Because when you aim, you aren't going to miss."

"Fine. Just dinner." Sam rose from her chair. He might think he'd won, but she knew better. This would be a working dinner. She would ply him with questions on his case in SLC.

They ended up at Sill's, and he ordered the mountainous hamburger and fries she always got when she was with D-Ray. Since Gage didn't play the game, she felt free to order the soup. It was almost a jubilant feeling.

"So, what have you been doing the past six months? Besides making waves in Kanesville," he asked.

"I don't make waves," she said irritably as she stuck her soupspoon in the bowl. She'd already crinkled up the requisite four hundred crackers into the tomato mixture, and now she stabbed at them with her spoon, crushing them into bite-sized pieces. "I get seasick."

He laughed, and she fought off the stirrings of attraction. What was wrong with her? She was acting like a bitch in heat.

"I'm serious. The only thing making waves is the fact I'm a woman and it's new ground for all these people. I'm just doing my job. Why don't you tell me about your case? The one that got you 'loaned' to us."

"Like a little soup with your crackers?" he asked, gesturing to her bowl.

She sighed. "I'm not here to be friends, Gage. Let's just talk about the case, okay?"

"I'm glad you don't want to be friends. That's not what I want, either."

Her stomach stirred again, and butterflies took flight. She shook her head. She could tell Gage was trying not to grin.

"The case?"

"The case. The suicides."

"Oh yeah, those. Well, they were a little different."

"Different how?" Sam asked, trying to be patient.

"Well, we knew it was a suicide pact. Everything pointed toward it. Two young boys. College freshmen. Roommates. Finally out of their parents' houses. They discovered they liked each other, and stopped fighting it. Until they got caught by one of their roomies. Then everything snowballed out of control. You know how mean kids are. The torture started, and the primo thing held over their heads was they would be outed to their families, church, student ward. Never mind that these other boys were screwing girls, and drinking every night, and these two were in love."

Sam cringed as she considered the two boys and how they must have felt. How they must have been treated.

"It culminated in two boys dying together, looking like a murder-suicide. The parents of the Smoot boy screamed that it *had* to be a murder-suicide and no son of theirs was gay. Tried to blame it all on the other boy. But evidence showed he was the shooter. Then they found a note. They had planned it. And the Smoot parents starting screaming lawsuit, if it wasn't hushed up. President Smoot sits on the presiding bishopric of the LDS Church."

"This is a horrible story. But I'm not seeing the correlation between that case and ours."

"There really isn't one. But no one understands suicide, so when they ask for help and you've dealt with it in any way, shape, or form they knock at your door."

Sam sighed with exasperation. She'd eaten only a few bites of the soup, and he was done with the burger and fries. And eyeing her suspiciously.

"Not hungry?" he asked.

"Too many crackers," she lied. "So they came and asked you for help? Because I sure didn't ask for help."

"Well, actually, I volunteered. Wasn't busy. And your chief was happy to have my expertise on suicide."

"Which you don't actually have," she said with a grimace.

"Hey, I had a case. More than one, of course. I've gone out on other suicides. This just happened to involve teenagers. Just like yours."

"Not the slightest bit like mine," Sam said, trying not to speak harshly. "You're going into this just as blind as we are."

"Maybe. But I'm a good cop. I can help."

"I'm a good cop, too."

"I know," he said, his face suddenly serious. "You're damn good. I'm just going to help you prove it."

"I didn't ask for your help."

"You never do, Sam. You never ask for anyone's help, and you never want it. But everybody needs it. We all need that interaction."

His voice was gentle, his eyes concerned, and she stared at him, fighting back the sudden urge to give in to him, to open up. That would mean falling apart. The price would be too great. She had way too much first-hand experience with what happened when people fell apart.

NINETEEN

Sam left Sill's Café alone. What she hadn't told Gage was that she was still working, heading to the home of Bethany Evans. Sam continued to try to reach her sister but had no success. She pulled up in front of the Evans home and stared at it for a minute.

It was one of the older homes in Kanesville, red-brick and small and square, with white window trims that were faded and cracked, peeling paint. The lawn hadn't been mown for a while. Weeds had invaded the flower beds. There were no homey touches that said "someone lives here and loves this house." It was probably a rental, and because of her Air Force enlistment Bethany's mom probably did a lot of moving. Little time to make a home, or feel like you fit in, especially during the important and emotional teenage years.

It appeared to be locked up tight, no one there. Sam sat in front of it for a while and pondered what she knew about the "new girl." Not much. Sam got out of her car and headed briskly up the front steps to knock on a obviously empty house.

While she was waiting her phone rang and she looked down to see a number she didn't recognize. She let it ring.

There was no answer at the door and, not surprisingly, no barking dog. Pets required care and stability. This looked like a situation that was as unstable as they came.

"Hello there." The elderly lady waving at Sam from across the overgrown bush was not someone she knew. "If you're looking for Martha, she's not home. TDY this week. I think Bethany is staying with some friends from her church group. They aren't Mormon, you know."

"Oh . . . thanks."

"I'm Elva Tippetts. You look official. Is something wrong?"

Sam introduced herself and soon found herself inside Elva Tippetts's house, eating food she did not want and listening to information she desperately needed.

The woman must not have a lot to do, because she was sure happy to find someone to listen to her talk. Her husband had apparently tuned her out years ago and instead watched *Wheel of Fortune* with the volume so high that Sam suspected he had permanent hearing loss.

Bethany Evans had moved with her mother to Kanesville when she'd been transferred to the large Air Force base nearby after a stint in Germany. Martha Evans was an enlisted soldier, and she worked on the base. She apparently chose not to live there because she had been an Army brat and didn't want the same for her child. And yet Martha still moved from base to base, dragging her teenage child along with her, probably reluctantly.

The Evans duo were not Mormon, did not attend any church actually, although Bethany had become involved with a youth church group through her new "private school."

Mrs. Tippetts wasn't sure why Bethany had left Smithland High. "Maybe that Assembly of God Church lured her in. I think they're one of those holy-roller churches, you know?" she said conspiratorially. "Did you know they wear pants to church? Can you imagine? What would God say?"

Sam considered the question for a moment. What would God say if she wore pants to church? Men wore pants to church. They had two legs. She had two legs. What was the difference?

Mrs. Tippetts stared at her anxiously, apparently not asking a rhetorical question. Since Sam was not on a first-name basis with God, she decided to sidestep the question.

"Were they friendly?"

"Well, not really, but she's always polite when we chat. I ask most of the questions of course. She just answers them. She has a weird accent. And sometimes she has parties and they drink beer in the backyard. I've never seen the likes of it."

"Have you ever left Kanesville, Mrs. Tippetts?"

"Oh, of course. Elmer and I went to Idaho Falls on our honeymoon. One year we took the kids to Yellowstone, and you know what? We didn't see one bear. I don't understand what all the hoopla is about bears up there, and boy, were the kids disappointed—"

"Uh, yeah, sorry about the bears. Does Martha Evans leave her daughter home alone a lot?"

"What?" Elva had apparently being thinking about the bears. "Oh yes, way too much if you ask me. Although she seems like a quiet girl. Never holds parties that I can tell. Not like her mom. Doesn't really seem to have friends. She did for a while, some of our good Kanesville kids, but she must have had a falling-out with them. Now she just goes with her church friends."

"You know it is legal to drink beer in Utah, right, Mrs. Tippetts?" Sam said, the words out of her mouth before she could stop them. "As long as one is of age, of course."

"Well, of course I know that. It's also legal to smoke, but our prophet let us know that is the wrong choice, and I guess it all goes down to free agency. Choices. Right ones and wrong ones."

The pursing of her lips left little doubt in Sam's mind which choices she considered right and which she considered wrong.

"I just don't get why people don't understand it," Mrs. Tippetts said, her look of disapproval turning to confusion. "It's so simple. God's plan is so easy to follow."

"Well, thanks for the cake and the information," Sam said hastily, standing up. This conversation was headed in a direction she did not care to travel. And, as always, assumptions were made because everyone knew Sam's family in Kanesville. She'd found out pretty early on in the conversation that years before her father had been "Sister Tippetts's" home teacher. Back when he left the house for things other than the grocery store and the doctor's office.

If Sam didn't escape now, the prying questions would turn on *her*. Time to go.

She said her good-byes and thank-yous and then made her way to her car. Sitting down in the driver's seat, she rubbed her stomach, groaning a bit, as three pieces of carrot cake settled heavily. She felt the familiar nausea and stomach rumbling, and she fought back against it. She tried to will herself to keep the food down, to not throw up, but the rich cream-cheese frosting was causing havoc with a system that rarely saw anything sweet or substantial.

She closed her eyes and thought of running, pounding the pavement, clearing her body of excess calories and sugar. The nausea passed.

Don't accept anything, especially food, from strangers, Sammy. Don't you know that is the best way to get into trouble? Mom and Dad taught you better.

"That could hardly include food from lonely little old ladies," Sam said aloud, to hush the voice inside her head.

She felt a twitch in her muscles and the urge to run, long and hard. She fought back the desire, knowing that even though she often indulged in it, running at night was hardly safe, even if she carried her small personal pistol in a fanny pack. Yes, this was Kanesville, but the recent rash of deaths should make it perfectly clear that tragedy and violence come to call no matter where you live or what God you prayed to. She also wasn't dressed for it, wearing her nice black pants and lightweight cream jacket that she often donned when interviewing witnesses. And her shoes were stylish, with enough of a heel that they would be murder on her feet. . . .

You're a little crazy, you know that, right, Sam? You can't really be thinking about jogging, the way you're dressed, and at this time of night?

"I'm not really thinking about it. It would just be nice," she said. Then shook her head. She didn't enjoy hearing from Callie—it made Sam question her own sanity, worry she was a little nuts. And she especially didn't like it when she felt compelled to answer back.

Sam would have to run an extra mile in the morning to make up for this indulgence. While it had been good cake, she'd eaten it because she had to, to keep Mrs. Tippetts talking. Was this why some officers got so fat? Food seemed to lower a person's guard, and the willingness to eat at someone's table—even a complete stranger's—often did more to make a person open up than any truth serum ever could.

Sam's cell phone jingled on the seat of the car. She reached over and snatched it up with her right hand, still navigating the car with her left as she pulled away from the curb.

"Montgomery," she said.

"Nixon," came the sarcastic retort, and Sam blanched as she recognized the nasal whine of the hard-edged reporter.

"Why are you calling me?"

"Guess," the woman replied.

"No comment."

"That's not going to work with me, Montgomery."

"Double no comment."

"I'm going to run this story, and you know it and I know it. You can either speak to me—on or off the record—or I go with what I have, a little tidbit that tells me Kanesville has a nasty little serial murderer running amok, killing teenagers before they even have a chance to try their first legal drink."

"By the time most of these kids are old enough to drink legally, they'll be married or on missions for the Church."

"Ah, you gotta love Utah. Still, you can either control how I play it or I can just unleash chaos on your department. You choose."

"You're a complete bitch, Nixon."

"Takes one to know one, Montgomery."

"I'll meet you at Juniors in an hour. You're buying."

TWENTY

Juniors, located in downtown Salt Lake City across from the police station, was half cop bar, half reporter bar. It was an eclectic mix. Cops and the media who wrote about them—often unfairly and with wrong intent—seemed an unlikely combination, but at Juniors it worked. A lot of give-and-take went on here. The media was a necessary evil, and more than one seasoned detective had learned to work the system to his benefit.

Pamela Nixon spent a lot of time at Juniors. Lots of secrets were given away here. Most of them were given out in partial allotments, some truth, a little spin, and a lot of desperation tingeing their dispersal.

Rumor had it that Pamela Nixon would sleep with just about anyone if the information was good enough. Sam had heard enough talk in the time she had been on the SLCPD force to know it was true, to some extent. She understood it, in a way only another damaged woman with aspirations could. Nixon had her eye on a network anchor spot in one of the big markets, unlike many of the other Utah reporters who were happy to live and report in the place they had been born and the culture with which they were familiar and comfortable. Nixon was willing to do whatever was necessary to make a move on something bigger, somewhere better— mostly somewhere different.

Sam slid into a chair on the opposite side of Pamela, placing both elbows on the mahogany table and then immediately regretting it as the stickiness ever present in a bar—that deep adhesive feeling that came from decades of spilled drinks—assaulted her arms.

She pulled first one, then the other from the table, wincing as she considered "just exactly where" these tables had been.

Sam, don't put that in your mouth. You have no idea where it's been.

That particular memory floated up, compliments of her mother, because it was one of the few things Sam could ever remember her mother having to say to her. Before Ruthie slipped away forever.

Her phone rang again, and this time she didn't look at it. It had continued to ring throughout the rest of the afternoon, and she had continued to decline the call. She knew it was Gage.

"Took you long enough to get here," Nixon griped.

"I don't exactly live around the corner, you know."

"Why the hell did you ever leave the only bright spot in this state, anyway? To move to Hicksville? What is *wrong* with you?"

"I can't explain it, and I'm sure not going to try to explain it to you. Besides, Kanesville is only twenty minutes from Salt Lake. That's hardly Hicksville. You'd have to drive a lot farther to get *there*."

"You know what I mean, Montgomery. Some places are better left behind, nothing but a distant memory."

"I guess I'm not done with it yet."

"You should have been done the day you left."

"There's still too much I don't understand."

"And you never will. I thought we went over this."

"Look—"

"You're not helping yourself, Sammy," Pamela said with affection. "You are skinny as a rail, and it's pretty obvious you are either working out too much or surviving on apples, coffee, and water again."

"What can I getcha?" asked the perky waitress, ignoring some good-natured hoots and flirting from the cops at the table next to them.

"Vodka tonic," Pam said.

"Diet Coke," Sam said.

Pamela raised an eyebrow at Sam as the waitress sashayed off, giving backward glances to the table of young cops—obviously patrolmen fresh out of the academy—who were enjoying the show.

"I have to drive," Sam said. "And this isn't a social visit, anyway. You threatened me, and I'm here to talk you out of doing something stupid like trying to blackmail a cop."

"It's not blackmail, Sam," Pamela said, a wry grin on her face. "It's reality. I have a job to do, too. My job is at odds with your job. But they can work together. They can. But let's get back to you for a minute. You're at least five pounds lighter than you were the last time I saw you. Are you eating?"

"Yes, I'm eating regularly. Well, kind of regularly. And using protein shakes."

Pam shook her head and Sam felt the anger rise up

in her gut. She hated having to explain herself to any-one, ever. Especially to someone like Pamela Nixon.

"I'm using them, but I'm eating, too," Sam said, her voice harsher then she liked.

"I'm just worried about you," Pam said, the sarcasm, anger, and haughty air suddenly gone. Their eyes met, and they were just two women, in a tough business, trying to survive. Trying to survive without starving themselves to death. They had met in an eating-disorders support group and had formed a bond that belied their very disparate careers.

"I promised you I wouldn't lose track of you just because you moved away, and I meant it."

"I'm okay. Let's talk about you. How are you doing? Eating enough?"

"Eating too much. I've gained five pounds and my boss called me curvy last week. Almost enough to send me over the top and back into a tailspin. I won, though. I didn't let it derail me. Three squares a day."

"I'm doing okay, too," Sam said, reaching out with her hand to touch Nixon's arm, the closest she ever got to physical contact with friends. And that was what Pam definitely was. A friend. Even when the other woman looked Sam in the eye and called her a bitch. Neverthe-less, she pulled her hand back quickly.

"Good," Pam said, a twinkle in her eye. Then her face hardened and her eyes narrowed. "Now, let's talk about this case. The dead kids. Something rotten in your neck of the woods, Sammy. Is it a suicide pact?"

"Not that I can tell. There's absolutely no indication that these kids—"

"But they were all friends," Pam said, ignoring the moue of disgust on Sam's face as she interrupted.

"They all hung out in the same crowd. They could have had a pact. Maybe you just haven't found the proof yet."

"No. That's not what this is," Sam said, her voice stubborn. She didn't intend to say more, at least not to Pamela Nixon. Friend or not, she was the press. Anything Sam said from this point on was fair game. She knew the rules, and friendship was on the back burner now.

"You have to give me something, Sammy, or I'm going to run with what I have. And what I have smells like suicide pact. Three kids. All from the same social group. All from the same little town. All the same age. All dead."

"That would be jumping to conclusions, and some pretty poor reporting on your part," Sam said sharply.

"Not really," Pamela said, her eyes ablaze with the future she saw ahead for herself, in the not-too-far distance. "It really makes sense. All that's missing is confirmation from the police that they found suicide notes at any of the three crime scenes. From there to suicide pact . . . Well, even if I don't say that, and just raise the question, people are going to read into it that way. Everybody is thinking it, Sam."

"People are going to think what they want. It doesn't change the facts," Sam said stubbornly.

"Yeah? I suppose so. But soon, you're going to have a little bit of an issue on your hands, because everybody is going to be wondering, 'Is my kid next?' They are going to want some answers, and they are going to be looking at *you* to give them those answers. If this is a suicide pact, and you know it, these parents deserve to know it. They deserve to be able to stop it."

Pamela's face was shiny, her eyes focused, concern and passion on her face. An act. She just wanted the story, and Sam knew it.

But Pamela was right. These parents were going to freak out, and soon—the parents of the kids who were still alive. What was worse? Thinking your child might be on the verge of suicide or thinking that a killer was creeping through the back alleys and side streets of Kanesville, murdering teenagers and leaving little trace?

"When I know, you'll know," Sam finally said.

"Exclusive," Pamela said, her tone harsh. "Don't fuck with me, Montgomery."

"Exclusive. Just keep a lid on it for a few more days."

"Good thing I trust you. Now why don't you have a real drink. And if you say 'too many calories,' I'm going to drag your ass to IHOP and make you eat endless pancakes."

"Fine, when the waitress comes back, order me a vodka tonic. Just one. I really do have to drive home."

"But first you have to let me tell you about my newest fling. He's a hottie."

Sam could feel the smile fighting to get out, anxious to escape her life for a while and listen to Pamela's wild escapades. She didn't relax very often. Maybe tonight would be different.

TWENTY-ONE

Sam pulled into her driveway and shut off the engine. A small white sedan sat at the curb in front of her house, a shadowy figure in the front seat. As soon as Sam stepped out of her car, she saw the driver's side door of the other vehicle open. She knew who it was before he even yelled hello and began walking briskly toward her. His stride was firm and his pace quick. He was lean and tall and very physically fit. She remembered back to their high-school years. He'd reached his height in their sophomore year, unlike many other boys. Maturity, at least physical, was not far behind.

"Hello, Paul," she said, her voice restrained and calm. She immediately wondered if her breath smelled of vodka and cringed that she should be bothered what this man—this long-ago boyfriend—thought of her.

Man of God. Seminary teacher. Widower. Sam knew his wife had died in a car accident several years before. Her father shared all that news with her. And of course she'd read about the horrible accident in the paper. Even worse, the toddler with Paul's wife had been thrown from the car and died and the baby inside her had lived only hours after it was delivered by emergency C-section.

One minute you have a family, and the next instant everything is just gone. How do you go on after such a thing happens? Sam had wanted to get on the phone, to call Paul, to ask him.

But she hadn't. And now he walked toward her and if she really wanted to, she could just blurt it out. Just ask. Even though they'd barely spoken in more than ten years.

The last time they'd had a real conversation . . . Sam couldn't even remember.

"Hey," Paul said softly when he got close enough. She'd watched him walk up her driveway but hadn't moved, still holding her keys in her hand. The moon was nearly full, and there was an eerie lightness to the evening, even though it was nearly 11:00 p.m. One drink had led to two, and then she'd drunk water for another hour while she watched Pamela drink herself into oblivion.

Sam had poured Pamela into a taxi and sent her home, listening to her mumble something about "exclusive."

"Why are you here, Paul?"

"Well, my mother always told me my Heavenly Father had a plan for me."

"Cute. But trite. What's the real reason?"

"When did you turn so bitter, Sam?"

"The day I saw my sister hanging from a tree in our backyard, and heard all the nice church folks explain how God had other plans for her and needed her with Him."

"You don't know there isn't a God, Sam."

"You don't know there *is,* Paul."

"Well, I want to believe there is. I want to believe that He's taking care of my wife and babies now, because I can't."

Sam swallowed hard as the grief and loss crossed his face.

"Why are you here?" she asked again.

"Because I wanted to talk to you. I couldn't really do that the other night. I wanted to talk about what happened with us, what—"

"That was a long time ago, Paul. Our lives went different ways. Bygones, you know?"

He winced. "You make it sound like I didn't matter at all."

"Oh, it mattered. But that was a lifetime ago. We both moved on. I'm sorry about your wife, and your kids. I never got a chance to say that. I'm sorry you lost them. But we live in two completely different worlds now."

"I didn't just walk away from you, you know, Sam. You had a miscarriage. I offered to marry you."

"You offered. I know; I remember. But it wasn't what you wanted."

"Can you blame me? I would have been the first male in my family not to serve an honorable mission."

"No, I can't blame you," Sam said, and turned away to walk to her house. "I don't think about it anymore. You and I were always different. You took your path, and I took mine."

He grabbed her arm to keep her from moving away. "We were young, and I was dumb, and I'm sorry it happened. I'm sorry I hurt you."

Tears came to Sam's eyes, and she fought them back, angry at her own weakness.

"Why are you here, Paul?"

"I . . . I just wanted to talk to you. To see if you were okay."

"It's been a long time for you to suddenly start caring, Paul. What's up with that?"

"Seeing you again—"

"I'm doing my job. That's all. We just crossed paths again because I am doing an investigation that you are peripherally involved in. That's it. Paul, I'm tired. I've had a long day and an even longer week, and it's just going to get uglier. I don't need this right now." She turned to walk away.

He gripped her arm tighter. "Sammy, please. Please just talk to me. Seeing you brought back a million memories, and most of them are good. The pain on your face when you look at me, that hurts. I don't want you to hurt. I'm sorry."

Sam met Paul's eyes and gently pulled her arm from his grasp. "I don't believe what you believe. I don't believe the Mormon Church is the only true church, and I don't believe Joseph Smith was a prophet of God. That's not hurt you see in my eyes. It's sadness for you and everyone else who has lost people they love. And all those things that you are teaching to those kids—all the crap that they filled our heads with as kids. We don't even know each other anymore. You married someone else, and had kids with someone else."

"And I lost them, too."

Sam winced at the thought of the baby-that-never-was, the pregnancy that had "spontaneously aborted." It wasn't really the same. She knew Paul's wife, toddler, and unborn child had suffered a violent death. Nothing like the cramping, and then the bleeding: the magic potion to undo the sin, to change what had been done.

She'd never understood why she cried at the loss. Why it mattered, when it had been so wrong. When it would have caused so much trauma, destruction, and despair—and put her in the firing range of all the gossip, the pitying looks, the judgment calls. Why did she mourn that baby-that-never-was, even now?

"What if I want to get to know you again?"

His words shocked her, and she stared at him open-mouthed. Then she furrowed her brow and said, "Did you just hear a word I said? I don't believe what you believe. I am not a Mormon anymore."

"Your name is still on the rolls. It's your culture. You can shun the tenets, but you can't remove the trappings. It's who we are, Sam, no matter what level of obedience you practice."

"I don't practice any obedience. It's your faith, and my dad's faith, not mine."

"You can't just walk away from it. It's not that easy."

"I never said it was easy. I just said it's the way it is. And who I am does not mesh with who you are. Apparently, it never did."

"I remember us meshing together really well," Paul said, sultry fire in his eyes, and Sam's stomach fluttered.

"Look, Paul, this is not good for you. You're a seminary teacher. The seminary principal no less. Flirting and sexual innuendo is counterproductive. And I'm never going back there."

"Back where? Back to your home? To your roots? And who says I'm flirting?"

"You're talking about us having sex back in high school. If it's not flirting, it's something close. Either way, I don't think that's in your job description, or conducive to my investigation."

"Sam, I wasn't talking about the sex act. I was talking about—"

"Paul, again, we went different ways. I'm sure there's a nice Mormon girl out there for you."

"What makes you think I want one?" Paul asked. Sam didn't like the sudden spark in his eyes, the reminder he had not always been so pure, so good.

"It doesn't matter. I'm not going there. You should go home."

"Not very neighborly," Paul said, his voice slightly harsh.

"We're not really neighbors. I knew you once. Things changed."

Paul turned and stomped away, and Sam watched as he got into his car and drove off. He slowed down, then raised his hand, but Sam didn't do the same in response.

All Paul Carson brought back was memories and pain. She'd left this town to be rid of the pain, then returned when she realized that some old ghosts needed to be settled before she would ever be at peace.

The strident peal of Sam's phone ringing made her jump. She pulled it out of her pocket and answered it quickly, glad for the reprieve from her thoughts.

"Hello?"

"Oh, Sam, please come. Please come now. It's my Whit. Oh God, it's my Whit."

Susanna's voice held a grief that Sam had only heard one time before.

TWENTY-TWO

Sam pulled in front of her sister's house, threw the shifter into park, and jumped out of the car before she had even turned it off.

The narrow street in front of the Marcusen house was littered with police cars, lining the road on both sides, including several Durangos with the Smithland County logo on the side, two fire engines, and an ambulance. The Durangos meant paramedics, and Sam's heart skipped several beats.

The phone call from her sister had been brief and panicked, and while Sam had tried to get more information out of her, Susanna had resorted to screaming and crying and then disconnected. Sam had tried to get a hold of Susanna repeatedly since then, but both her cell and house phone went to voice mail.

Sam knew something was horribly wrong. She felt it deep in the pit of her stomach, and Callie was screaming in her head.

Move, Sam. Go. Now. Go! She needs you now. Don't

*let it end. Don't let her come to me. It's not her time.
She's too young. I was too young. It's not what you
think. It's not the white light and the beautiful angels,
and the singing. It's just—*

"You shouldn't be here, Sam," said D-Ray, who was
already inside when she pushed her way through the
door. His face showed pain and grief, and she knew it
was bad. Worse than bad.

"Don't even fucking think about trying to keep me
out," she said, pushing past him, knowing he was only
trying to keep her from getting hurt. Knowing that this
was real. That this was her family, once again, torn
apart.

She ran into her sister's house and found Susanna
collapsed on the floor, a paramedic attending to her.

The main chaos came from a room at the back of the
house. Whit's room. Sam pushed her way through the
wall of cops standing around, fighting off the arms that
tried to keep her back, knowing only that she had to get
to Whit and try to save her. To do what Sam hadn't
done for Callie.

Inside the bedroom Sam stopped cold. All sounds
seemed to disappear as she viewed the montage before
her. The smell hit her first: bitter and acrid, the coppery
scent of blood, along with feces and urine. There was
blood on the carpet, vomit, and other bodily wastes,
and Whitney was already loaded onto a gurney, a por-
table ventilator breathing for her, moving her chest up
and down. Her face was nothing but a white death
mask.

Three-quarters of a pink satin tie hung from Whitney's open closet door. The rest of it was nowhere to be
seen, but the color and the similarity to Jeremiah

Malone's death hit Sam in the chest like a sucker punch. She found it hard to breathe as she watched the paramedics work over Whitney, try to keep her alive. She already looked dead.

A stepstool lay on its side at the base of the door. Sam breathed in and out as she considered the scene. It looked like a suicide attempt, but . . . She felt the arms around her and someone pulling her into his chest, strong, and a familiar voice said, "Your sister needs you."

D-Ray pulled her from the chaos, and his words broke into her consciousness, making her realize the tableau before her was not a chimera but cold, hard fact. Her niece was near death and might never recover.

And Sam's sister—the one who had cared for her for so many years—needed her. Now.

She turned and walked into the other room without saying a word to D-Ray, but she could feel his presence behind her. Susanna was sitting up, a blanket draped around her, shivering. She hadn't stopped crying, and she looked up just as Sam came toward her, though she seemed to be seeing beyond her. Then Sam heard the noises and voices behind her and saw that they were wheeling Whitney out of the bedroom and headed for the front door.

Susanna jumped up and threw off the blanket. She headed toward the gurney, but Sam held her back.

"Oh my God, my baby. My baby. How could this happen? How could this happen? My baby." Tears streamed down her face and she clutched her sister as though she were going to disappear into thin air and Susanna was going to do everything she could to stop that.

"You have to save her, Sammy," Susanna said, turning to her. "She has to be okay. You can't let her die. You have to save her."

Sam knew that the words were not rational, that at this point there was nothing she could do for Whitney. That would be up to the paramedics, doctors, and nurses. But Sam held her sister closely and said, "I will. I will."

"They're going to Life Flight her to Primary," D-Ray said, and Sam turned to look at him for the first time. Lind Harris stood behind him, a sour look on his face, his lips tight.

What did he feel as he witnessed this personal tragedy? Did it make him hate her more? Pity her? It didn't matter. Nobody mattered right now but family.

"I have to go with her," Susanna said, trying to control her gasps and sobs.

"You can't, Sissy. They won't let you."

"I'll take you both in my car. It's outside," D-Ray said.

"But she needs me. She'll be so scared. She'll—"

Sam knew that Whitney was completely unaware of everything that was going on around her. And possibly always would be, if she even survived. "Sissy, you can't go in the helicopter. D-Ray will take us. We'll get there fast. I promise."

"We have to go now, then. Now please."

Susanna started looking around for something and finally spotted it. She picked up her purse off the side table and headed for the door. She wore a pair of pajama pants and an old T-shirt. Her feet were bare. Her hair was standing on end, and there was a dark stain on the T-shirt, possibly from hot chocolate or something she drank to calm her nerves before bed,

"Sissy, go change. Fast. Put on some jeans, a shirt, and shoes and socks, and comb your hair."

Susanna looked down at herself, a perplexed look on her face, as though such simple things as dressing and wearing shoes were beyond her comprehension.

Sam guided her toward her bedroom. It would be a long night. Possibly a long week. Maybe longer. Sam helped Susanna dress as though she were a child, helping her pull on a clean T-shirt, a pair of sweats, and some socks with a pair of sneakers. Sam leaned down to tie the sneakers and heard gasping noises coming from her sister.

"Sissy, where is Roger? He needs to be here. He needs to be helping you."

Sam looked up to see tears still streaming from her sister's eyes and a look of total despair on her face.

Sam finished tying the shoe and rose, pulling Susanna to her feet and hugging her close. "Tell me where he is, and I'll call him. I'll take care of it. You don't have to. I'll call on our way to the hospital."

Susanna still didn't answer her question.

"Sissy? Where is Roger?"

Silence.

"Don't you want me to call him? This is his family, too. He should be here."

"I don't want him here. Or at the hospital. I'm done with all of this. All that matters now is my children. Please don't let her die, Sammy. Please."

This time Sam didn't answer. And she didn't question Susanna further. Not only because she didn't know what to say but also because she didn't trust Roger Marcusen and hadn't for years, since the day he had tried to feel her up when she was only seventeen. That was the man her sister had thought would save her. Sam didn't blame Sissy. She blamed the world. She blamed the culture. She blamed a mother who crumpled up and went away when one of her four children died.

"Are you sure you don't want me to call him?" Sam asked Susanna.

"I'm sure. Let's go. We have to save Whitney. She's worth saving."

TWENTY-THREE

The parents of children in the Primary Children's Medical Center Pediatric Intensive Care Unit all seemed lost. They pushed the button that opened the doors leading out of the PICU and walked through, then stood there, unaware of the doors closing behind them with a whoosh, looking first left, then right, trying to get their bearings.

Where did they go from here?

It didn't matter how many times they walked out the same door, they still stopped and looked around as though to say, "Where am I? How did I get here? Where do I go now?"

That was a question that had no answer. Even if they were just heading to the cafeteria to shovel down tasteless food, or to the bathroom, they stopped and looked around, trying to get bearings that might never be regained.

Several times in the past few hours Sam had watched the young polygamist wife—with the long braid down her back, large puff of hair at the front, and modest dark blue dress with puffy sleeves, black stockings, and sturdy, plain black shoes—go in and out. She walked through the doors, her eyes filled with loss and isolation, and even more timid and withdrawn, gripping the hand of her husband—dressed in jeans and a long-sleeved pin-striped western shirt—as they entered and exited the PICU. It was unusual to see polygamists here.

Families like the Clarkston polygamy clan usually just let the frail, interbred babies die, because they didn't want to answer questions about who had sired the children. Those who lived were listed as fatherless, and all their care was ministered by the state through Welfare. Sam had seen this firsthand, before Gage had her removed from the case that hit so close to her heart.

But here, obviously, this father cared about his children with this wife. Sam wondered just how many other children he might have—and how many wives. How many children? How much he could really care?

Right now Susanna, Sam, and D-Ray were waiting for news about Whitney. Unable to do anything but waste time, and think, seeing the polygamist woman brought back memories of Mary Ann Clarkston. Painful memories.

"Code Blue in PICU. Code Blue in PICU," said a woman's voice over a loudspeaker, and Sam jumped.

They'd been waiting in a family conference room while the doctors had situated Whitney in the PICU. Until she was settled there, and while the doctors fought to save her life, no one would be allowed in.

"Oh God, no, please don't let it be Whitney," Susanna said, tears streaming down her face. "Please, oh please."

"Code Blue canceled. Code Blue canceled," the same voice repeated over the loudspeakers, and Susanna looked first relieved, then anxious, the tear marks still staining her face.

There were numerous children in the Pediatric Intensive Care Unit at Primary Children's Medical Center, and the Code Blue could have been any one of them. Every parent who wasn't standing next to their child probably felt their heart stop every time there was an announcement.

Susanna paced back and forth, her arms wrapped tightly around her chest, shaking her head and crying. They'd been at the hospital for well over an hour, and all they'd been told was that the doctors were still trying to save Whitney and things did not look good.

Sam sat in a chair, D-Ray next to her.

She stood up and let go of his grasp, and he stood and followed her out to the drinking fountain. They both watched as the young polygamist wife and her husband walked to the door, picked up the phone, and asked for admittance into the PICU.

And then Sam saw him. Gage, standing outside the door of the family conference room. She watched him for a moment, fighting the urge to both throw herself into his arms and pummel him on the chest. He looked uncharacteristically anxious, the tension showing in the lines around his mouth, hunched shoulders, and crossed arms. His eyes darted around, as if he was looking for someone—or deciding whether or not to walk in.

Finally, he spotted her; his eyes widened in obvious concern, and he uncrossed his arms. Sam walked slowly to him.

"Why are you here?" she asked, instead of screaming like she wanted to do. Life seemed so wrong, so off.

Mary Ann. Whitney. Callie. So many losses.

"I don't know," he answered softly. "I thought . . . you might need me."

Sam took a breath. "I . . . I don't know what I need." The words had come out slightly louder than she intended. The young polygamous wife and her husband turned and stared at Sam. She blushed. The husband put his hand on the small of the woman's back and guided her into the PICU before the automatic doors closed.

Suddenly Sam felt herself being whirled and then pulled tightly into Gage's chest. She didn't fight, because she couldn't. She could barely speak.

"They were probably from a different plig group," he said, knowing what she was thinking. "Clarkstons don't care for their ill children. Brings too much focus down on the group."

"I know," Sam said, her voice muffled as she let him embrace her, disgusted with herself that she was so weak and he felt so solid, comfortable.

When she finally felt stable enough, she pulled back and stared him down.

"I know what you're thinking and . . . . ," he started.

"No, Gage, you don't know what I'm thinking. You can probably guess, but you can't know. My niece is in there fighting for her life. Whatever small thing happened between us before means nothing, really."

Gage lifted a hand and smoothed a piece of hair from her forehead.

He spoke in a soft voice. "Except she died. Mary

Ann died. We've never once talked about it. You just left. But I know you think about it every day. And blame me."

Sam could tell he meant it. She could still feel his fingers on her face, like they'd left a mark. She couldn't speak for a moment. Then she looked down at the speckled tile floor.

"No. I blame myself."

TWENTY-FOUR

Everyone knows the young should not die, and yet so many of them do. It was easier when they were someone else's child, someone else's niece or nephew.

That's the way it usually was.

But Sam watched as an almost-lifeless Whitney breathed in and out, deep and methodical, her chest rising and falling without a hitch, the way a machine would. A tube snaking around and into her mouth provided the mechanical breaths.

Sam had promised her sister she would stay with Whitney—hold her hand and not leave her side—while Susanna tried to get some rest in the "sleeping room" they'd assigned to her and Roger. Roger had opted to go home and sleep in his own bed, even with his youngest child hovering on the brink of death.

"The man could sleep through an earthquake," Susanna always said. This was an earthquake of epic proportions. Was he sleeping? Was he even human? Susanna had never said where Roger was when Susanna discovered Whitney hanging from the closet door. Sam didn't ask.

She had a gun. She knew how to use it. She preferred not to go to jail. It was probably best she didn't know.

It had been twenty-four hours since Susanna had found Whitney hanging. Sam knew it would take a lifetime to recover from that trauma, if Susanna ever did. Whenever Sam closed her eyes, she saw Callie's dead, lifeless face, blue and distorted, blood spilling from her ears. Whitney had looked the same. Sam remembered the smell, the blood, the vomit.

Her stomach roiled and she fought off nausea. But she couldn't leave Whitney. She'd made a promise.

Whit's eyes were closed and unmoving, her lashes not twitching, her brows not furrowing, the way they had so often when she was younger and angry about something.

Whitney had always been able to raise one eyebrow in a quizzical manner, a talent Sam had long admired and never been able to emulate. Whit's mother, Susanna, had also been able to do the trademark move, so Sam convinced herself it was a genetic Montgomery gift, and one she had not been blessed with.

But nothing on Whitney's face indicated she was even there anymore. There was no raising of the eyebrow, no pouting lips or angry eyes. Just closed lids and white, ashy skin.

Next to the sterile hospital bed, hoisted on a large metal stand, myriad beeping and flashing machines displayed lines and arcs. The only proof that a live person was in this hospital bed.

A nurse sat quietly in the corner, a rolling tray in

front of her, taking notes and writing on charts, watching the monitors by the teenager's bed closely, noting each alarm. She'd nodded at Sam when she came in, but didn't speak.

A lump filled Sam's throat as she stared at her niece and thought about Whitney's disappearance the other day. Was Whitney the fourth teenager in the suicide pact? The fourth one Sam had not believed existed. She'd been so sure that these were all murders, yet her own niece lying before her on this hospital bed made her feel as though it had to be something else. How could a hanging be an accident? But suicide?

And what about the note that said: "Bethany"? Sam shivered and scrubbed at a rebellious tear that had fallen down her face without permission. *Not again, not again, not again . . .*

The nurse stood up, stretched, and whispered, "Be back in a minute," to Sam, who nodded in response. She looked back at her niece, who looked like a wax figurine. No, not a wax figurine, but one of those mechanical bodies that you see at Disneyland or other amusement parks.

"Why, Whitney? *Did* you do this?"

"I don't think so," Gage Flint said, and Sam turned to see him standing in the doorway. He must have gone home for some rest. For once, Sam didn't tense up at his presence. He made her feel less alone. She nodded and looked back at Whitney.

And nothing more needed to be said.

TWENTY-FIVE

Sam refused to leave Whitney's side until her sister returned, so Gage sat beside her and they both stared at Whitney, watching for some response. Some reaction. An indication there was still a person inside.

When a shell-shocked Susanna wandered in, Sam hugged her and then told her she would be back later.

Susanna didn't acknowledge Gage. She barely looked at Sam. She only had eyes for her daughter.

"Let's get you some food," Gage said, leading Sam out of the room. She pulled her hand out of his instinctively, though it felt uncomfortably right there.

"Gage, I don't want to sound ungrateful, but what is this? Why are you here?"

"You're a friend, and you need me."

She felt like she should make him leave but didn't have it in her. She wanted to totally bend, to give in to his pushiness, let him lead her around so that for once she didn't have to think or feel. Or live in the agony of the past.

Except he didn't believe in her—her skills, her strength.

"So you're here just to be a friend."

"Yes. Is that so hard to believe?" He looked into her eyes and looked so earnest, almost childlike, that she wanted to reach out and touch his face, stroke his cheek. Put her lips on his and feel the five-o'-clock shadow rasping against her own skin as she trailed kisses down his neck—

Stop it! You have a case to solve and a sister to support.

"Yes," she whispered, in answer to his question. "Yes, it's hard to believe. I've been on my own for so long now it's the only way I know how to be."

"Let's go to the cafeteria. People say it's the best hospital food in the state."

"Isn't that an oxymoron?" she asked.

He grinned. "Follow me. I'm sure they have crackers."

Sam settled for coffee and a chef's salad. Vegetables made her more comfortable, if one could be comfortable around food.

Gage ordered coffee and a grilled cheese sandwich, with fries.

They ate without talking. Sam was surprised at how hungry she suddenly was. She was never hungry. Right now she felt almost ravenous.

"It's nice to see you eat something. You're too skinny," he said between bites.

"Apparently you haven't been paying attention to movies, television, or fashion magazines. Skinny is in," she said.

"Today's media is stupid. Ever take a peek at Marilyn Monroe? Now that was a woman."

Sam winced. She would be lucky to gain another five pounds, let alone curves. Every day was a fight.

"You look lost and terrified," he said quietly.

"It's a place I've been too many times in my life," she said, quite sure he didn't know how close to home he was hitting with his comments.

"Why are you so determined to do it alone, Sam? You know it doesn't have to be that way. You can let me in. I'm begging you to let me in, but you just keep pushing me away. I want to be a part of your life. Just . . . let me help you."

"I don't know how," she answered softly, then went back to eating her salad. Her hunger was gone. But she intended to finish every last bite while he watched.

"No, I want to be there for you, Mary Ann. Just tell me when. What should I wear? And actually, where is the wedding being held? Where should I be?"

"Hell. You should be in hell, sinner!"

"Huh?"

"And now, because you have sinned, an innocent will die—"

"Huh? What is happening, what is—"

Why was there so much blood? Why was Mary Ann curled up in a ball, sobbing, sobbing, then suddenly quiet? How did this happen? She'd just infiltrated the most notorious polygamous clan in Utah. She was invited to the wedding! How had this happened? The blood . . . The blood was Mary Ann's. And she was dead.

Dead.

Sam looked down at the gun in her hand and wondered how it had got there. What had happened?

"You did this," her father said to her. "This was you, Sammy. It was always you."

Sam sat up with a start, her heart pounding, sweat slicking the T-shirt to her body. Her underwear was soaked through, and she got up from the bed to change, shivering a bit. It had been a few months since she'd had this dream, reliving Mary Ann's death. Of course, in real life, Sam had shot no one. But she had wanted to. She had wanted to destroy the man who had let an innocent girl die. And Sam wasn't convinced that Gage hadn't signed the girl's death warrant by removing her from the case.

But it was you, Sam. You gave her hope. You let her think you could get her out, and that wasn't your job. That wasn't what you were there for. Gage isn't to blame for that.

Great, now even Callie was taking sides.

"What do you know?" Sam huffed at the empty air, and headed into her bathroom, turning on the shower and stripping bare to wash off the sweat and bad dreams.

After showering, she found a new pair of dry, clean underwear and opened a second drawer to pull out an oversized T-shirt.

One that said it was from Wasatch Brew Pub. One that she had "stolen" from Gage.

"So what, it's a perfectly good T-shirt," she said to herself, and crawled back into the bed, moving to the other side to get away from the dampness of the sheets. Of course, her thoughts moved to Gage, and she immediately knew putting this T-shirt on had been a bad idea.

"What's up with you girls, anyway?" D-Ray had complained one day while they were sitting in McDonald's, D-Ray snarfing down food, Sam just picking at a salad. "My girl, she comes over and she steals my T-shirts and pajama pants. She takes them home. Why can't she just buy her own? Don't get it. It makes no sense."

And Sam couldn't explain it to him, because a man wouldn't get it. Because even after three or four washings a man's T-shirt still had that man smell, and a significance that could not be duplicated by buying a man-sized T-shirt and some pajama pants. She wished she could still smell Gage on this shirt, but she'd had it for at least a year. Too many washings. And yet she could feel him. And it was keeping her awake.

"Dammit," she swore as she got up and stripped off his shirt. She found another, left over from a 5K run. "Dammit."

You want him, Callie's voice said from inside Sam's head. *You want him here now. And he wants you.*

Talking to Callie again. All cops were a little crazy. That's how they ended up on the job.

"Good night, Callie. I'm going to bed now. Please let me sleep."

There was no answer. Because there never was when Sam spoke back. Callie only told her what she didn't want to hear.

A sharp rasping noise from the back part of her town house made her still. She listened carefully, all her instincts on alert. It was quiet, all but the roaring of her heartbeat in her ears, and she slowly calmed down.

Probably the damned cocker spaniel from across the street.

She turned back to her bed and a sharp rap on glass caused prickles to run up her spine. She grabbed her sidearm from the table next to her bed and carefully eased out into her living room, shadowing the walls to the kitchen, trying to make out any shape in the dark night.

The glass patio door was closed, but she could see something smeared across it. Someone or something had been there and left behind a trail. A dark trail. They might still be there.

She eased back into her bedroom and picked up her cell phone, quickly dialing Dispatch. Only when two uniformed police officers had covered the backyard did she flip on the inside kitchen light and the patio light.

The two officers, both young, stared at her through the glass. One had a look of distaste on his face. The trail was blood.

A dead rat body, minus its head, was on the patio. The head was about a foot away, perched on a stick that had been driven into the grassy ground.

TWENTY-SIX

Sam slept little and woke early, heading out for a run with a cloudy head and a heavy heart.

Her footsteps pounded on the pavement in the early light of morning, and the rhythmic beat reminded her of the ventilator that was keeping Whitney alive. Sam cringed and tried to think of something else, but the case had become too personal.

Personal. Her shoulders sagged as she fully realized what this meant. With her niece one of the victims, the chief would most likely remove Sam. The only chance she had was to keep it together, not betray any sign of weakness. This wasn't a big-city police department, and they didn't have a lot of detectives to turn to: just her, D-Ray, and a cop who was already nearly semi-retired, whose only desire was *not* to leave the office—or to leave as little as possible. And Gage. Her only hope to stay involved was to play nice and by the chief's rules.

She'd played off the dead rat as teenage vandalism,

and both young officers seemed inclined to believe her. It would go in the reports, of course, but maybe the chief wouldn't see it. A harmless teenage prank. Harmless, unless you were the headless rat.

Was that a message? Who would stoop to that level?

Oh, maybe Lind Harris?

The force was small and didn't have a lot of other options, so as long as she didn't let it become personal she should be just . . . But how would she do that? Not let the fact that her niece was lying in a coma, hooked up to a ventilator, affect her?

How was she supposed to pull this off?

Lie your ass off, and stay on the case.

Sam made her way into work an hour later, a cup of Starbucks coffee in one hand and the newspaper in the other. It was a cloudy, rainy summer day, perfect for her mood. The sky had been threatening all morning, but the rain hadn't started up until a few minutes before she pulled into the Kanesville Police Station parking lot.

Now she sat in her chair at her desk and tried to focus. In front of her were various reports, all pieces to the puzzle, none of them fitting together. The crime lab hadn't come back with anything positive on the necktie. There were lots of prints on the computer from the seminary building, but none that were registered in the BCI database. Not surprising, considering this was not *CSI* and life rarely happened like it did on television. Every once in a while, just occasionally, Sam wished it would. Everything except hearing from her dead sister, like that one show on television that she could never sit through. The dead should not talk. It was unseemly.

Whit's evidence was not here, of course, and Sam

would be lucky if she didn't get pulled off the entire case before getting a chance to look through it. She'd already talked to D-Ray and he'd told her there was nothing that indicated Whitney's injury was anything but an attempted suicide. Nothing.

"Nothing," Sam said with disgust, throwing the report on her desk and rubbing her eyes, then instantly regretting it. Now she would have black mascara rings. Always an attractive look.

"You said there wasn't going to be anything," D-Ray reminded her, his voice rising above his cubicle walls.

Sam stood and walked over to the entrance of his enclave, trying to ignore the smell of grease and the general disarray on his desk. D-Ray worked best this way—it was his MO. How, she didn't know.

"I have nothing on Jeremiah. It looks like a suicide."

"The tie wasn't around his neck," D-Ray reminded her.

"Yeah, only because our favorite dickwad removed it."

A dickwad who might be taking his personal hatred toward me even further than sneers and nasty comments.

"You don't know that for sure."

"Yeah, I do. And you do. And so does anyone with a brain, and if the press were to get a hold of it—"

"Sam," D-Ray said, the warning in his tone unmistakable, raising her hackles. "I see that look, and I know what you're thinking. You're thinking I'm siding with Lind Harris and all his idiots, but I'm not. You get the press in on this and you'll just complicate things. Make it ten times worse. Throw a raccoon a scrap and you know what happens? They come back for more.

And more. And when they don't get what they want, they get ugly. They dig holes, and turn over garbage cans, and make messes, and worst of all, if you confront them, they will attack. There is no real purpose served by that tie being around his neck. Either way, you know how he died."

Sam turned away angrily, knowing that part of D-Ray was right and part of him was morally, repugnantly, unethically wrong . . . unfortunately, all characteristics the rest of the system shared with him.

She retreated back into her own cubicle with a huff and sat down heavily in her chair. She heard D-Ray move in behind her, and she took slow, steady breaths, determined to be cool and calm when she faced him again.

But her desk phone rang, and she picked it up, pulling on a professional face.

"Girl, you are running out of time." Pamela Nixon. Right now she was pretty close to being the last person Sam wanted to talk to. "I get no calls. I get no e-mails. I get no text messages? Where is the love?"

"Ugh, Nixon, this is not a good time."

"When is it ever a good time for this kind of shit, Sammy? But I have a hot story, and I have to run with it. Suicide pact it is, since you've given me nothing else—"

"Oh, knock it off," Sam said, knowing the irritation in her voice was thick and terse. "You and I both know that this is no suicide pact, and writing that it is will do nothing more than cause mass hysteria in this town. Is it really worth it to you to have the story?"

"To have first dibs at this *huge* story, Sammy? Of course it is. The only thing holding me back is my genuine love and respect for you."

Sam snorted and D-Ray stood up and gave her a quiz-zical stare over the top of the cubicle wall. She waved him away.

"You have twenty-four hours, and then I'm writing this one the way I see it. With a little bit of both. That, of course, is only going to make you look like a fool and totally incompetent at your job, which I have no desire for. Thus, consider this your heads-up. I need a call in twenty-four hours, or the story goes live, and your reputation goes with it."

There was a click on the other end of the line, and Sam cursed at the phone. D-Ray stood up and looked over at her again, then quickly popped back down into his chair, apparently not liking the look on her face. She didn't imagine it was good.

Pamela Nixon *was* a bitch. But if she didn't write about the story, someone else would. Sam had to find something. The press would quickly turn into that rav-ing pack of raccoons if she didn't.

Wait, D-Ray is in his cubie! Then who is standing behind me?—

"You ever hear of the choking game?"

"Huh?" Sam asked, twirling around in her chair, the question surprising her. Gage stood in her cubicle entrance, larger than life, and she felt a flush on her cheeks. She tried to steel herself against reacting to him. He was standing so close, just inches from her. In her cubicle. Uninvited. Granted, there was no door, but still . . .

"I asked you if you'd heard of the choking game."

"No, I haven't heard of it," she said rapidly, looking at him through tired eyes. She hadn't slept well after getting back from the hospital. She'd cried the whole way home, thoughts of how terrified Whitney must have been hammering her mind.

The rat incident hadn't helped. Salty tears pricked her eyes. She pursed her lips and fought them.

Gage seemed to notice her near loss of composure and his eyes softened. Then he seemed to make a decision—to continue with work as if nothing were out of the ordinary.

"Leave it to kids to always come up with new and innovative ways to get a rush or get high. When the thrill rides at the amusement park don't do it anymore, they move on to different things. Sometimes those things are very real, very illegal drugs. And other times the thrill can seem so innocent. Like sniffing glue, or even spray paint cans. They know it's not safe, but they do it anyway. The choking game is one of those things."

"And how does this choking game work?"

A part of Sam wanted him out of her cubicle and far away from Kanesville, but a bigger part of her realized that wasn't going to happen. It had come down to need. They needed him on this case, as much as it rankled.

But that didn't mean Sam had to engage with him on anything else. *Just the case.*

And she wanted to know what he was talking about. A "game" would answer a lot of questions about how three—four, with her own niece—relatively healthy, seemingly happy teenagers just decided to commit suicide one day. It would also mean there was no serial killer. But that was too easy. And Gage had already told Sam he believed these were murders. But a theory like this one might be enough to keep Pamela Nixon off their case, while they investigated the real story.

D-Ray appeared behind Gage—apparently interested

in what he had to say. "Can we use a conference room? I'd like to sit down," Gage said.

Sam nodded her assent and stood up. They followed D-Ray down the hall and bumped into Chief Roberson as he came out of his office. Gage invited the chief to join them, and Sam fought back the desire to scream childishly, "Don't forget, this is *my* case!" That would go over well.

"You grow up round here, Flint?" the chief asked conversationally as they headed down the hall toward the lone conference room in the small station.

"Utah's Dixie, actually. Lived right in Saint George. Not far from Zion."

"Oh, you're from Dixie, huh? My mom and dad retired down there. Lived there till they died. Still have a little place in Washington, just outside Saint George. I go down there when the snow gets too high and the wife gets too loud," Chief Roberson said, instantly turning into the good old boy Mormon small-town police chief. Sam wanted to smack the chief between the eyes.

"Oh yeah?" Gage answered. "Where in Washington? I grew up just off Saint George Boulevard, but my aunt LaRae lived in Washington until they finally moved her into a home in Saint George."

Great. He has an aunt LaRae, a perfect Mormon name.

The tradition came from taking the first syllable of both parents' names. "Larry" and "Raylene" became "LaRae." And it would give Gage immediate Brownie points in the chief's eyes.

"Oh, it was just a ways off that first exit, you know, by the Maverick—"

"Uh, I think we have some work to discuss," Sam said, interrupting their little stroll down memory lane.

Chief Roberson gave her a dirty look, and she cursed the moment Gage Flint weaseled his way into the good graces of the man who held all the cards as far as she was concerned.

"Sure, Sam, let's head on in here." The chief's tone was kind, but his facial expression was stern. He was not pleased with her. She knew she'd better play along. The look was a warning.

As they settled into the room, Gage took control of the conversation. "Here's what I'm thinking. This choking game, kids are doing it for thrills, and sometimes, they die. I did some Google searches late last night and I found some pretty scary stuff."

"Is it like autoerotic asphyxiation?" Sam asked, wincing a little. Masturbating while choking definitely held no attraction for her, but it obviously did for some people. She had been involved in at least two investigations while with the SLCPD.

"Same concept, but without the sexual component."

"Are you suggesting this is what Whitney was doing?"

"No, I'm not. But what I am doing is looking at all the options. What if one or any of these were actually connected with the choking game? It's becoming a real problem in some areas, and that could be what we're dealing with here. I just figured you would want to cover all your bases, before the media gets ahold of it."

Damn Nixon. Somehow she knew, and had already talked to Gage. Sam felt her blood boil.

"Tell us more," Chief Roberson said, and Sam sat back, feeling as though the case were a runaway train and she was the incompetent engineer, unable to do anything to stop it.

"The choking game goes by a variety of names, including 'passout' and the 'fainting game.' Both girls and boys do it, although usually the girls do it in groups at slumber parties and other events and use chest compressions. Boys usually use their hands to choke each other."

"But why in the hell do they do it?" Chief Roberson asked.

"It's the same concept as autoerotic asphyxiation," Sam said, jumping in before Gage could completely take over. "When you have restricted oxygen and blood flow to your brain, you get a rush."

"Right," Gage said. "Kids have described it as a fuzzy feeling, where your vision goes black and you get very woozy. That's the sensation they're looking for, and once they feel it, the pressure is supposed to be released. When the blood rushes back into the brain, it gives them a secondary rush."

"Damn," D-Ray muttered. "Where do they come up with this shit?"

"It's crazy, I know," Gage answered. "And it seems like boys are more likely to try it alone than girls, which means their fatality rate is drastically higher."

"But neither girl was with anyone else," Sam pointed out.

"That we know of," Gage answered.

The name Bethany rang through Sam's brain. The friend who became the enemy: the girl they all turned on. But how could Bethany have managed to convince these two mean girls they were still friends and get them involved in the choking game?

"So, you're thinking someone else was there?" Sam asked.

"I'm just pointing out the obvious. We don't know. We don't know that they were alone, even though all indications point to suicide. Were they just suicides? Or was Jeremiah Malone's case a botched encounter with the choking game?"

"This is giving me a headache," D-Ray said.

"What we need to consider," Gage said, "is that these kids don't realize that once they've decided to use a ligature to reach the sensation, it's only mere seconds before the sensation turns from exhilarating to lethal. They lose consciousness, and their own body weight kills them."

"So you think we need to do some asking around to see if kids are doing this?" Chief Roberson asked, and Sam felt a rush of despair in her chest. It was going to happen. He was going to take this away from her. It wouldn't be her case anymore. "And I'm guessing you think this because it will give us some time to figure out what's really going on."

D-Ray's mouth dropped open and Sam turned to look at Roberson with surprise. They all liked the chief, but he wasn't really known for his policing skills. At one point, he'd gone to a local Kanesville girl's house and threatened to arrest her if she didn't return some seriously overdue library books. The librarian was a friend of his.

"Exactly," Gage said. "It's just a precaution, and to cover all the bases. It's possible, although not probable, that the first two girls and Jeremiah were either suicides or victims of the choking game. And maybe Whitney just decided to kill herself because she was pregnant."

"What the hell? How did you find that out?" Sam asked angrily, clenching her fists and rising out of her chair.

"She was pregnant?" D-Ray said incredulously.

"Calm down, Sam. Your sister told me."

"When did you talk to my sister?"

"This morning, when I went to check on Whitney. The doctors had just told Susanna the news."

"She doesn't even *know* you and she told you that?"

"I have a face that inspires confidence."

D-Ray guffawed, and Gage gave him an angry glare.

The implications of Whitney's pregnancy, along with her accident, hit Sam then, like a gut punch. "The baby?" she asked him.

He just shook his head.

"Oh, poor Susanna." Was it a relief or an answer to a prayer? And what kind of prayer would that be?

"There is good news, though. Whitney is starting to respond, squeezing her mom's hand, and reacting to pain. The doctors are cautiously optimistic."

"That's good. But . . . I find this out from you?"

"Of course. You would rather the news come from someone else. Anyone else. Well, sorry, but I'm what you've got." His lips thinned in anger, and his face flushed. Sam saw something else there: pain. She'd hurt him. Well, good. It was his turn to be hurt.

Roberson looked from Gage to Sam and then back to Gage. He turned to D-Ray, who just put his hands up in the air with a "don't ask me" posture. Once again, the chief surprised Sam.

"This is why I don't like having female officers," he said. "You think it's because I'm sexist, or a chauvinist, but the truth is, sometimes when men and women work together, there's friction."

He pointed a chubby index finger at Gage. "You came here as a favor, but take this as my warning. While I welcome your opinion and help, I am not that old and stupid." He looked at both of them.

Gage rose, gave Sam a smoldering look, and then said a polite good-bye to the chief and D-Ray, offering each his hand. "I have some phone calls to make. I'll be in the empty cubicle on the other side of you, Sam. In case you need to find me." He turned and walked from the room without another word.

The chief turned to Sam. "And you, missy, you need to be professional here. You're walking a damned thin line on this case, especially now your family's involved. If we had more detectives, you'd be off it so fast your head would spin. But I'm willing to give you the benefit of the doubt."

" 'Missy'?"

"Oh, don't give me that crap. You and I both know I'm as fair as they come. I hired you, and not because it made me look good, either. I hired you because I have an instinct about good detectives and I know you're one. I've worked with a few in my time, and even though we don't see a lot of stuff here in our town, it happens. And when it does, I want it solved, and I want it solved fast. Got it?"

Sam blinked and nodded, and he got up and wandered out of the conference room, muttering something about a donut and another "damn stupid mess with red tape."

Sam sat silently in her chair for a minute, then looked at D-Ray. He got all wide eyed and innocent. "Don't be looking at me. I didn't say squat to him about Gage. Still think it's a pansy-ass name, but he seems like an okay dude."

This is the answer you needed, Sam. Until you find the real one. It's all you've got, but it will keep the wolves at bay.

"Sorry," she muttered, listening to Callie's words of caution float away. "I was just a little surprised to hear he knew Whitney was pregnant."

"Did you know?" D-Ray asked.

"Susanna told me she thought maybe Whit was pregnant. She said, 'A mother knows.' But she didn't have proof. She just suspected it. But she did say that Whitney was dating Jeremiah Malone."

"Okay, this just gets more and more complicated. Do we have a killer? An innocent choking game? A suicide pact? Maybe all three," D-Ray said. "Or maybe none of it is tied together. Uh, no pun intended. I mean, the first two girls sure looked like suicide. Boys are more likely to die from accidental choking than girls, and Whitney—"

"Whitney wouldn't kill herself."

"Sam, she was seventeen years old and pregnant, and the father of the baby just died. If anybody had a reason to be suicidal, she did."

"As much as I don't want these to be murders, D-Ray, my gut tells me they are. The slide show was the killer's way of saying, 'This isn't what you think.'"

"Yeah, I mean, I know coincidences happen and all, but this is a hell of one." D-Ray scratched his head. "Somebody wants to keep us guessing. It's working."

"And we don't have any choice but to do the leg-work. So get prepared to put in some OT. Follow this possibility up. I have a phone call to make. I'll meet up with you at Winger's at noon."

"And what would you like me to order you today?" D-Ray asked innocently. "I think the soup is French onion. One of my favorites."

Sam just shook her head and walked away, listening to his soft chuckle.

She had to give Pamela Nixon just enough information to get her moving on a story, completely in the wrong direction. Sam felt slightly guilty about that.

Why are you feeling guilty? You don't know squat. You have an instinct these are murders. Gage just handed you something to keep the media busy while you figure out what is really going on.

"Right," Sam said aloud.

She walked outside, flipped open her cell phone, and dialed Nixon's number.

"Time's almost up, friend," Nixon answered. "What do you have for me?"

"It's called the choking game, and it's killing kids across the United States. I'm not telling you more, and I'm an unconfirmed and unnamed source. You name me, you never get diddly from me again."

"Choking game?"

"Choking game. Google it. You'll find hundreds of entries on it." Sam clicked the phone shut and hoped she was telling the truth. She would be Googling it herself later, but right now she had a girl named Bethany to find.

Sam walked toward her car, then stopped abruptly when she saw an angry Gage leaned up against it, arms crossed and folded across his chest.

"You look pissed," she said. "Mind telling me why?

Because from my viewpoint, you don't have any reason at all to be mad." She fought the hot flush she felt rising in her face but wasn't successful. She knew he would see the emotion she could feel pulsing through her veins.

"You're a detective; figure it out," he said, terse words filled with strong emotion. She just wasn't able to tell which one it was.

"You like me, and you don't know the difference between wooing a girl and stalking her, so you're just hanging out until I define that for you?" He winced, and Sam knew her words had struck home. For some reason, the fact that she'd hurt him made her flush. Guilt filled her. And panic.

What if he really leaves?

It was what she wanted, wasn't it?

"Stalking?" He laughed harshly, but there was no humor on his face. "Sam, I'm doing what I should have done last time. Walking you through this, instead of knee-jerking it and not giving you a chance to finish what you started."

"Huh?" Sam said, momentarily derailed. It was not the answer she expected.

"Figure it out," was all he said, and then reached forward and stroked her cheek, his fingers warm. Sam jumped back, a hot sensation she couldn't control running down through her body. He turned and left before she could say anything else, getting into his SUV and driving off without another look back at her.

Confusion filled her mind, and she ran her fingers through her hair, which suddenly felt heavy and in the way. She fought the urge to pull it back in a ponytail, like the old Sam would have done. She wondered if she should follow him and run him down. Pull him over, lights and sirens, and find out just exactly what he was up to.

D-Ray made sure that didn't happen. He walked out the front door of the station, his dark brown sorrow-filled eyes meeting hers. "We've got another one."

TWENTY-SEVEN

Fourteen-year-old Milton Needham had been discovered by his mother, hanging from his bunk bed, a belt around his neck. Her screams brought her husband and older son into the room, and they quickly got Milton down and began doing CPR. By the time the paramedics arrived, they could detect a faint heartbeat and he was Life Flighted to Primary Children's Medical Center, where he would be treated in PICU, the same place where Whitney slowly healed.

Pictures of Milton in various stages of growth were framed and on the walls of this newer home in West Kanesville. One set upon the mantelpiece featured Milton with his father. Milton was pimply and gangly, with thick glasses, a large beaked nose, and a braces-filled grin.

In the picture, he wore his Boy Scout uniform while his father beamed beside him. Obviously, the picture had been taken when Milton received his Eagle Scout award. His father looked proud. Milton's smile looked fake and miserable.

Mormons always placed a special emphasis on Boy Scouts, and getting to be an Eagle Scout was a sign of accomplishment within the community, almost as important as baptism and serving an LDS mission.

Milton was right on target. And according to his mother, he also *was* a target—for bullies.

"I haven't been able to get him to go to school for the past week. The kids are so mean, just so, so mean," she said, sobs slipping out between each word. "I offered to go talk to the principal, but he wouldn't let me. Nobody should be allowed to do that to someone. No one should be that cruel."

The scene was almost a repeat of the one at Susanna's house, only it was Marsha Needham's husband trying to get her dressed and her things together so they could be rushed to the hospital—only to stand by helplessly as a machine breathed for their son.

Any interviewing the police did would have to wait, but Sam's gut instinct told her that this was exactly what it looked like. A teenage boy's suicide attempt, one who was tired of being tortured, teased, and ignored by the pretty girls. There was a note that explained this in detail. He was hanging from his own belt. The other deaths—and Whitney's near death—happened to the very kids about whom Milton's mother complained. Someone was targeting the bullies, not the victims. Nothing about this attempted suicide resembled the others; while there was a good chance this boy had been "inspired" by the others, Sam knew instinctually that Milton had brought about his own near death. But she would follow up every report and piece of evidence.

"You need to stop whoever this is. Find whoever did this to my boy!" Marsha Needham said, shocking Sam out of her thoughts.

"Ma'am, this appears to be a suicide attempt," she said soothingly.

Marsha Needham was having none of that. "I've heard what people are saying, and I know the truth. The truth is, somebody else is doing this. We have a killer here in Kanesville, and he's going after our children. You need to stop it or find someone who can. Find the person who did this. *Fix this!*"

Gage walked through the front door just as Sam was being told to "fix" the situation, and he quickly came over to stand by her.

"Who are you?" the distraught woman asked.

"This is Detective Gage Flint," Sam told her. "He's helping us on this case."

Gage raised his eyebrows for a minute as he made eye contact with Sam, and then turned to the distraught mother.

"We've dealt with this kind of thing before," he said, his voice a calming tone in the midst of all the medical hustle and bustle and raised voices. "We know what we're doing."

"Fix it," the woman implored him.

Sam and Gage watched as Marsha's husband urged her out the door. "Well, so much for keeping the killer theory quiet," Sam said to D-Ray, who just shook his head.

"Why did you do that?" Gage asked her after D-Ray walked away to confer with the head of the Kanesville

Fire Department, who always responded on medical calls.

"Do what?"

"Tell her I was helping you. You haven't exactly been a member of my cheerleading section."

"You have cheerleaders?"

"Funny. You know what I mean. What changed your mind?"

"Who says I changed my mind? She's a Mormon woman in a patriarchal community. She's distraught. She's not going to look to me to save her. She's going to look to a man. You just happened to be standing there at the right time."

He looked at Sam and shook his head. She didn't know if he was hurt or genuinely puzzled. She didn't know how she felt, either.

"So you don't really want me on this case?" Gage asked. "If I said I would leave right now, would you tell me to go?"

At that moment, D-Ray came back to join them. All three stood and watched as the paramedics and police officers loaded up their gear and prepared to leave the Needham house.

Only a few would remain behind to process any possible evidence.

"This is a mess," D-Ray said. "Do you think this was the Vengeance killer?"

"Don't say that out loud," Sam told him. "All we need is for the media to give this a name."

"They're out there. Channel Five and Nixon, and a few from the local papers," Gage said.

"Well, don't talk to them," Sam said.

"I'm not stupid, Sam," Gage growled back at her.

"I just mean . . ." Sam stopped talking. She didn't want anyone to know she was doing her own form of playing with the media, hoping that Nixon would be squawking about the "choking game theory" loud and profusely and that would head people off in a new direction. But if the media got to Milton's mother . . .

This would hurt her. But there was no way around it. Who wanted to think their own child could take his life? Who wanted to realize that someone they loved so much was in that much pain that the only answer appeared to be death? Hanging was not a cry for help, like drug overdose or slitting of wrists. People who hung themselves were done.

Sam sighed and rubbed her temples. While this wasn't going to make her job easier—in fact, it muddied the water—Gage had given her the answer she needed to stave off a little time. She flinched as she realized she owed him one. Maybe she'd drop a six-pack off at his front door and call it good.

That would work, right?

Not even close.

"You didn't answer me," D-Ray said insistently. "Do you think this is the . . . uh . . . same killer?"

"No," Sam said. "I think a sad, lonely, emotional boy decided he'd had enough of being bullied, and since other kids were doing it, why shouldn't he? I think he hung himself because he figured he didn't have much else to live for."

"Yeah, me, too," D-Ray said, then chucked Gage in the shoulder like men do and walked away from the scene.

"You didn't answer me, either," Gage said to Sam

once they were alone again. "Do you really want me to leave?"

"I don't know," she said truthfully.

"Well, maybe you better go looking for that answer." He turned and followed D-Ray over to talk with the responding officers.

TWENTY-EIGHT

Mark Malone sat in a large recliner in the Mormon room of his house and held his face in his hands, leaning forward, rocking like a small child seeking comfort. The traditional Mormon room was a small sitting room where LDS families entertained church visitors—those like the visiting teachers or the home teachers. This room held a piano, a portrait of Jesus, a gold-painted bust of Joseph Smith, and muted green and maroon rugs and table coverings.

It made Sam distinctly uncomfortable to be here, in the room of the house normally reserved for the believing, but this was where President Malone had asked to meet.

They had waited a lot longer than normal to interview the man, mainly because the chief had made her give Malone "time" to absorb his grief and cope. In fact, Chief Roberson had insisted on coming along for the interview, leaving both D-Ray and Gage out in the cold.

And she knew what this meant. She would be sabotaged. No matter what she said, it wouldn't be the right thing, and she wouldn't get the answers she was looking for, because the chief was going to protect his own. And his "own" was not his detective but one of the members of his dogged faith: the only true church. No matter how fair he seemed, she knew the ropes here in Mormon country, and priesthood authority trumped all other hands.

Sam didn't want to do this now, even though a few days had passed. She never did. It was one of those things that would be wonderful to put off for as long as possible—say, forever.

It was not hard to question a perp, thief—or, worse, a murderer, the scum of the earth. But working the family of a dead victim, or a live victim for that matter, gave her nightmares.

Malone's wife, Lydia, had been given a sedative by the paramedics the day of the incident. She was still nowhere to be seen, and President Malone claimed she was unwell and in her bed—probably the slumber of the undead, those left behind by someone they loved more than life itself. And yet, as with her mother, Sam questioned the depth of a love that was so fragile a woman could disappear into herself or, even worse, become a shell, an outer body, a host for the organs inside with no real brain or feelings or love. Disappear while her children were still alive, needing a nurturing parent. In Sam's mother's case, while her other children were still alive.

"I'm sorry to have to do this now, President Malone," Sam said, anxious to get it over with. "But unfortunately it's part of my job, and I have to ask these questions."

He shrugged his shoulders and removed his head from his hands, leaning his head into the back of chair, eyes closed.

Sam took his silence for assent to continue. "Did you have any indication that your son was suicidal?"

Malone's eyes popped open, and he sat forward in the chair. "My son would not kill himself. Ever. This was not a suicide."

"I understand you want to believe that, President Malone," Sam said in her kindest, most understanding voice. "And it may very well be that you are right. But first we have to follow all the proper steps and make sure that it wasn't a suicide or an accident. He was found strangled with a tie in your computer room. Unfortunately, this could be something that is currently really common among boys. It's called autoerotic asphyxiation, and often ends in death. There is another game they call the 'choking' game, and sometimes that ends this way as well."

"He did not kill himself. This was an accident. Your assumptions are wrong."

The man's words were calm, but his demeanor belied his ease. He leaned forward, tense, angry, eyes flashing sparks that were directed in her direction. She knew he was used to running the show, to asking the questions. This went against the grain. She didn't care. She couldn't.

It was her job to get the truth, and she was going to get it, no matter what she had to do. So he was a man in authority, a stake president, leader of the faithful in many local wards. She was the law. It shouldn't be a question.

But it always would be a question. And it spurred

her on. "I know you don't want to think he killed himself. But the truth is, it looks that way. So give me something, please, to help me believe you. Tell me why your son would not do this?"

"He was the captain of the football team, for hell's sake," the man burst out. "He was popular and had lots of girls after him. He was being looked at for a full-ride scholarship for Brigham Young University. Quarterback. They don't just hand those out, you know."

"I know that. But this happened, and I have to get through all of this to find out why. Are you absolutely certain nothing could have been upsetting enough he would kill himself? Or that he didn't regularly participate in the practice of autoerotic asphyxiation?"

"What the hell? What the hell is that anyway? You keep saying that. What does it mean?"

Sam had no desire to explain the hows and whys of choking yourself while masturbating, or the supposed extreme rush it gave you. She would if she had to, but there had been no sign of masturbation at the scene, leaving the two options: either suicide or the choking game.

Malone began again before she could start. "Didn't you hear me? He was going to BYU. Full-ride scholarship. They have an honor code there. Nothing could be more exciting or important than that. Nothing. He's a good Mormon boy. A good boy. He doesn't do that kind of thing. That kind of vile . . ."

Vile thing. Malone was a stake president and heard lots of horror stories. He was not innocent to this, she realized. He knew what was being implied.

"President Malone, all teenage boys do it. Even good Mormon ones."

"Don't you tell me that, missy!" He glared at her, denial, anger, and harsh reality spreading quickly across his face. "You have no right to say that to me, or to say that my son was responsible for tying that tie around his neck because he was trying to get himself. . . . aroused. I don't know who you think you are."

"President Malone, my title is Detective Samantha Montgomery. It wouldn't bother me if you called me Sam. But I do not answer to 'missy.' "

The chief started to move forward, perhaps to intercede, but then thought better of it. He stepped back and let Sam continue.

"I'm a police detective, trying to solve a crime. Do I enjoy this? No. I would rather be running a marathon. But it's my job. So please tell me what you know. Was that your tie? The one he used?"

"No, God no. I've never seen it before. It wasn't even a good-quality tie. And I never wear dark blue. Are we done now?"

Sam stood up and turned abruptly away from him. She knew this tactic would work, because she'd been a subservient Mormon girl for most of her life. Walk away and they would try to woo you back. Whether through force, fear, or sheer desperation—a Mormon man could not bear for any woman to walk away from him or to treat him as though he were lesser than her. He had to have the last word. No one turns their back on the holy priesthood.

"Wait, why are you going? You haven't even come close to figuring out what happened."

Sam decided to gamble, while she had the upper hand. She turned and stared back at him.

"We already have an idea, President Malone. Jeremiah was caught up in a game, if you want to call it that, that teenagers sometimes play. It's all part of growing up, but sometimes they get caught up in it, and that's it. They take it further. Sometimes, too far."

"Sam, I think that's enough," Chief Roberson said, and she looked up, thrown completely off her game by his intrusion. She'd almost forgotten he was there.

Embarrassed to be derailed, though it shouldn't have surprised her, Sam blinked, breathed, then spoke. "I am trying to solve a case you've assigned me to solve."

"Well, I think you are just going a little too far with this, Detective. Obviously, this man knows nothing."

"Obviously, we won't know that if we never get to question him like we would any other—"

"Detective Montgomery, would you like to find yourself on suspension?"

"Well, Chief, if that is what you feel is necessary."

Not used to being called out by any of his officers, his mouth dropped open a little, and Sam knew he was thinking long and hard about what to say next. She decided to help him.

"These are dead teenagers. And the intricacies and covenants that these people are intoning are not going to change the fact we have dead children. Children. That is all they are. But maybe you are right; maybe we should discuss this elsewhere. I'm totally amenable to that," Sam said, knowing the look on her face had to convey just how desperately she wanted to take this elsewhere and give the chief a piece of her mind—even though that would undoubtedly result in her suspension.

And then she remembered Gage's words. She remembered that he believed, like she did, that this was a serial murderer and not suicide. And this man, no matter how arrogant, had just lost his son. And she could hardly solve the case with irrational, emotionally charged behavior.

Chief Roberson caught her eye, and she put up her hand, asking him to stop without words. He waited a moment, then gave her a brief nod.

"President Malone, I know these are hard questions. All I want are answers. Don't you want them, too? Don't you want peace of mind, not always wondering what happened? I can tell you from personal experience that not knowing is the cruelest fate of all."

Stake President Mark Malone, a blond, distinguished man in his late forties, looked her straight in the eye, then reached into the pocket of his shirt. He pulled out a picture and held it out to her. She stepped forward and took it.

Then the man collapsed, consumed with a grief he couldn't explain. Chief Roberson gave her an alarmed look. Sam looked down at the picture and saw two teenagers, naked, laughing, the girl's arm up as she took the picture. It was obvious this was a sexual interlude. The girl's long hair covered her breasts, but there could be little doubt what these two were up to.

It was Jeremiah Malone and Sam's niece, Whitney.

"Where did you get this?" Sam asked Malone.

He didn't speak, his hands covering his eyes. "President Malone," she said again, softly but firmly. "Where did you get this?"

"Someone left it on my doorstep," he said, his voice a mere whisper, the words coming out choppy and terse.

"I'm sorry," she said. No one wanted to believe their

child could do such a thing. Especially the morally rigid. She followed her instincts and went to Malone, knelt down by the chair, and gripped his shoulder as he shook.

And she knew it would never be spoken of again.

TWENTY-NINE

The peaches were mushy, the lemons didn't smell fresh, and the green peppers were way too small. Sam had decided to assuage the emptiness inside her by filling up with a healthy meal, except nothing at the grocery store looked appetizing. It wasn't food she wanted or lacked. It never was.

All she'd thought about since leaving President Malone's home was the distinguished man's breakdown. She'd bagged the picture and dropped it off at the crime lab, but she knew it had been handled too much and this killer—and she knew it was a killer—was too careful to leave behind evidence.

And the fact that the stake president had allowed her to comfort him had no place in her psyche to be compartmentalized. What was she supposed to do with that image? She didn't know. She wanted a strong drink and mindless sex. That immediately turned her thoughts to Gage, which made her flush.

Sam turned away from the peaches, annoyed with her own weakness and chiding herself for not focusing on the case. That's all Gage was—or could be—to her. She pushed her cart forward and almost bumped into two women whispering to each other, carts side by side, blocking the aisle. Their heads were together and eyes wide and glistening, a look of surprise and superiority on both faces. Gossipmongers. The same kind that she had encountered for years—and still did.

She looked around the women, in the direction they kept turning, and when she saw the ratty bathrobe, the uncombed hair, and the blue slippers her breath slipped out of her and didn't return. She put a hand on her cart for support and forced herself to breathe deeply, refusing to allow herself to return to the past, to a place where her mother made hamburgers for every meal, every day. The same meal she had made the day Callie was found hanging from the tree. Hamburgers over, and over, over, every day, dressed in an old bathrobe and ratty slippers, until one day she just stopped functioning completely.

Breathe, Sam, breathe.

How could Ruthie Montgomery have escaped the hospital? Her father watched her so closely, so diligently, that he no longer had any health left, all of his energy and support going to care for the woman who didn't even seem to know he existed. But the hospital— surely their care and guard was even closer than Sam's father's, who had slept through four noisy girls, slumber parties, and movie night with Mom.

Movie night. When Mom and the four girls sat down and watched the late show, Nightmare Theatre, *something their father would never have approved of. But their mother was every bit as enthralled in it as the daughters were.*

But this ratty hair was not laced with gray. The body was a bit larger, the slippers a color of blue that no one in her family would have bought—they were the color of Callie's eyes. That color caused keening and wailing that wouldn't stop without medication. The only response from a catatonic mother they had managed to get in years. It was never allowed in the Montgomery house.

This lost soul was not Sam's mother. It was Lydia Malone.

Sam approached Lydia and said her name softly. The woman stood in front of the grapes, picking up first one bunch, then another, and staring at them help-lessly, as though it was impossible to decipher which bunch was better. Or as though they held some invisible message that would make everything right again.

"Lydia," Sam said again.

She didn't respond to Sam at first, then turned to stare at her dully, through eyes that only saw what she wanted to believe was real.

"I need grapes. Jeremiah gets so upset if there aren't any grapes. He says they are fuel for his body. He only likes the sweet ones, though. Do you know if this kind is sweet?"

"No, I think these aren't good grapes at all. I think they are out of season. I bet if you come back another time, though, they would be better."

The two women who had led Sam's attention to Lydia Malone had gotten a little brazen and moved in closer, probably hoping to hear the conversation and have something to tell all their friends and ward members.

"Why don't you let me take you home," Sam said, her voice soft, her face close to the other woman's ear. Sam fought the impulse to wrinkle her nose as the woman's unwashed state hit her senses. It was a familiar smell.

"Oh, I can't leave without grapes. Jeremiah will be so mad. Do you know where the good ones are? Are they keeping them in back?"

"No, they probably don't have them here. I heard they carry them at Smith's, though. I'll take you to get some," Sam said, taking Lydia by the elbow and steering her away from the prying eyes and toward the door.

"But . . ."

"You want the best grapes, don't you? Let's go."

"Okay," the woman said meekly, allowing Sam to guide her out of the store.

Although she thought it was possible Lydia Malone had driven herself to the store, Sam did not attempt to find her car and, instead, drove her home. Sam parked in front of the Malone house and let herself out of the driver's side, hurrying around to open the door for the other woman. But Lydia Malone was in no hurry to leave Sam's car, even though she had not spoken a word on the ride home.

The Malone home was dark, and Sam wondered where President Malone was now. Sam also wondered if she would be chastised for her small lie—not taking her to Smith's when she had promised—but Lydia did not react. Sam, used to this silence, let her be. Now the woman stared at the house, almost fearfully.

"It's okay, Sister Malone; I'll help you inside," Sam

said, using the familiar title LDS Church members used to address each other.

"I can't go inside," the other woman whispered. She didn't take her eyes off the house. "There's no one there. No one is home."

"I'm sure your husband will be home soon."

"No one is home."

"Not right now, but—"

"No one is home!" The words came out as a shrill scream, and Sam jumped back.

She waited a moment, watching the other woman, who stared at the house with longing and desire—and repulsion. To step inside this house would be yet another reminder that her son was dead and would never come back. Every time she saw a place where he had once stood, she would be reminded of him. In this small town, no place would be safe. And yet she probably wanted that as much as she dreaded it.

"No, no one is home," Sam said softly, compassion filling her. Lydia Malone had been mentally ill before Jeremiah died, for reasons Sam didn't entirely understand and probably never would, but this . . . from this she would probably never recover.

"I can't go inside if no one's home. It scares me. It scares me."

"I'll go inside with you," Sam said. "I'll wait until your husband comes home."

"He never comes home," the other woman said, not looking at Sam, still staring with fear at the large house. "At least not really. His head is somewhere else. His heart, too. No, no one lives here anymore. No one at all. Especially not me. I can't. There isn't a place here for me."

Sam saw the desolation in her face and knew she had to make a call.

"I think I'll find somewhere else for you to stay," she said lightly, not wanting to tip the woman off to her real purpose. "Someplace where people are home."

"That would be nice," Lydia Malone said, still not breaking her gaze from the house.

Sam stepped away from the car and moved to the sidewalk, quickly dialing Dispatch and requesting an ambulance for a 5150. She gave the name and the address, and the dispatcher asked no more. Perhaps the only surprise was that it had taken this long.

Before the scene became chaotic—which Sam knew it would—she returned to the side of Lydia Malone. The woman turned to look at Sam, finally, breaking her gaze from the house she feared, the memories that haunted her.

"I'm crazy, aren't I?" she asked, tears streaming down her face.

"You just need a little help to get through a tough situation."

"No, I was this way before. So depressed. So sad. I didn't even get out of bed. I wasn't there for him. I wasn't the mother he needed. Now he's dead, and I don't get the chance to fix it. I don't get the chance . . . I lost me. I didn't get to achieve any of the things I wanted to do, because of my duties. And I let it drive me crazy. Maybe he thought he wasn't enough. That I didn't love him enough."

The truth had already broken this woman, spreading the fissure that existed in her brain. Would more truth do more damage? Possibly irreparable?

"You didn't wish it on him, Sister Malone."

"Don't call me that, please. Call me Lydia."

"Okay, Lydia. Jeremiah's death was not your fault."

"It was. It had to be."

"No, it didn't."

She reached forward and put her arm on Sam's shoulder. "You don't understand. You're not a mother. It's your job, as a mother, to keep your kids safe. I was in bed when he died. When he took his own life. I was sleeping, too sad to even realize my own son was worse than I was."

"I don't think he killed himself," Sam said, deciding the truth could not hurt any more than the pain Lydia Malone had already endured.

"You don't?" Shock filled Lydia's gray eyes—clear gray eyes, Sam noted. Eyes that didn't look crazy or lost, at least right now.

"No."

"Someone killed him?"

"It's something we are looking into. Either that, or it was an accident." She didn't want to have to explain the nasty games boys could play, games that sometimes ended with a funeral and insurmountable grief.

"But who would want him dead? Everyone was his friend."

"I'm not sure right now, but if someone is responsible, I'll find them."

"Who would do this to me? Why? Why would anyone do this?" Her gray eyes became cloudy again, and the woman looked away, back toward the house, fear filling her gaze once more. "I never knew it would be like this. One day you're tucking that sweet child, with big blue eyes, into bed, and he looks up to you and says, 'Mommy, will you marry me?' And when he wakes up, he can't even stand to look at you. He hates you. The venom is so real. And you just wait for the day when he will love you and adore you again, when he outgrows the hatred and embarrassment, and I'll never . . . I'll never have that. I couldn't handle the hate. It was just a phase. He was a teenage boy. He would have gotten over it, right?"

"I'm sorry, Lydia."

Sirens filled the air as the ambulance pulled onto the street, followed by two police cars. Lydia Malone didn't seem to see or hear them.

"My son died hating me."

THIRTY

Late-summer nights in Utah were hot and sultry, some-times breezy, but generally still and quiet. Tonight was no exception.

Sam ran through the tree-lined streets of Kanesville, the small, old houses a blur as she passed them, con-centrating on her rhythm and the shadows around her. Her feet pounded the pavement, her heart beating rap-idly.

There were only a few lights on; some just illumi-nated a porch or house number. She ran uphill, toward the mountain, although she knew she wouldn't go that far. The climb gave her something to concentrate on; just breathing was an effort. That was what she needed tonight.

She needed to keep moving, so she wouldn't give in to her demons. As a precaution, she hadn't put her iPod on tonight, so she could hear everything should some-one try to accost her. After all, there was a killer loose in Kanesville. And even though teenagers seemed to be the targets, a killer was a killer. And she was a woman alone, running at night. This town, which should be so safe, was a hotbed of violence right now.

Safe? Are you kidding me? Have you forgotten what happened to me? And that was twenty years ago.

But it was safe. Bad things hardly ever happened in this small town. Occasionally, of course . . . But for the most part, crime was low.

There's evil everywhere. Just because a town is small, or religious, it doesn't mean it's safe. This place has never been safe.

Sam shook her head as she ran, pushing harder, faster, her calves aching as she neared the top of the road that led to Highway 89. There she would stop and turn around, if only she could shut her mind off. Stop Callie from talking.

No one you love is safe. And this place killed me. It swallowed me whole.

You have to believe me. You have to know I didn't kill myself. I was so scared. So scared.

Sam stopped cold in the middle of the street, a sudden chilling awareness running through her body, making the sweat on her skin icy cold, as though she'd just run through a snowstorm. Callie's haunted voice seemed to echo in the dark around her.

"But you killed yourself. You hung yourself from the tree, right? It was—"

No, it wasn't. Suicide had a feel, a desperation, a dark, pulsing need.

Callie's scene hadn't been that way. Sam didn't remember a lot, except how stoic her father was. He'd been the one who took Callie down, her body cold and stiff. Sam remembered bits and pieces of that night. She had run over to Callie—after her father pulled her down from the tree—and touched her face. Freezing cold. Her father pushed Sam away. Where was her mother?

Sam had no memory of that. No screaming—unlike Jeremiah's mother, Lydia Malone, a beacon calling them to the scene.

Where was Mom?

Sam remembered all the people traipsing through the house. The look of pity on the faces of the ward members and neighbors. And how cold, dark, and empty she felt inside—a feeling she grew up to know as empathy with the victim.

The scene at Milton Needham's house had felt completely different from the other recent hangings—and, now, from what she remembered of Callie's death. Sam had known from the moment she walked into the door of the Needhams' house that it had been a genuine suicide attempt. None of the others had reached out and talked to her this way. She'd sensed the despair on all of them, but there'd been no terror around Milton's. Just a sense of complete and total failure. And anger. The boy had given up. And just think how sorry everyone would be.

I didn't want to die.

Callie's death, no matter how little Sam remembered of it, did not have the same feel. Despair, yes—but terror, too.

Oh my God, please help me. Please help me. I'm scared. I'm so scared.

Terrified. The realization that Callie had been terrified hit Sam in the chest like a solid, physical punch. She gasped for breath and felt a tear on her cheek. She covered her mouth with her right hand to hold back the sobs as the brutality assaulted her. Callie had been terrified as the rope tightened around her neck and her legs swung helplessly, back and forth. She'd struggled to free herself, her hands and arms pulling at the rope around her neck. Blackness seeped into her brain as the rope tightened and her throat ached and the world faded from view. There was no air, no air, no air. . . .

Save me. Somebody save me. Oh my God, please save me. I don't want to die.

Was the voice even Callie's? Did this voice belong to Whitney? Did it belong to Sam herself?

The sobs took over Sam's body as she thought of her poor sister, so scared and unable to do anything to save herself. Hanging was a brutal death. They didn't even use it for the death penalty anymore.

Sam struggled to get control of her body and emotions and took off running again, the tears drying on her cheeks. The fear and terror—Callie's terror, or perhaps Whitney's—followed Sam. As she ran she scanned the bushes and sides of dark houses for shadows that might move. She could hear the crickets chirp and her feet crunching on the gravel as she scanned the empty streets. Occasionally she would pass a house with a light on inside, but for the most part, all was dark.

It was nearing 1:00 a.m., the time for all good residents to be in their beds, fast asleep. And yet Sam was up, jogging past midnight, headed to the cemetery, where she always ran the best, the fastest. As though she could outrun all the death that had stained her life.

She reached the black wrought-iron gates of the cemetery, only to realize that was not what she wanted. She didn't want to talk to Callie tonight. It was already too raw, and Sam couldn't take any more. She ached for a place to go to escape the pain, and when Gage flashed into her mind she angrily tried to brush the thought away. He would just think she was weak and be even more convinced that she needed his help to do her job. But she couldn't face any more of Callie's anguish tonight.

Sam turned away from the cemetery, framing an apology to Callie in her head as she ran back toward her house. *Wasn't thinking straight, Sis. Just wanted to talk to you. Just wanted your help to figure out this huge mess.*

Sam certainly hadn't planned to be hit with the realization that her sister had been murdered. How did one plan that?

From behind her, she heard the sound of a car approaching, as she saw the shine of the headlights lighting up the pavement in front of her. She instinctively moved closer to the side of the road for the car to pass, and glanced behind her to see the car had slowed and moved closer to her side of the road.

She could taste the fear as it washed into the back of her throat, and she quickly surveyed her surroundings. Across the road, to the south, there was a deep gully where no houses could be built, due to the water level. To the right was a subdivision of small two- and three-bedroom houses: homes that had been there as long as she could remember, much like the one she had grown up in, where her father and mother still lived.

In this subdivision all the lights were off, except for an occasional porch bulb. Directly ahead was a streetlight, and Sam continued to run, determined to stay in the light, hoping this would keep the car behind her from running her off the road. If that was what was intended. Maybe it was just some teenagers trying to scare her. Or an old person unable to sleep, out for a drive. Maybe a middle-of-the-night run to the grocery store for a sick child. Maybe a drunk driver trying to find their way home after a night of partying.

A woman jogging this late would catch all of these people off-guard.

As these thoughts streamed through her head, she kept turning and watching the car, which was keeping pace with her as she ran.

In the dark of the summer evening, all she could tell was that it was a light-colored four-door sedan and whoever was driving it was traveling about the pace of her running. With deadly intention.

Suddenly, deciding that taking action was her only course, Sam sprinted across the road and dove down into the gully, listening as the driver of the car gunned the engine and screeched across the road following her. She tumbled down a steep incline, wincing as twigs and rocks scraped her bare arms and legs and a large stick tore across her cheek.

She reached the bottom of the gully and splashed into a small creek that ran through the ravine, gasping at the sudden shock of cold water on her hot, sweaty body.

She heard a car door slam and chose to stay low, getting onto her knees and crawling over to the side of the creek, where a large tree towered over the rushing stream, branches reaching out across the divide. She quickly moved behind it and waited, reaching into her fanny pack for her off-duty jogging weapon, a Walther PK380. It was lightweight and sleek but packed a powerful punch.

She could see and hear nothing but the rushing of the stream and the intense pounding of the blood in her head as adrenaline rushed through her body. She scanned the hill above her, the gun aimed at darkness, looking to see if whoever had run her off the road—and tried to run her over—was coming down. But she could see nothing.

After a moment, she heard a car door slam and a squealing of tires, but she still didn't move. Her eyes had adjusted to the darkness as much as they would and she listened to every cricket's chirp, every crunch, every crack, struggling to hear them above the sound of the creek and her own frantic bloodstream.

Finally, she convinced herself that the danger was gone, and only then did she realize how wet her clothes and shoes were, from crossing—rolling through, really—the creek. She began to shake, and instinct kicked in. She put the gun back in her pack and pulled out her phone, calling the first number that came to her.

Why that was Gage Flint's she didn't want to know.

She only knew he would come and, for a moment at least, she would feel safe.

And she also knew that the car that had run her off the road was a light-colored four-door sedan, just like the one Paul Carson drove.

THIRTY-ONE

Gage wrapped Sam in a blanket and handed her a cup of tea. She was shivering head to toe, despite the fact that it was sixty-eight degrees outside. She knew the soaking in the creek wasn't the cause. Maybe she had freaked herself out, but more likely . . .

Someone had tried to kill her.

Even as a patrol officer on the streets of Salt Lake City, right out of the academy, she had never faced this. A lot of cops didn't. But tonight someone had tried to run her over with a car. Or make her scared enough to think he intended to kill her.

He? How do you know it's a he?

She tried to get the mug to her lips, but her hands shook too badly, and Gage moved in and took it from her, holding it gently up to her lips so she could take a sip.

"You know we need to report this."

"I can't."

"Why the hell not, Sam?"

"Come on, Gage. You know how it works. This case

became personal the day that Whitney was found. If it were another jurisdiction, with more officers, I'd have been taken off it immediately. But the more that happens, the more personal it gets, the greater the chance they'll remove me. You obviously gave me the choking game idea for cover, to delay the inevitable. And so Pamela Nixon would be satisfied. But that's not going to last forever."

He was silent as he pondered her words. They stared at each other, Sam wondering about the look in his eye. She couldn't interpret it. Was he angry? Condescending? Disappointed in her, yet again?

"Sam, maybe it's just not safe. Maybe you shouldn't be—"

Sam took a sharp breath. "Look, Gage. I need something from you. I need you to do what you didn't do before—just believe in me. Give me the chance you never did on the Clarkston case." She threw off the blanket and stood up, moving until she was face-to-face with Gage. "Please. Help me by letting me do this, hands off. Don't let anyone or anything make this about me. I must be getting close to something—I don't know what, but I think someone is scared. Very, very scared."

Gage was silent for a moment. "This goes against everything I am trained to do," he said, stepping around Sam. He picked up the blanket and wrapped it back around her shoulders. He had gently removed her shoes when they'd first got to his condo and given her a pair of warm thermal socks. She was sure she was quite the fashionista but didn't care.

As much as she wanted to stop shivering and to be warm, she wanted to figure this case out more. She wanted it with all of her being.

"Please. I promise I'll be careful. And if things get too scary I'll call you. But I have to keep going and find out what's going on here. You owe me that."

"I've always believed in you, Sam. I'm sorry you think I don't."

"Actions speak louder than words, Gage. Show me. Don't tell me."

Gage gently pushed her back into the recliner, which he had settled her in when they first arrived, and then walked away, over to a closet near the front door.

He opened the door and reached to the top shelf, then turned and came back to her with a prettily wrapped package.

A gift. Wrapped in a small box, black, with a large red metallic ribbon. It was slightly dusty and had obviously been there awhile, unopened.

Gage walked toward her and reached out with it, trying to hand it to her.

Sam stared cautiously, not moving, not reaching out. In her experience, gifts meant something was expected from her in return, and Gage was a heart-wrenching reminder of everything she'd never managed to have.

Plus this was a girlie-girl-looking gift and everyone knew she wasn't one of those. She'd never had the opportunity to be one, and it was too damn late to be starting now.

Yet Gage stood in front of her, holding it out, and she didn't know whether to take it or turn on her heel and walk away. Why was she even tempted?

"Sam, please. Just open it."

Finally, she reached out and took the package. She pulled off the large ribbon gingerly and opened up the box to see a pink-handled Smith & Wesson .38. It was a perfect carry weapon, lightweight and from the Small Frame Airweight series.

She shook her head as she stared inside the box, then looked up at Gage.

"A pink gun?"

"Yeah, a pink gun. It's a .38, so it still packs a powerful punch. But it sends a message. Because you think you aren't feminine, but you are. You are one of the most beautiful women I've ever met. There's beauty in power, and you're strong."

"And you've been holding on to this since the Clarkston case?"

He nodded, his eyes darkening, his intent serious.

"I didn't get the chance to give it to you."

"But you ruined my career." Sam tried to put the pieces together in her mind.

"I didn't ruin your career. You're still working. You're still a detective. You were headed in the wrong direction, and I didn't want to see you go there."

"*There* where, Gage? There where you are? Because that's what drew us together—we've both already been there. The dark side. And once you go there, you don't come back without some nasty little parasites clinging on just for fun." Gage took a breath to interrupt, but Sam put up her hand. "I'm not a girlie girl. I need to be able to handle the dark side, so I can stop bad people. I'm just like the kindergarten kid who tells you, 'I wanna be a cop when I grow up, so I can kill the bad guys.' I don't necessarily want to kill them, but I will if I have to."

"I know that," Gage said, moving back toward her. "I know you have a gun. I've been worried more than once that you've wanted to use it on me."

She half-smiled as she considered his words.

"I've fucked up enough in my life for both of us, Sam. So this is advice from someone who's already been there. Don't let your demons get ahead of you and trip you up."

He stood close enough that Sam could smell his musky male scent, and need pulsed through her body. She wanted more than anything to just grab his hands, let him pull her in, and collapse into his embrace. After all, what was stopping her? Stubborn pride? Morals? One step and she would be in his arms. One step and they could breathe as one, and he could touch her in places that she wanted to be touched, and . . .

She shivered and fought off the desire. One step was too much. She wasn't ready to forgive him for altering her whole life. She wasn't sure she ever would be.

"What did you do? How did you fuck up?"

Gage backed away and turned from her as soon as she asked the question.

"Long story, long time ago," he said tersely, staring at a picture on his wall. A picture of one of the Arches in southern Utah. The desert. A place to look that was anywhere but at her.

You aren't the only one with issues, Sammy.

Sam looked at him and saw genuine regret and hurt on his face. They stared into each other's eyes, neither one speaking for a minute.

"That day? The day in the lieutenant's office? I know you want me to take it back, and say I was wrong, but I won't. I can't. Because the truth is, if I hadn't pulled you off the case, you would have died. You would have been dead, along with Mary Ann. And that's not something I could live with."

* * *

Sam remembered standing in front of the lieutenant's desk, Gage casually lounging in a chair to her right. She'd been offered a seat but refused it.

"So what do you think, Detective Flint?" the lieutenant had asked, his furry eyebrows down low over his eyes as he pondered her fate.

Gage paused and looked over at her, pretending not to see the angry simmer in her eyes. She wanted to yell out, to scream, but she knew that would only work against her. The best defense was to stay cool. Then he looked back at his senior officer.

"I think she has gotten a little too close to this girl, and this other guy is way too interested in her," Gage said. "I feel like her involvement, at this point, would be detrimental to the case. I don't think it's helping, and I think we can close it without anyone inside."

"Bullshit," Sam said, the word bursting out of her mouth like an angry bee. She couldn't contain it and immediately regretted it, but she had to speak up or she would be gone and not able to bring justice to Mary Ann and all the women like her.

"If I disappear now, they're going to be suspicious. They're expecting me. Owen is planning something for me. I know it makes you uncomfortable, and it makes my skin crawl. But I have to do this. Pulling me now is the dumbest thing you can do."

"Well, Detective Flint seems to think you're too close."

"What's 'too close'? You have to be close to get the answers. That's what undercover is all about. Yes, I'm close, but not too close to get hurt or make a mistake."

"But I understand you did make a mistake."

"You say it was a mistake. I say it was the right thing."

"It jeopardized the investigation."

"This is a real girl, a human being. She needs to get out of that environment, and she doesn't want to marry her uncle. My God, would any of you want such a thing for any of your daughters? I just contacted Tapestry Against Polygamy so she could have a chance to live a normal life."

"But as an undercover operative you weren't authorized to do that. You didn't even check with Detective Flint."

"He would have said no. He wants this case won. Hands down. Regardless of the human cost."

"You directly disobeyed orders and put an entire investigation, and the millions of dollars involved, in jeopardy."

"I was trying to save a young girl who was being enslaved into—"

"That's enough, Montgomery. I think we've heard what we need to. Detective Flint, do you have anything to add?"

"No, I think this says it all."

Sam shook off the memory and looked at Gage, who stood watching her with an odd expression on his face.

"What?" she asked.

"You look a million miles away—sort of like a lost little girl." He stepped in closer to her, and she felt the need to push him away, at least emotionally.

"Well, I'm not a little girl. And I don't need rescuing. Is that your thing, Gage? Rescuing lost little girls? They say all cops have a thing, a reason they do the work."

"I'm fucking good at it. That's why I do it," he said harshly, his eyebrows knitted closely together. The furrows on his face made him look older than his thirty-some years. He was close enough Sam could smell him. She didn't want to, because it would stay with her the rest of the night. "I know what people willingly do to each other. I might as well be the one who does the tough stuff, because I'm already dirty. My hands are already covered in blood."

"Should I call you Rambo?"

"I've been called worse."

"Well, Rambo, I've got my own bloody hands."

"It's not the same, Sam. War changes you. It's like nothing you've ever dealt with. Once you've looked a kid in the eye and shot him, you're different. It doesn't matter that the kid was half a second away from blowing you to fucking hell. It doesn't matter that he would tear you from limb to limb if he got close enough. The only thing you can think of is 'he's just a kid.' And when he's lying there on the ground, eyes staring but sightless, you want to pray for forgiveness because this was someone's *fucking kid*. And he won't be going home to dinner tonight. He won't be listening to tunes and playing video games."

Sam watched Gage without speaking. She wanted to cry for him but knew that wasn't what he wanted. And she considered how little she really knew about this man. The fact that he had just shared something intensely personal with her scared her. She needed to get out now, before—

Before what? You're a coward, Sam.

"Well, I've been fighting a war since the day my sister hung herself from a tree in our backyard. It might be a different kind of war, but it really sucks to not know the enemy. How do you fight a war—and win—against your past?"

"You let it go."

"Well, isn't that an easy answer," Sam said, her stomach roiling. He made it sound so simple, and she felt incredibly stupid. Embarrassment flooded her body. He'd been in a true war zone, and she'd been in sweet, charming little Kanesville. He'd fought against teenagers who were not even old enough to know about guns, let alone use them. As far as she knew, the teenagers in Kanesville only viewed her as a deterrent to their fun. How could they compare?

"I think I need to go," she said abruptly, and threw off the blanket, leaving it where it fell on the floor. She walked to the front door, picked up her soggy shoes, and walked out into the night without another word.

And he let her.

Once outside, Sam stood there, cursing the fact that she had called him. Now she was here in Farmington, and while she really enjoyed running, it wasn't all that pleasant in wet shoes and oversized socks. No car. Why could she never make a great exit? All the really cool girls could do it. Certainly, all the best actresses in movies managed to do it. Julia Roberts, Greta Garbo, Kathleen Turner.

She was the Lucille Ball of leavers. She walked out the door without options.

Without usable *shoes,* for hell's sake.

The front door opened. "So," Gage said from the doorway, his athletic profile silhouetted in the light behind him. "Would you like a ride home?"

"Dammit, Gage!"

"It never pays to swear at your ride."

THIRTY-TWO

Bethany Evans had beautiful long black hair and deep brown eyes, which were large, with long lashes. Her lips had that plump look that Hollywood starlets paid major money for. She was extremely petite and had an elegance that most teenage girls wouldn't find until their twenties. She also had a "no trespass" look on her face that Sam had seen before, usually in kids who had no real tether in life. Moving from base to base with her Air Force mother undoubtedly resulted in the distancing tactic Bethany used to keep people at bay.

Sam was used to trespassing on personal space and a sixteen-year-old girl might have scared her off twenty years before—or at least brought out the fighting desire in her—but not today.

Bethany's mother had been on her way out the door, headed to a function up on Hill Air Force Base, so she left her daughter to talk with Sam with little complaint. It was a very telling insight into their relationship. A distant, busy mother, a lonely teenage girl who was tired of having to fit in every time they moved. A parent could step in and stop a police officer from talking to a minor, but Bethany's mother seemed to have no such concerns, even when Sam quizzed her.

"Oh, Beth will be fine. She's mature. She can stand up for herself."

Bethany just stood and stared at her mother, and Sam recognized the look of want and need on her face—the need to have someone care, support her, step in, and be a parent.

No doubt, Bethany had been an adult since she was very, very young.

"So Bethany, I have some questions for you."

"Aren't you Whitney Marcusen's aunt?"

Sam arched her eyebrows. "Well, yes, I am, but how did you know that?"

"Because she told me that she was going to get me in trouble with the cops, and that they would believe her over me, because her aunt was a bigwig on the force. That's how. I didn't even do anything. It wasn't my fault Jeremiah asked me out."

"Get you in trouble how?"

"Oh, she had all kinds of ideas. She wanted to make me look like a creeper, just 'cause she was jealous. I didn't even do anything with Jeremiah. I didn't even like him. But the fact he liked me was enough to turn Whit and the others against me. But I guess they got theirs, huh?"

Bethany raised her chin and blinked hard, trying to look tough. But the tears sparkling in her eyes told Sam she was terrified. And not really all that happy that her tormentors were dead.

"That kind of talk could get you in trouble, Bethany.

It could make people wonder if maybe you had something to do with the deaths of these girls and Jeremiah."

"Oh, please. Look at me. I weigh ninety-five pounds and I'm only five feet tall. Like I could hang any of them. I think they just realized what creeps they all were and so they killed themselves. Good riddance."

"There are such a thing as accomplices, Bethany," Sam said, her voice low and steady. "Teenage boys have been known to do just about anything for pretty teenage girls. Even kill."

Then the tears spilled over. "I didn't kill anybody. I hated them, because they made my life miserable at that school. I had to transfer to a private school. Did you know that? I had to go to the same place all the geeks and nerds go who can't get along in regular school, all because your niece was jealous. My mom can't even afford it. She had to call my dad and beg him for the money, and since he doesn't give a crap about me, he sent it to her, just to shut her up. And I never even did anything. Jeremiah came after me. He asked *me* out. Next thing I knew they were calling me slut and whore. Writing things on my Facebook page. Spreading rumors I'd already had sex and had an abortion."

Bethany was looking everywhere but at Sam while she said this, avoiding eye contact. Sam reached out a hand and touched her wrist, and the tiny girl startled, finally looking straight at her. The tears had smudged Bethany's makeup.

She stilled for a moment, and they looked at each other, and Sam saw a little bit of herself in the hollows under Bethany's eyes. High school was ruthless, teenagers were brutal, and fitting in or finding a niche was often downright impossible.

"That must have been hard. Kids can be so mean. Believe it or not, I know how you feel. And I appreciate you talking with me like this. I'm just trying to find out what happened. I'm sorry I have to ask all these questions, but it's my job to find the facts."

"Well, I can tell you one thing right now. I know they aren't suicides. All three of those girls are too vain and selfish to ever kill themselves. They think they are God's gift to earth. And they all thought they were better than me, too, even though they were all screwing around with guys." She hesitated, swallowed hard, and then corrected herself. "Were too vain, I mean. And Jeremiah did, too. He thought he was so hot and irresistible. He's just a stupid small-town Utah Mormon boy. And Whitney was just a slutty Utah girl."

Bethany's chin went up again, and only a few tears remained.

Sam kept her voice soft, unthreatening. "You realize that one of the reasons I'm here is because you are a person who had motivation to want them gone, right?"

"I'm not stupid."

"Okay, well, can you tell me where you were Saturday morning?"

"Here. In bed. It's my only day to sleep in, and Mom always stays at her boyfriend's place on Friday nights, so if you're going to ask me for an alibi, you aren't going to get anyone to back me up. I don't even have a cat. Are you going to arrest me?"

"No, I don't have any proof that you did anything, Bethany. Just that your name came up more than once. What about last Wednesday? The night Whitney was found hanging at her house?"

"I was at my youth group that night. Up at my

church. You can ask Pastor Jeff. And who the hell would be pointing a finger at me anyway? That slime bag who calls himself Slick? 'Greasy' is more like it."

Sam fought back a smile at Bethany's description of the arrogant Devin. Instinct told Sam this girl was not involved. It also told Sam that being close to these kids could make Bethany a target as well.

Sam asked Bethany the name of her church, wrote it down on her notepad, along with the name Pastor Jeff.

"Is your mom gone a lot, Bethany?"

"Yep. She's busy. Never really planned on having me. It just happened."

"Well, for now I'm going to take your word for it that you had nothing to do with these murders. And they are murders. I'm not trying to scare you, but I want you to think about this. I want you to be careful. Lock the doors. Look behind you when you're walking. Do you have a car?"

"Yeah, I have a car."

"Do you park it in the garage?"

"No, my mom parks hers there and the rest is filled up with boxes we'll never get around to unpacking before we have to move to the next crappy little town. Saves us time, at least."

Sam felt a pang of emotion for the beautiful girl who was obviously lonely and tired of a nomadic lifestyle. Sam also knew that no matter what her instinct told her, she had to investigate this girl closely and look into every nook and cranny of her life.

"Well, maybe you should move those boxes somewhere else so you can park in the garage."

"There's a lot of boxes."

"I'll arrange for some help. And I have a few other questions I have to ask you."

"What?"

The look of defiance came back, but not as fiercely as it had before, and Sam thought she had found a way through to the girl, despite her very impressive suit of armor, built from years of starting over in strange places with strange people.

"Have you ever heard of the choking game?"

Bethany looked away, pursed her lips, and then looked back at Sam.

"Maybe."

"I'd like a yes or no answer, Bethany."

"Maybe I don't want to answer."

"You don't really have a choice."

"Okay, fine, so I've traveled a lot, you know. I've lived in other countries, and more states and cities then any of these other Podunk Mormon kids. I've seen a lot."

"And you've seen the choking game?"

"It's not called that. That's stupid. It's called passout."

Sam could see the tears building up in Bethany's eyes again and knew she had hit on something.

"And have you played this game, Bethany?"

"Ya."

"Did you play this game with Whitney and her friends?"

"Maybe."

"Yes or no answers, please."

"Why should I tell you anything?"

"Because I'm the good cop here. I'm sure you've watched enough television to understand the difference between good cop and bad cop. If someone else has to question you, they might not be as nice. Especially since you don't have an alibi for the morning Jeremiah died."

"I didn't do anything wrong. You can't pin something on me I didn't do."

"What makes you think I'm trying to pin anything on you?"

"Because I'm not stupid. You have to solve this case. It's your job. And you'll do whatever you have to do to solve it, even if you get the wrong person."

"But most people think these are just suicides, Bethany. They aren't looking to pin them on anyone."

"Nobody thinks they're suicides. You should hang out in the hallways of the school. Then you might hear what people really think."

Sam sighed. She had no doubt the community was buzzing. She was surprised there hadn't been more vocal outbursts and demands for justice in a case that was as clear as mud. That, undoubtedly, would be coming soon. "I'm not looking for the wrong person, Bethany. I only want to stop your friends from dying. I want to understand. I want the truth."

"First of all, they *weren't* my friends. They used me for my mom's alcohol cabinet, and a place to party and hook up, and then they screwed me over and tried to destroy me. They tried to make everyone hate me. I'm glad they're dead."

Sam winced a little. "They aren't all dead, Bethany. Whitney is still alive."

"Yeah? Well, I hear she's just a vegetable in a diaper. So what? Maybe she deserves it. Maybe she should have treated people better. And you want the truth? I think that's a lie. You *want* me to tell you Whitney was a nice girl who was attacked and assaulted. The truth is, she was a bitch."

Bethany's lips pursed, and a spark of anger flared in her eyes. Sam knew why this girl had been targeted. Not only was she not a Mormon, like just about everybody else at Smithland High, but she also was extremely beautiful. And she didn't just sit back and take it. She had an opinion and wasn't afraid to share it. The other girls would not have liked her encroaching on their turf. They wouldn't have liked her independent spirit.

They wouldn't have liked the fact that she was different.

"They all deserved everything they got."

"You don't really mean that, Bethany."

"Maybe I do."

"You want to go visit Whitney in the hospital? Her eyes are closed, but a machine breathes for her. In and out. It's a tube they shoved down her throat, so that her brain won't get starved of oxygen and cause permanent damage. Of course, they don't know how long she went without oxygen, so it might already be too late. She might spend the rest of her life on that ventilator, never knowing who or what is around her. She might wake up, but be different. She might *really* have to wear a diaper for the rest of her life.

"She will probably miss homecoming and prom, and all the football games that are coming up. She might not ever go to another high-school activity. She might never even open her eyes again."

"*Shut up!*" Bethany finally yelled. Her eyes had filled with tears again as Sam talked, but as hard as it was to continue, Sam knew she'd needed to push Bethany, to find out everything she knew. "Just shut up. I didn't do it. I didn't have anything to do with anything. I just wanted to make friends, okay? I wanted this place to be different. Instead, it was worse than anywhere I've ever been."

Sam felt the beginnings of a headache at the base of her neck. "It's hard to fit in, isn't it?"

"What do you know? You're obviously from around here. You're probably Mormon, too. Everybody is Mormon, except for a few of us, and as soon as they figure out you aren't going to join their church they either use you for what they can get or turn on you and abandon you. This is the worst place ever. I wish my mom had never made me move here. I wish I could go live with my dad in California. At least there you don't feel like so much of an outcast, because just about everybody is an outcast. Of course, he doesn't want me. An outcast from my own dad. Great, huh?"

"Bethany, teenagers are the same everywhere. I'm sorry you've had a rough time here."

"You don't know anything. I bet I've been more places in my life than you've ever even thought of going."

Short of a cruise she had taken with some friends and a trip to New Orleans, Sam had not been anywhere, so she could hardly argue with Bethany.

Sam leaned forward and waited until Bethany met her eyes. "You're probably right. And you know what else? I haven't been inside a Mormon church since I turned eighteen. I turned my back on what everyone else around thinks is the only true thing. That makes me a bigger outcast than you could ever be. That makes me what they call an apostate. Exiled to Outer Darkness."

Bethany blinked and then asked, "Why do you live here, then? Why do you stay here where people look down on you? I mean, you're an adult. You could go anywhere. Why would you stay here?"

Good question.

"My family is here. My parents are getting old and they need me. And I guess because I'm too damn stubborn to let anyone drive me away."

Bethany looked her up and down and then smiled, a tentative gesture, but it lit up her face like a spotlight was shining on it. She had perfect dimples in both cheeks. Oh, the girls must have hated her beauty.

"I didn't hurt them, or try to get someone to hurt them. I hated them, but I didn't hurt them."

"I believe you," Sam said softly. She also knew she had better get some protection on this girl. "But you need to be totally up-front with me. You need to tell me about passout."

Bethany hesitated for another moment, and then finally said, "We only did it once. It was at a slumber party over at Whit's house. They were all making fun of me because I had a weird accent and I didn't belong to the church they belonged to and I thought getting baptized for dead people was creepy. So I told them they were dumb and immature and didn't even know what it was like in the real world. Whitney kept pushing me, so I finally told them about the game. I just wanted them to feel as dumb as they made me feel. They'd never heard of it, and then I felt bad I told them. Because the one time I did it in North Carolina, I didn't like it. It's just a stupid head rush. I was sorry I said it. But of course Whitney made us all do it."

"And how do you do it?"

"There's lots of ways, I think, but I just knew the one where you all just get in a big group and hug someone tight, until they can't breathe. Then just before they pass out you let them go."

"And you all did this?"

"Yeah," she said reluctantly. "Then Jeremiah and Devin and another guy, Mark something, came over. Whitney told them about the game. They wanted to do it, only they had this great idea." Bethany paused, as if embarrassed. "Thought it would be cool if we were giving them blow jobs while they were light headed."

Sam tried not to wince at Bethany's words. "I thought you said that you had never had sex, Bethany."

"A blow job's not sex. Everybody does it."

In Sam's mind, the act of oral sex was more intimate than actual copulation. But she'd seen research that showed oral sex was very common among high-school kids, at least for girls pleasuring boys. She didn't think it happened the other way around. She tried not to react as the girl talked. "So you gave them blow jobs?"

"We all took turns. And then the guys wanted to do it again, and Jeremiah . . . Jeremiah, he turned to me and said he wanted me to do him, because I did it best. And that made Whitney mad. And she and Jeremiah got in a fight, and then everyone left. And that was it. After that they started spreading rumors. No one was my friend anymore. And even though I was the only real virgin of all of them, they told everyone I was a slut."

"And did Jeremiah ask you to do it again after that?"

"Yeah, all the time, but I wouldn't. He was part of them. He spread the rumors. But he wouldn't let it go."

"What about the other girls, Tawny and Madison?

Were they at the slumber party, too? Did they do the game with you?"

"Yeah, of course. Wherever Whitney went, those two nitwits went with her." Bethany's eyes filled with tears again, and they spilled, unbidden, down her cheeks. "It's my fault, isn't it? I showed them the game, and now they're all dead. Even though they were mean to me, I didn't want them to die. I lied when I said I wasn't sorry. I *am* sorry."

"I know, Bethany," Sam said, wanting to pull the girl into a hug. Instead Sam reached out and squeezed Bethany's shoulder for a long moment.

As Bethany cried, Sam pondered what she had learned. She was looking for a serial killer among a group of kids who were practicing a potentially fatal sex "game." If it weren't for the slide show, she might now be thinking these were, at the least, accidents. Attempts for a cheap high.

But if that were true, who finished up the slide show? And who put it in the seminary building?

And was this girl crying into her hands really innocent?

THIRTY-THREE

"Hi, Momma," Sam said, sitting by the side of the hospital bed, in a metal-legged chair she had scooted as close to the bed as possible. She had left Bethany as soon as the girl was calm, giving her a card that had all the numbers where Sam could be reached. Then she drove to the hospital to sit by her mother's side.

Sam reached out and grabbed her mother's left hand, placing it in her own and stroking it gently as she talked in a gentle voice.

The room was sterile and cold, the smell of antiseptic almost overpowering. A vase sat on the night table to the side of the bed, filled with drooping daisies and petunias, undoubtedly brought here by her father, so "Ruthie could feel like she was at home, and not all alone."

Other than that, there was nothing in this room that spoke of Sam's mother, personalized her, or even evoked any memories of the woman she used to be. It was just a standard, psychiatric room in a hospital.

Sam's mother lay in the bed, staring straight ahead, not moving her eyes, seemingly looking off into the distance, gazing at who knew what.

"There's a lot going on, Momma. I know Dad doesn't like me to say anything, but Susanna is having some trouble. Whitney is in the hospital. She had an . . . an accident. Jace hates his mission, and wants to come home, and Roger Junior is having some of his own issues. I never hear from Amy. I don't even know where she is. And you know what happened with Callie. That's why you're here."

"You sure of that?"

Sam jumped up from the chair and turned to look at Roger Marcusen, one of the last people she wanted to see today. Her brother-in-law had red, bloodshot eyes and unkempt hair, and he was wearing a wrinkled shirt and old khakis that obviously hadn't been pressed in a while. Susanna always took the utmost care with her family and their clothing. She was more worried about appearances than anyone else Sam had ever known— probably because Susanna had spent her teenage years trying to be mother to two needy girls and dealing with a mother who was completely vacant.

Roger's hair, always thin, was now sparse on top and stuck out at odd angles, like he had run his fingers through it numerous times. It screamed angst. His jowly face was lined, and dark shadows were permanent fixtures under both eyes. He'd gained weight over the years, and he had a good-sized gut sticking out. He was nothing like the football player/stud he had been in high school.

And that probably ate him alive.

"What do you want, Roger?" Sam had never much

liked her brother-in-law, and his actions in the years following the marriage simply proved her instincts true. Both she and Amy had figured out pretty quick that they didn't want to be left alone with Roger, as he would somehow manage to feel them up.

Susanna pretended not to know all the things that were said about her eternal mate, but Sam knew she couldn't be that blind.

"I came to see my mother-in-law. Came to see how she's doing."

"Your daughter is in the hospital. That's probably where you should be. My mother's condition hasn't changed in years. So, again, Roger, why are you here?"

"Fine. I came to see you or your dad. I knew someone would be here. I need you guys to talk to my wife. Susanna has thrown me out of the house. She seems to think she can handle all this better by herself. I'm not dumb enough to think she came up with this idea on her own. You told her to do it, didn't you?"

"She *can* handle it better without you. You've never helped her before. All you've ever done is make things worse."

"Oh, please, you know as well as I do that she's not capable of making any decisions on her own. Never has been. She needed me to take care of her, and that's why we got married. You know she cried for a week after we got married? Just wanted to come home and take care of you, like it was her job. I needed a wife, and I got a bawl baby. She left me on my own to raise these kids."

"Left you on your own?" Sam looked hard at him, knowing that hatred sparked from her eyes and hoping he wasn't too dense to see it, to feel it. In a way, he was responsible for the decimation of their family, too. He took Susanna away when the family needed her most. Or maybe when Sam needed her most. Maybe that could have been forgiven if he'd been a good husband and father, but he wasn't and never had been.

"Well, Roger, you have done a fine job. Just fabulous. One of your children is near death, one is desperately homesick and miserable in a foreign country, and the other one's addicted to pornography. Yes, you've been a fine example for your children, having an affair with your own sister-in-law. Why don't you—"

Sam felt the sudden movement from her mother's hand, a squeeze, and Sam turned back to her. "Momma? Momma? You just squeezed my hand. I felt it. I know you moved." She turned back to Roger excitedly. "Go get a nurse, now. Hurry."

"I'm not your little slave boy, Sam. I have something to say."

"Anything you have to say I don't have the time or desire to hear. Just go."

"You'll listen to me, because I said you'll listen to me." He took a step toward her. Sam didn't move from the bed. Using her free right hand—the other held her mother's hand tightly—Sam reached back and pushed her light jacket aside, displaying the service weapon she wore holstered on her hip. Roger stopped advancing but didn't move or leave.

"I'm prepared to do whatever I have to to protect myself, Roger, and don't you forget it. My name isn't Susanna, and you can't do whatever you want to me."

Roger's eyes widened, and he took a step back, then shook his head. "I just want my wife back. Tell her to come back."

"She isn't coming back, jackass. And you have no one to blame but yourself."

His eyes hardened again. "You're a little bitch. Watch out, Sam. That's all I have to say." Then he turned and left the room, and she sighed with relief.

Turning back to her mother, Sam grabbed the call button strapped to the side of the hospital bed and then tried to remove her hand from her mother's, but Ruthie Montgomery's grip just tightened.

Sam hit the call button with her right hand, still holding her mother's hand with her left.

"I'm here, Mom. And you're here, too. Thanks for letting me know." She continued to talk to her mother in a soft voice.

Sam heard, rather than saw, someone enter the room and turned her head. "Did you need something, ma'am?" asked a young nurse. "First time the call light has gone off in this room. Kinda surprised me."

"She's holding my hand. Grasping it. She won't let go. I think she's responding to me being here. I think she wants to tell us something."

"Oh, well . . . Are you sure?"

"Yes, I'm sure. I know what it feels like when someone squeezes my hand."

"Well, sometimes these patients have reactions—"

"Look at her hand. She's squeezing my hand. She won't let go."

"Well, it does look like it. Maybe if you give it a moment—"

"Call the doctor. Now. Get somebody in here. My mother is responding. She's trying to tell us something. And no one is listening."

"Well, it's not that easy—"

"Can I speak any plainer? Get the doctor. *Now.*"

"Fine," the young nurse said, scrambling out of the room, but not without giving Sam several nasty glances as she exited.

"Momma, I know you hear me. I know you are listening. I know you're in there. Talk to me, please. Talk to me."

She doesn't have anything to say. She lost her mind the day I died.

Sam wasn't sure she was hearing Callie's voice. She'd never been sure. Maybe Callie was wrong: There was that month Ruthie made hamburgers for every meal. Before she stopped functioning completely. She stood over the stove, sobbing, making hamburgers, waiting for Callie to come in and say thanks for making her favorite meal.

No one could console Ruthie. Sam remembered wrapping her arms around her mom's legs and crying with her, but Sam's father just sat at the table and waited for the meal.

Why did he do that?

You're finally listening to me. Finally you see.

"No," Sam said out loud. "No!" She didn't want her mother to be lost forever. Okay, so Sam had already been raised as a motherless waif, but there was still time. There were stories to be told and laughter to be shared and games to be played.

Random thoughts of Chutes and Ladders and Candy Land roamed through her head. She'd spent countless hours, as the youngest child, begging her older siblings to take some time out and play a game with her.

Most of the time, the answer was no. But every day after her older sisters shuffled off to school, Momma would take a break from the cleaning and ironing, and sit down on the floor with Sam, playing at least one game of her choice. No matter how busy Momma was, she always played at least one game.

"Remember when we used to play Candy Land, Momma? I always wanted to go live in Candy Land, and you always told me it wasn't a real place. You told me that it was imaginary, but there was nothing wrong with going there, to that imaginary place. That I could visit that place anytime I wanted, and that would be okay. Everything there would always be okay. I just had to remember to always come back home, because I was loved and needed. You told me that all the time."

Sam felt the tears sting her eyes as she remembered the days they spent on the floor, Sam lying on her belly, feet up in the air, the old, worn shag carpet tickling her tummy where her shirt rode up.

"Is that where you are now, Momma? Are you in your imaginary place? Where everything's fine? Because I understand that, but I need you to come back home."

Sam laid her head down on the bed beside her mother's hand and let the tears flow. Her grasp on Sam's hand suddenly slackened, and Sam raised her head and looked up to see there was no change on her mother's face. No indication she even knew anyone else was in the room.

"Please come back, Momma. Please."

"She's never been gone, Sammy," her father's voice said behind her.

Sam jumped and turned to her father. "Dad, she squeezed my hand. I mean really hard. She responded to me. I think she might be coming out of it."

"Now I wouldn't get your hopes up, Sammy. She's in there. I always told you kids that. But as for getting well enough to walk or talk again, well, that just isn't going to happen. She squeezes my hand, too, sometimes. It's just an involuntary reaction or muscle spasm, the doctors say."

Sam's hand was still in her mother's and again Sam felt a squeeze.

"Dad, she's responding. She is; I know it."

"Well, what's going on in here?" said a harried young doctor as he came through the door and walked to the side of the bed where Sam stood. "I understand you had some kind of reaction from the patient? Of course, I'm sure you're aware that often these reactions are involuntary or muscle spasms."

"She squeezed my hand. And wouldn't let go. She's responding. We need to do something, run some tests."

The doctor gave Sam a sad but polite look, then asked her to move as he took over her position, holding Ruthie Montgomery's hand. "Ruthie, this is Dr. Farr. Can you hear me? If you can hear me, squeeze my hand. Okay? Ruthie?"

He stood over her for a moment, looking at her expectantly, but nothing happened.

"Ruthie, can you hear me?" he asked again.

He stood up and shook his head, saying to Sam, "I'm sorry. I know you wanted to believe it was more. But it isn't. I think we should all go now so she can have some time with her hus—" The doctor had been holding Sam's mother's hand while he spoke, and his eyes suddenly widened.

"Uh, she just squeezed my hand. You're right. She is reacting. She is hearing us."

Sam's chest tightened up as she considered his words. Her mother could hear them. Maybe she would come back to them. Maybe she could regain those lost years.

"You're all making too much of this," Sam's father said gruffly. "She's been squeezing my hand for years. Now I think it's time for her to rest. You've been bugging her too long. You're tired, aren't you, Ruthie. Don't worry; I'll make them leave."

"She squeezed my hand again," the young doctor said excitedly. "I'm going to order up some more tests, see if these are real responses, and not just quirks—"

"We don't have that kind of money."

"I will pay for the tests. Whatever they are. Just do it."

"Sam—"

"Dad. Just let me do this, okay? Please?"

Her father turned and walked from the room without another word, and Dr. Farr excitedly explained what he had in mind.

Sam listened closely as he told her his plan. But the words were hard to comprehend, because all she could think about was that her mother was finally responding.

About time, Callie's voice said in Sam's head. *About damn time.*

THIRTY-FOUR

The call Sam received at midnight woke her from a dead sleep. She'd been dreaming about little girls with beautifully curled pigtails and immaculate braids, dancing around her as she cried in the center of a circle of torment. No one was there to help her. Her father was standing just outside the circle, holding Susanna's hand, but not looking in Sam's direction.

The tears on her face were real, she realized as she scrambled for her cell phone.

" 'Lo," Sam answered.

"Sam, this is your father. I'm sorry to have to wake you so late, but I'm afraid your mother . . . well, your mother has passed away. She went peacefully in her sleep."

Sam shook her head, unable to process or believe what her father was saying. Just earlier that day, Ruthie Montgomery had been grasping Sam's hand, holding it, communicating.

Passed away? Went peacefully?

Sam sat up and looked at the clock, scanning her room, looking for any sign that this was a dream, that at any moment she would wake up and her mother would still be alive, albeit catatonic and in a hospital bed.

"Sam, can you hear me?" His voice sounded ragged and old and stressed, but not alarmed or panicked. Had her father ever been alarmed or panicked? She couldn't remember a time when he was anything but stoic.

"She can't be dead. There was nothing wrong with her. Well, nothing wrong with her body, anyway. How could she just die? Are you . . . Is this a dream? Are you kidding me?"

"No, Sam, I'm sorry, it's true. They called me about an hour ago. One of the nurses discovered her when they did their regular bed check."

Grief clutched Sam's chest, and she fought back the tears as the reality of her father's words hit her. Dead. Really dead, this time. Not just a ghost of the person she used to be but no longer talking, breathing, walking.

"I'll be there in ten minutes," was all Sam said.

Then she hung up the phone and fell back in her bed, hitting the pillows, crying like a baby for the first time in years. She didn't know why she was so distraught. In reality, she had lost her mother years and years before. Apparently, some part of Sam had always believed she would get her mother back. That somehow, those years would be made up.

Now it would never happen. Now, Sam truly was motherless.

It wasn't so different from before. So why did she feel so empty?

Why did she feel as though she had lost so much?

THIRTY-FIVE

Sam spent the next morning with her father, making funeral arrangements, picking out caskets and burial plots, and putting together the clothes that her father insisted her mother would want to be buried in.

It was standard Mormon practice to bury active temple-going Mormons in the same attire they wore to practice their sacred ceremonies and rites. Sam cried as she pulled out a new pair of temple garments, obviously never worn. Her father must have bought these with the hope that someday her mother's mind would return and they would again go to the temple, like all the other good Mormon couples their age. Sam's father had already laid out a plain white long-sleeved dress, white stockings, an unworn pair of white shoes, a white slip, and sitting next to it a small packet of ritual temple clothing.

Other than a trip to the Salt Lake Temple to participate in a "baptism for the dead" ceremony—an experience she found both abhorrent and ethically wrong—she had never participated in any temple rituals and did not understand the meanings of the clothes in the packet: a robe, an apron, a sash, and a veil.

Her father had told her that two of the "sisters" from the ward would be coming with her to the funeral home, as only other temple-endowed Mormons were supposed to dress the deceased in their sacred clothing.

Sam stared at the clothes in front of her and felt her stomach churn. She did not understand this religion she had been born into; she never had.

The garments had four marks on them, one shaped like a reverse L, over the right breast. Another, shaped like a V, appeared over the left breast. There was a horizontal line about three-quarters of an inch long in the midsection, and a similar mark just above the hem of the right leg.

Sam knew that before old garments could be discarded the marks she was looking at now were supposed to be cut out and destroyed. Her earliest memory of this was a year or two before Callie died, as Sam happened upon her father in the backyard, burning trash in a barrel.

She watched as he dug into his pocket and then tossed small white pieces of fabric into the burning pit.

"Daddy, what are you doing?"

"Nothing, Sammy. Just throwing some kindling on the fire."

"That doesn't look like kindling."

"It is. Now go find your mother and see if she needs help setting the table for dinner."

At the time, Sam really hadn't thought more about the incident, but now she wondered why her father hadn't explained. Why was so much of this ritualistic religion a secret? It was like being the outsider on an inside joke, over and over and over again.

When Sam was sixteen she had questioned Susanna about the temple garments and ceremonies and had received no answers. "You will find out when it's your time to go to the temple, Sammy."

Now, she still knew little about this strange clothing and was even more offended that strangers were to come with her and actually do the dressing of her mother's body, just because they were "inside" and Sam was out.

"Sam, the sisters are here," her father called from the living room. She gave the odd clothing one more glance, then put it all into the small colorful flowered suitcase her father called her mother's "temple" bag and zipped it up.

"I'm coming," she called back to her father. On a whim, she opened her mother's closet and pushed hangers aside as she looked at some of her mother's old dresses. Everything dressy enough was out-of-date and faded; Sam's mother had worn nothing but housecoats for years now.

Yet, for reasons Sam didn't understand, her father had never emptied the closet of her mother's church clothes. In the middle of the sad, old-fashioned dresses Sam saw a vivid purple dress that was festooned with dark purple daisies with yellow centers.

Memories of her mother putting on the dress filled Sam's mind. She remembered looking up at her mother as she combed her hair and put on some lipstick, readying herself for a Sunday church meeting.

The four girls had been bathed and dressed first, and everyone was waiting for their mother, who was just finishing up the last touches of hair and makeup. The other girls were in the living room, already fighting over who was going to get to sit on the end of the pew during Sacrament meeting, but Sam loved watching her mother get ready for Sunday meetings.

Sam's father walked into the room, straightening his dark blue tie, and grabbed his suit coat jacket off a chair. He shrugged into it, then turned and looked at her mother.

A look of dismay came over his face. "You're wearing that?"

"Well, yes," Sam's mother said, her face going from lighthearted and carefree to worry filled in just seconds. "You don't like it? I thought it was so pretty and colorful, and it was on the sale rack at ZCMI."

"It's a little bright, I think. Maybe something you could wear to a party, but not really church appropriate."

"To a party? When do we ever go to parties?"

"Well, you know, the Church has parties."

"The Church has no parties. Not the kind of parties that you're talking about."

"You understood all this when you became a member, Ruthie. Mormons do things differently. We wear our best clothes to show our respect to God, and we don't want to look gaudy or garish."

Sam's mother turned away and pursed her lips tightly, a stray tear escaping out of the corner of her eye, and then she saw Sam, sitting on the floor, forgotten as they had their exchange.

"Go ask Susanna to comb your hair again, Sammy," her mother said roughly. "I have to change."

*　*　*

"You were a convert to the Church," Sam murmured softly, wondering why she was just remembering this now. Or why it had never sunk in. Her father talked about his pioneer roots constantly. But her mother had been . . . something else.

Sam walked over to the round mirrored vanity, where her mother had always sat to brush her hair and put on her lipstick. She remembered a pair of purple beads that perfectly matched the dress. She also remembered her mother taking those off before changing into a staid blue suit for church.

Sam opened up the drawer and sorted through the clumps of jewelry, none of it expensive but all of it bright and colorful. She couldn't remember her mother wearing any of it. As Sam scooped through the masses of beads, looking for the purple necklace, she saw a brown book at the bottom of the drawer.

She dug it out of the mass of costume jewelry and read the word "Journal" on the front.

She opened it up to browned pages and a back-slanted handwriting that she knew belonged to her mother. Sam wasn't sure why she knew this, but these writings were a part of Ruthie Montgomery. A part of the Ruthie she didn't know.

"Sammy?" her father yelled again. "It's time to go."

"Coming," Sam said, tucking the journal into the front pocket of the floral suitcase, intending to remove it first chance she got. She grabbed the bag and walked out into the living room, where two women waited— women she vaguely recognized but couldn't call by name. One burst into tears and grabbed her tightly, hugging her close. Sam shrugged away from her, stiff, not returning the embrace. Not only did Sam not really know this woman, but she was pretty sure her mother didn't know her, either.

Sam's mother didn't even recognize her own children.

The woman looked around uncomfortably and then stepped closer to the other woman, who was more grim faced and didn't look likely to hug anyone spontaneously.

Sam decided to stick close to her for the rest of the time, so the Crier wouldn't get ahold of her again.

These two women, women who barely knew her mother, were going to be responsible for dressing her in the last clothing she would ever wear.

While Sam did not cherish the idea of dressing her mother's dead body, she also did not feel that anyone had the right to take it away from her.

"I'll follow you," she told her father as he let the other two women into his car. He gave her a look that she knew well from her youth. A "why make this so difficult?" look. But Sam needed space and time. She needed an escape. She sure as hell didn't need to be trapped first in a car, then in a funeral home with the Crier and the Grim Reaper. And her father.

Funny, she had never looked at her father that way before.

Her cell phone rang as she started up her car.

"Montgomery," she answered, her voice clipped and abrupt.

"Sam, it's Amy. I just heard about Mom."

Sam left the car running, so the air-conditioning would cool it off, and sat speechless. Amy. Sam barely remembered her. The one who escaped. Sam tried to remember what Amy looked like; she couldn't even remember her face. Her father did not keep old family pictures around. Where were those? Where were the memories?

Sam had no idea what to say to the sister she hadn't heard from in years. How had Amy found her number?

"Sammy? Are you there?"

"How did you find me? How did you know my number?"

Amy was silent for a moment, then said, "Professional courtesy."

"What the hell is that supposed to mean?"

"It means I know the same kind of people you know." *Cryptic, isn't she?*

Right now, Sam didn't care. She had too much to deal with. Too much to deal with on her own. She needed help.

"Are you coming home for the funeral?" The words were out before Sam could stop them. She didn't ask Amy where she had been or where she was living. Sam had been abandoned so many times in her life that she no longer had any faith in the ties that bound a family together. This person, her sister, was nothing more than a stranger to Sam.

"I don't think so," Amy said. "I'm not really welcome there. I just wanted . . . Hell, I don't know what I wanted. Let's be honest. Mom's been dead for years. A beating heart doesn't make a person alive."

"Actually, technically, it does."

"Technically? Always the dogged one, Sam. Always so literal."

"Where are you, Amy?" She hadn't intended to ask, but there was a twang to her sister's voice that she'd never heard before.

"Texas. Married a cattle rancher. Spend most of my days out farming. Never thought I'd love it like I do. Never. Oh, but you and I have something in common. I'm also on the police force out here. Part-time. Turns out I'm a crack shot."

Sam pulled the phone away from her ear and looked at it like it had just been possessed by the devil or contained some kind of hallucinogenic mind control drug that made her hear—

She put the phone back to her ear. "Cattle? Ranching? Texas? You're a cop?"

"Part-time. Sheriff's deputy, actually."

"Amy, why don't you ever call? Why don't you come home?"

"It's not my home anymore, Callie. It hasn't been my home for years."

"Uh, I'm not Callie. I'm Sam. Callie's dead."

There was a silence on the other end of the line. "Sorry, Sam. Freudian slip. Was just thinking about how first Callie died, then Mom died emotionally. And you were so little you didn't understand any of it."

"You're only eight years older than I am."

"Sam, I'm a lifetime older than you. But I don't have time to explain. Tell the family I won't be coming back. I'll send flowers. But I won't be back. I can't ever come back."

"But how did—"

"Good-bye, Sam. Look me up if you're ever in Texas."

"No. You don't get to do this. You don't get to just walk away again! We need you." *I need you.*

There was silence on the other end of the line, which encouraged Sam to continue speaking.

"Did you know Susanna's daughter, Whitney, is near

death, from hanging? She was pregnant with a baby from a boy who's dead now. She's barely alive. Susanna is a shell. Now Mom's dead. There is nothing left. This family is near extinction. And still you won't come back?"

"Whitney hung herself?"

"No, she was hung. I don't think she hung herself. I think someone is killing these kids. And now it's in our family again. It's a part of us."

"Is she going to die?"

"We don't know. But Susanna could sure use her family around."

"Susanna never wants to see me again, Sam. She thinks I lured her husband. She thinks I . . . Well, at this point it doesn't matter. In Kanesville, everybody believes what they want to believe anyway. I'm sure nothing's changed. I'm sorry about Whitney. But my coming back there isn't going to help anyone."

"It would help me," Sam said quietly.

"If you want the answers, Sam, I think you know where to look."

"What the hell is that supposed to mean?"

"It's a patriarchal society, Sammy. It all starts with the priesthood holder. You want the answers, go to the source."

"You want me to interview the president of the Mormon Church?"

Amy laughed, a harsh bark that was far from amused.

"I don't even know you," Sam said quietly, not sure how to take her sister's reaction.

"No, you don't. But you can trust me. And you need to trust me on this. If you want the answer, go to the source. Go where it started. But let me guarantee you, you aren't going to like the answer you get."

"Why don't you—"

"Gotta go. Look me up if you ever get to Texas."

The phone disconnected, and Sam didn't even get a chance to say, "But I don't know where in Texas you are. Awfully big state to just 'look someone up.'" And Sam didn't have any idea how Amy knew she was working as a cop, unless she kept in touch with her father. Sam knew that Susanna would not be the connection. So why had her father never said anything? *Go to the source.* Was her father the source?

A horn honked, pulling Sam out of her reverie, and she looked over to see her father's stern face, staring at her from the driver's side of his car. Next to him sat the Grim Reaper, and she didn't even bother to turn her head, her lips pursed so tightly Sam thought they might remain frozen that way.

She nodded. Her father took off and she pulled out onto the road, following him the eight blocks to the local funeral home.

Susanna was in the hospital with Whitney. Amy was apparently raising cattle and chasing bad guys in Texas. That left Sam.

In two days she would bury her mother.

Let them dress the body. Let them do their rituals and say their prayers and look down their noses at her, because Sam knew the real truth: Ruthie Montgomery had died years ago.

But what had she been before she converted to the Church, married Sam's father?

It was time to find out. Sam slipped the book out of the front pocket of the suitcase and tucked it under her seat.

Tonight, she was going to get to know her mother.

THIRTY-SIX

Sam sat in her cubicle at work and chewed on the end of a pen as she leaned back in her chair, swiveling it slightly from side to side.

"What, you retired now or something?" D-Ray said as he came in from the break room, holding a donut in one hand and a steaming cup of coffee in the other. She knew D-Ray thrived on their repartee, but she had too much on her mind to respond.

D-Ray looked down at his mug, then back at Sam, then shook his head. "You need a warm-up?"

Despite the Mormon environment, every police department across the state, with the possible exception of the one staffed by the polygamists in southern Utah, had a coffeepot or coffee machine. Sam survived on coffee.

She had a mug sitting on her desk, but the coffee had gone cold long ago.

"No, I'm good," she said. A very puzzled D-Ray walked away.

As she pondered the intricacies of the case she was involved in, she found she also had a lot of questions about her mother's history. The unknowns and missing pieces swirled in Sam's brain like a puzzle that just wouldn't fit together.

Her mother had been an only child, born and raised in abject poverty in Manassa, Colorado. Manassa's claim to fame appeared to be the fact that Jack Dempsey, a famous boxer, was the local hero. Sam had no idea who he was.

Sam's grandfather Ezra Bean Paulsen had been a miner and had died of black lung disease when Ruthie Paulsen was only a child; her mother had struggled with her health and barely managed to put food on the table.

Sam opened to the next entry and positioned the diary among the papers on her desk.

Pigweed for dinner again tonight. I went out and picked as much as I could find, because Momma is sick. It grows up close to the Conejos riverbanks, and the ones closest to the water are the best. There's no other food, but we are lucky. I can pick this just about anytime in the spring and summer and it makes a good meal.

We still have a little salt left from when those nice ladies in town brought us some food, and that makes it taste really good.

My mouth waters when I think of the bread they brought us, but that was months ago. When they found out Momma was sick because I passed out at school. The nurse said I just wasn't eating enough. I didn't dare tell her I rarely eat at all, but she must have known. She had kind eyes that looked at me with pity, but I could tell she cared.

The next day a group of three ladies came to our door. They didn't tell me who they were, but just dropped off some food, and invited me to come visit their church, First Assembly of God in Manassa.

I never went there, of course. Although I was tempted to go, just to see if they had that good bread. I pictured elegant ceremonies and a man who looked like Jesus standing on a podium, and everybody just waiting for the chance to eat the good bread.

But I didn't have a dress to wear. Not one good enough for a church where a man like Jesus would be preaching.

Momma had a Bible, and it had some pictures in it. That man looked glorious to me. I wanted to reach out and touch him, and I stroked the pages over and over again, as though some of his beauty, his light, would find its way into my pitiful small body.

I sometimes thought about passing out again at school, even if I just had to fake it. Anything to ease that gnawing ache in my stomach during lunchtime, when everyone else had a lunch bag and I went outside as though I didn't care. Most days Momma didn't even know I was gone. She barely woke when I came home.

I could only get her to eat a few bites of the pigweed, no matter how hard I tried.

No matter how good I told her it was.

I usually finished it all myself.

Sometimes I got a stomachache after I filled myself up too much, and then I had to throw up in the backyard, crying and sobbing as the food came up. I didn't *seem to know when to stop, because I was always so hungry.*

Sam rubbed her eyes. Her mother, eating too much—then having to vomit it up—made Sam uncomfortable. Surely this couldn't be hereditary? This inability to keep food down.

Sam knew her anorexia/bulimia had a psychological basis, but she was a little stunned at this revelation.

She didn't even know what pigweed was, but she had grown up with a healthy meal on the table every night, even if it was just corn fritters and syrup. What would it be like to have to go pick weeds for dinner?

The Mormon missionaries were here again. The cute one with the dark blue eyes and nice smile was extra kind to me. They brought bacon and some beans, and some flour, sugar, salt, and some of that maple syrup, along with a recipe card with directions on how to make pancakes. My mouth waters just thinking about it.

They keep talking to me about their church, and how the Lord blesses those who live the Gospel, and part of those blessings are enough food to eat. It certainly seems to be true, because every time they come to see me they have more good food than I have ever seen in my life. Last time they came, in addition to the other stuff they brought a plate of cookies. With real chocolate chips. Well, chocolate chips. I'm not sure I would know what a real chocolate chip was, but they sure tasted good. After the missionaries left, and after they gave Momma a blessing, I ate the whole plate of cookies.

Then I got sick.

But I couldn't stop myself. They tasted so good. I must be a bad person that I can't eat good food and keep it down. Something must be wrong with me.

But I swear on everything that is holy that if I have kids they will never, ever go hungry. I will do whatever I have to do so they have food, and never know that gnawing ache.

Momma wasn't better after the blessing. She muttered and tossed and turned, like always, and I put a cool washrag on her head. It seemed to soothe her. She is nothing but skin and bones. I know she is dying. No preacher blessing is going to change that.

I remember when I was younger and she sat with me every day, an hour before school started, and went over my grammar lessons with me.

"We might be poor, Ruthie, but we are smart. And we will never act stupid or take charity."

She'd been a schoolteacher before she took sick, and before my daddy died. And I knew that what these missionaries were doing was charity, but I couldn't say no. How could I say no? I didn't want to die . . . I knew she was already close to gone. Did I have to go, too? Was that how life worked?

And if I didn't, what would happen to me when she died?

I would be completely, utterly, alone.

The missionaries continued to bring food to Ruthie and her mother and even arranged for a doctor to pay several visits, but there was nothing that could be done. A bad heart, they said, a result of a bout of untreated scarlet fever as a child. And after Sam's grandmother—a woman she had never known—died, the missionaries arranged for Ruthie Paulsen to live with a Mormon family in town. She'd been just sixteen years old. She didn't say much about them but wrote about the food they served for each meal and the sack lunches that she was able to take to school.

She never wrote about feeling loved or accepted or even named the people who she lived with. But they had what, to her, was a bounty of food, and she wrote about it in great detail.

Eventually, the missionaries who had befriended her finished their callings and returned to Utah. And they arranged to bring Ruthie Paulsen with them.

In Utah, she lived with another Mormon family, was baptized, and a year later married one of the missionaries who had been responsible for bringing her to Utah.

The cute missionary with the dark blue eyes was Sam's father.

Sam, who had inherited those same dark blue eyes and blond hair, reread the passage she had marked with a torn scrap of paper from a notebook, much later in the journal.

Why? This question needs an answer. And what? What does this God expect of me? The brothers and the sisters of my adopted community come to me, and they say, "It was God's plan. God wanted her. He needed her." God needed my daughter to hang from a tree? He needed my daughter, barely a teen, to be cut down? Literally. A hacksaw chewing through the rough cord that bound her, dangling, lifeless, hanging from a tree. In her prime, just a girl still, although she wanted to be more. She had a body she didn't understand, a core she couldn't reason with. God wanted her to die like this, her face blue, her ears bleeding, because she spread her legs for boys who tempted her with the wiles of this world?

This is what my husband tells me. The man who brought me to this community. To this belief system. And God help me, I believed. For a long time, I really did. For the God they spoke of brought me food, and children, and a home, and a peach tree in my backyard that bore the most luscious fruit I had ever tasted. All I had to do was go to the temple, to swear to never reveal the secrets, to praise Him, to pay a full tithe. All it took to have this life, this paradise, was complete obedience.

Except this is no paradise.

Now, all is bitter, all false. Even the beautiful peach tree bears nothing but rotten fruit, for my daughter died hanging from it. Died because she couldn't live up to what someone else wanted to her to be. It was nothing but a façade.

Who is this God? Why did I ever believe in Him? I don't understand how any God could expect this of any mother. I've lost my daughter, and he acts as though this is all a part of God's great and glorious plan. He feels like it was all good. God's vengeance for the things that are wrong.

What plan? How could this be great or glorious? How could this be predestined? How can people pray to find their lost keys and claim, 'Hallelujah, after I prayed I put my hand in my pocket and they were there,' and yet my daughter dies hanging from a tree, probably praying for help the whole time? Praying to a deaf *ear. What kind of world is predestined anyway, that people cling to it as though it were glue? What sort of God would help someone find their keys when they are lost, but let a child die without stepping in to save him or her? What's so important about choosing who or what you were or are?*

What's wrong with just coming into life and seeing what happens?

What would be wrong with that?

I guess what's wrong with that is my daughter is dead, and I'm supposed to believe that God had something to do with it.

This. Is. Not. My. God.

Sam put the book down so it lay open on her desk, and wiped away a tear. She didn't know this mother. This was not the woman Sam had lived with for so many years.

That woman played board games with Sam, and worked on her lessons before school and stopped to hug her when she caught her daughter watching her. Reaching out and just pulling Sammy in, holding tight, laughing as she tried to squirm away from her mother's kisses.

Why did Sam have so few memories of this mother? Why was it all coming back now?

Sam's mother's writing was clear and literate, and it belied the rural education she had undoubtedly received, growing up poor in a small town.

Circumstance had left Ruthie where she was alone and vulnerable. And it went a long way in explaining to Sam why her mother had converted to this church.

The more complicated answers to her past had died with her, unless there was more in the journal.

Sam heard D-Ray getting out of his chair and slammed the diary shut.

"Man, Sam, what is up with you?" D-Ray said, poking his head around the corner. "Normally you'd be all over my ass with a comment like that. Instead, you just ignore me. I think I prefer you as a smart-ass. At least I know I'm real, and not a ghost like Bruce Willis in that one flick."

"What comment?"

"I asked you if . . . Never mind."

"Look, my mom just died, D-Ray. Not sure why you expect me to be normal."

D-Ray looked chagrined and looked away for a moment, then made eye contact with her, and she saw his sincerity. "I'm sorry 'bout your mom."

Sam didn't know what to say, so she ignored his comment. Her cell phone rang. She answered, "Montgomery."

"Sammy. Oh, Sammy, She's waking up. She's opening her eyes."

Susanna's voice rang loud and clear through the phone line, and it seemed as though a miracle had happened.

Or it did it just mean life and mortality was random? Gambling. Sometimes you took a hit when the cards were seventeen and you got an ace or a two or, best of all, a four.

And sometimes you got a ten.

Sam and D-Ray rushed to Primary Children's Medical Center, and Sam jumped up and out of the car as D-Ray pulled into the roundabout in front of the hospital. She left D-Ray to park the car, and hit the stairs running instead of waiting for the elevator. She made it to the PICU, where she had to stop and call in through a phone on the wall.

"PICU," said a voice on the other end.

"I'm here for my sister. I mean I'm here for my niece. Whitney Marcusen."

The door buzzed. Sam dropped the phone without replacing it on the base and made her way to Whitney's room. There Sam saw a body, or the shape of a body, covered under a sheet, no machines beeping life. No movement. No hope.

Her heart seemed to stop—literally, like she'd read about in books—and she felt the blood drain out of her face.

"Hey, can I help you?" asked a kind-faced nurse with dark hair, a harried but concerned look on her face, and a clipboard in her hand.

"My . . . my niece. They said she was waking up. They said she was doing better."

"Name?" asked the nurse.

"I'm Sam Montgomery."

"No, no, the patient's name."

"Oh, sorry, Whitney Marcusen."

"Oh yes, Whitney. She's over here in room two-oh-four. Sorry, in PICU we move them around all the time. We need different rooms for different stages of care."

Sam's heart started to beat a regular rhythm as she stared at the small sheet-draped body on the bed.

"I . . . I thought she—"

"Yeah, sorry. It happens a lot. I'll show you where your niece is."

"Who is—"

"I can't really say. I'm sorry. Patient confidentiality and all that."

Sam nodded and followed the petite nurse to Whitney's room, where she encountered a wild scene.

She was glad to see Whitney active and thrashing, not a small, dead shape on a gurney. But Susanna was distraught.

"She wants me to help her," Susanna said, staring at Sam, boring through her with sleep-deprived eyes and the angst of a helpless mother. "She wants the tube out, and they won't take it out."

Sam moved forward and grasped Whitney's flailing right hand, holding it in hers. Stroking her fingers, Sam moved in so Whitney could see her eyes.

Her niece looked back and forth, back and forth, frantically, trying to find solace somewhere. Finally, her eyes connected with Sam's.

Help me, Whitney mouthed around the vent tube that was down her throat. *Help me.*

"Whit, they are helping you. You couldn't breathe, so they had to put this tube down your throat to help your lungs. To keep oxygen going to your brain. I know you want it out, and that's a good sign, but calm down. Calm down and breathe."

What? Whit mouthed. *What hap?*

"You had an accident. Somehow you hurt yourself, and . . . and now the doctors are trying to help you recover. The tube is down your throat to help you breathe. Your lungs aren't strong enough."

Help me, Whitney mouthed again.

"Oh, Whit, we are helping you. The doctors are helping you. You're going to get better."

Help me, Whitney mouthed again, this time more

ardently, and she began to thrash around, fighting against the blankets and tubes that kept her tied to her hospital bed.

"We're going to have to sedate her," the nurse whispered to Sam. "But this is good. All very good. She is responding so well."

"Then why do you want to sedate her?"

"So her brain can heal. It was a very serious brain trauma, and she needs the time to get better. But I've seen a lot of these. She's on the road to recovery."

Susanna soaked in the nurse's words, as though she were a barren desert and the nurse offered much-needed moisture. "Recovery," Susanna muttered. Then she sank to the floor and put her head between her knees.

THIRTY-SEVEN

Sam took her sister to a hotel close to Primary Children's, checked her in, ordered her room service, then told her to shower, eat, and sleep. In that order.

"I can't leave my daughter," Susanna had protested, after the doctors pronounced her suffering from trauma, shock, and exhaustion.

"You can't take care of her like this," Sam had said. "Now she's getting better, soon she will be going home, and she's going to need you then. So you need to take care of you. Shower. Eat real food. Sleep in a real bed. As soon as I get you settled, I'll go back and I won't leave her side until you come back."

"Promise me, Sammy. Promise me you won't leave her."

"I promise."

Sam had grabbed the bag of clothes that Roger brought to the hospital for Susanna, and they opened it after she got out of the shower. Susanna wrapped herself in a large towel and began picking at the chicken tenders and Caesar salad Sam had ordered.

Inside were four pairs of temple garments, Mormon sacred underwear, two pairs of jeans, and a toothbrush.

"Well, he certainly gave that a lot of thought, didn't he," Susanna said wryly.

"Asshole," Sam responded.

"I need a lawyer, Sam. I'm not playing this game anymore. We've been married for twenty-two years, he's cheated on me God knows how many times—once with my own eighteen-year-old-sister—and I've tolerated it because I've been striving for the eternal family, and to keep my church covenants. Twenty-two years, and he shows up with *this*? Four pairs of garments, no clean panties, no bra, two pairs of jeans, and a toothbrush. And you know what's the worst part of it?"

"What, Sus?" Sam asked gently.

"There's no fucking toothpaste. And this isn't even my toothbrush. I think this is the one I use to clean the grout in the shower. I'm divorcing that bastard and I'm never looking back."

"Sus?"

"What?"

"I'm not so sure Amy was really the one to blame in all this. I'm not so sure Roger didn't force himself on her."

"What the hell are you talking about?"

"Well, I saw him more than once. I saw him corner her. At family parties and events. It's been in the back of my mind for a long time, but I just sort of shoved it away. Like everything else. I mean, why the hell else do you think Amy ran? Left our family and never came back?"

"Because she had an affair with my husband?" Susanna asked, her voice hard and brittle.

"Did she? Or did he just make it all up? Force himself on her, because we were all little more than orphan girls. Just motherless children with no real guidance. Where do you turn when your sister's husband does that? What are you supposed to believe in?"

"What the hell, Sammy? Where is this coming from?"

"Susanna, Roger is a cheater and a serial adulterer. You know it, I know it, and the whole damn town knows it, even though he goes to church every Sunday, and you pretend like nothing is wrong. Maybe Roger drove Amy away because no one believed her. Even now he's trying to blame everyone else for the fact you want him gone. He came to the hospital and confronted me."

Susanna looked confused, her pale face withdrawn, and bright pink spots showed up on her fair cheeks. "I . . . I . . . The hospital? When? I didn't see him there. I've been with Whitney for so many hours straight I can't count them anymore, but I know if my husband had walked in I would have seen him."

Sam looked at her sister with compassion, realizing exactly how exhausted—both mentally and physically— she must be.

"Different hospital. Never mind, Sus. This isn't the right time. We'll talk later."

"I need a lawyer." Susanna's voice was weak and her eyes dim and withdrawn.

"I'll find you a lawyer, Sissy."

"Okay."

Sam made a quick trip to Walmart to get her sister the few essential items missing from her bag of clothes.

When Sam returned to the room, Susanna promised to try to sleep. She accepted the money Sam gave her for a taxi without complaint. She'd endured too much, and her pride was gone.

"The first thing Whitney said when she woke up was that girl's name, Sam. I forgot to tell you. She said, 'Bethany.' You need to look at that girl. She is behind all of this."

Sam pictured the petite girl, crying so abjectly, and considered her instinct. She just didn't see Bethany being involved in this.

"I've interviewed her, Sissy. I'll talk to her again."

"She's responsible. Mark my words. You have to arrest her!"

"I'll do my job, Sissy. Now you need to sleep."

Sam worried about Susanna recovering completely from this—knowing what had happened to their mother—but knew that right now Whitney had to come first. Then Sam would worry about fixing Susanna. Sam had applied a Band-Aid. For now, that was all she could do.

She returned to the hospital to find Whitney quiet and sleeping. "She's sedated," the nurse said softly. She was the same one who had said she believed Whitney would recover. In the PICU, each patient had their own nurse, necessary as they hovered on the threshold of life and death.

Sam took her niece's hand and squeezed it tightly. There was a small response, enough for Sam to know that Whit was in there, somewhere, sedated or not. Would she come out of this the same mean and spoiled child? Would she still taunt and tease those who were not thin and beautiful and talented? Or would she be different for her touch with death, whatever that meant?

Had Whitney passed her grandmother Ruthie like two trains passing each other in the night? An image danced in Sam's brain: one of her mother, dressed in her white temple clothes, alive and active like she hadn't been in years, hand pressed to the window of a train; Whitney, in a hospital gown, going the other way, also pressing her hand against the glass.

Sam's mother crying out, saying, "Don't believe! This is not my God!"

Whitney squeezed her hand again, and Sam jumped. Whit's eyes fluttered open and then closed again, and Sam felt the tears stream down her cheeks. Was Whit trying to tell her that yes, Ruthie had seen her, and that she was finally at peace? Or was that just old mythology and religion talking?

And why was she crying now?

Why couldn't she stop?

The nurse came up to her and offered a box of Kleenex. She took some with her free hand and wiped her face, never letting go of Whitney's hand.

"Sometimes these things go really, really bad, and this one is looking positive. I know it's hard not to cry. Get it out. But just remember, this has a good outcome. Not a bad one. I'm just the nurse, so don't quote me, but I see all the things here that we like to see in recovering patients."

"Thanks," Sam said through her sobs, angry at her weakness. She knew she was crying for more than Whitney. She was crying for Susanna, whose marriage was a sham; for Amy, who had run from a dysfunctional childhood; for Callie, who had died too young; for Ruthie, who had died after years of not even coming close to living; and for herself.

That made her cry more than anything else, mostly because she was angry she would waste tears on herself. She was fine. Just fine. She didn't need anybody or anything.

Yeah, right, Sammy.

Sam stared at Whitney's sleeping face and wondered again what kind of person she would be when she was well, healed, back to normal. Would she be normal? Would she be brain damaged?

We all have it in us, Sam. It's just how we use it.

Who is talking? Callie? Ruthie? Whitney? Or maybe, maybe, just me. Maybe it's been inside of me all this time, and I just didn't figure it out. Maybe no one is out there but me.

Sam felt more alone than ever before.

THIRTY-EIGHT

Sam needed to talk to someone who would listen without judgment, and she had no idea who that was. But for some reason, Gage's name kept running through her mind. No-nonsense, practical Gage.

Maybe this was just an excuse to be near him again.

Maybe that was why she was sitting in his driveway, wondering if she should walk up to the door or just drive away. That decision was made for her when his Jeep pulled up alongside. He gave her a slight wave.

There would be no quick escape.

He didn't ask why she was there, just ushered her inside, his hand on the small of her back, pushing her forward through the door gently.

"Something to drink?" he asked her as he took off his outer shirt and removed his service pistol and holster.

"You have beer?"

"I have beer. Chick beer or real beer?"

"Chick beer? What's chick beer?"

"Oh, you know. The good old three-point-two Utah beer in some sort of 'lite' version."

"Why do you have 'chick beer'? Do a lot of entertaining?"

"Yeah, I've had a few barbecues this summer, and the guys bring their wives and girlfriends. They turn their noses up at real beer. I think I might even have a bottle of wine left over from the last one."

"I'll take a real beer."

He laughed and walked into the kitchen. She surveyed the room, looking a little closer than she had last time she had been here. It was decorated in warm browns and tans, very male and masculine.

There were no feminine touches here. No vases with flowers or ornate frames. Gage was all man, and he obviously did not share his life with anyone else. The butterflies in her stomach surprised her.

"You look like you've seen a ghost," Gage said, walking back into the living room with two beers bearing a label she didn't recognize.

"If you only knew," she answered.

"I can't stand that look on your face," he said softly. "You look so . . . scared."

"I *am* scared. I don't understand what's happening."

"In Kanesville?"

"In Kanesville, in my family. I'm not up to it. I don't think I can handle it."

"Yes, you can. You're brave, and you're courageous. And you have the most honest heart of anyone I've ever met."

He reached out and grabbed her hands, pulling her up to him until they were facing each other.

Sam was still in her khaki capris and the colored

tank she wore to the hospital, with a light sweater covering it up.

It didn't feel substantial enough as she leaned against him. She could feel him—all of him. She might as well have stripped down naked and walked in the front door.

Gage wore a pair of tan cargo shorts and a T-shirt similar to the one she'd absconded with two years before.

Sam looked up into his eyes and almost came undone. There she saw his true self, vulnerability, and maybe just a hint of the arrogance that had led to Mary Ann Clarkston's death. And Sam forgave him right then, just a little bit, because she saw it in his eyes. She saw that he had made the mistakes he made because of her and because of the roles they both held in society. And she wanted him. Needed him.

"You were trying to protect me. You shouldn't have done that."

"When?"

"The Clarkston case. Pulling me off. You were trying to keep me safe."

"It's what I was raised to do."

"It's not what I want."

"It's not what I want, either. I want you, as a partner. An equal. You *are* my equal. This last year has been a nightmare. I don't ever want you to leave again."

"I . . . I'm not exactly a part of your life, Gage."

"I want you to be."

"I still think about Mary Ann. All the time. It's not going to go away quickly."

"Mary Ann died for a lot of reasons. If you want me to apologize I will. But it's not that simple. There are a lot of things you didn't know. You didn't know that she was counting on you, planning on you to get her out.

You didn't know that her father discovered the note she wrote. You had no control over the fact that he beat her to death and left her body in the desert."

Sam stared at him, a lump in her throat. Did she want Gage's apology? What difference would it make?

"I gave her hope. I might have been able to help her. If you had let me go to the wedding—"

"I couldn't, Sam. I had inside information."

Sam closed her eyes as the implication hit her. "You knew she was going to run, to try to get me to take her out of there."

He sighed heavily. "I knew. At the wedding. And it would have blown your cover."

"Ruining your case." Disgust tinged her voice as she stood up.

"No, Sam. You are not leaving, and you are going to hear me out." He grabbed her arm and pulled her in front of him, holding her there with both hands. "The Clarkstons aren't like that man and woman you saw at the hospital. Caring for their children. Holding hands. I don't like polygamy, but there are some good people involved in it who really believe they are living the life God wants them to. But not very many. It's a big damn game. Women and children are nothing but a ticket into Heaven, and the one with the most wives wins. If you had tried to get her out of there, like she was planning on asking you to do, they would have killed you along with her. And then they win."

"I might have been able to save her. I'm a cop, for God's sake."

"You wouldn't have been carrying. They pat down everyone that goes inside their buildings, and they all carry guns. They own property. Landfills. Garbage dumps. And people just disappear, Sam. One day they're there, and the next they are not. The only reason Mary Ann's body was found was because we were looking for her, and because you gave her the courage to fight back. Most of the people who they kill just disappear. And no one ever reports them missing.

"You didn't know that they had every single room in that store bugged. Including the women's restroom. That's how they operate. You blew your cover the minute you told her you would help her."

Sam stood in stunned silence. She'd been so angry at him for so long when, in reality, she had made all the mistakes. She'd been nothing but a rookie cop.

"I . . . But . . . That's a violation of so many laws I don't even know where to start!"

"And you really think these people care?"

"How did you know this?"

"Because I had someone else on the inside. I have for years."

"Who?"

"I can't tell you. I can't tell anyone, because she would die. You don't want to know. And you're just going to have to leave it at that. And trust me. For once, dammit, Sam, just trust me. I pulled you because if I hadn't, you would have died."

Sam considered his words. "Why didn't you tell me this before?"

"When did you ever give me a chance? Plus you would have demanded an explanation, would have wanted to know the source. You never would have let it go. You were angry and bitter."

"I grew up angry and bitter."

"And I want to ease the anger, make you whole again."

Sam started to cry, silent, hot tears that she couldn't

stop. "This doesn't mean I'm not still pissed at you. You should have at least given me a chance."

"I wasn't going to let you die."

"I might have surprised you."

"I spent two years investigating these men before you ever came on the scene, Sam. You would have died. And I would have lost you forever. Better for you to hate me, and know you were still alive, than that."

"You're too good for me."

"You have no idea. I told you before, I am only good at two things. Killing, and making love. I joked about it, but it's real. The rest of life I suck at. I have no real talent for just being human, or just walking out among the masses and acting normal. I think war took that away from me. Or maybe I was always that way. I don't know. But I do know that I *want* you. And I can protect you from anyone, anywhere, anytime."

"Gage, I could walk out in front of a bus tomorrow and die. You can't stop that."

"That's not the same thing. I can't control acts of God, Sam. Or acts of nature, or whoever you worship. But if someone comes after you with deadly intent, they *will* not walk away from it."

Sam felt that electrical pulsing she always felt when Gage was around. He was so unlike any other man she had ever met.

A thrill shimmied down her spine, and Sam stared into his eyes.

Then Gage leaned down and kissed her, without warning, surrounding her with warm lips, his distinctive scent, the scratch of stubble—each sense hit Sam separately and all together. And for a long moment, she couldn't think—didn't want to.

One hand moved to her waist and gripped her there. The other tangled into her hair, pressing the back of her head to change the angle, deepen the kiss.

And finally, there, Sam broke away.

"I don't know if I'm ready for this. I've been so angry at you for so long." Her voice came out rough, barely above a whisper. She looked up into his eyes again and saw everything: a wide-eyed hunger and vulnerability that she knew instinctively he would never want anyone to see.

"You're ready. You've been ready since we met. You know as well as I do that you can't fight this. You won't win, so why try?" He smiled. Then kissed her again, his lips soft on hers at first, then more insistent. Her lips parted and he explored her with his tongue gently, then with more vigor.

Sam's body tingled with electricity as adrenaline coursed through her bloodstream. Gage ran his hands up and down her spine, and she could feel the heat and intensity through the thin fabric of her tank, shivering as his hands traveled lower to cup her buttocks. Then he moved his hands upward, pulling her into him closer, touching the small of her back with both palms.

She put her arms around his neck as he pushed against her, ground his mouth against hers, and Sam felt her whole body go weak. She took her arms from around his neck and reached under his T-shirt, needing that contact. Needing to feel his skin against her skin. She ran her hand up his spine and felt his shiver and knew he was feeling all the same things she was.

Gage pulled away from her and took her hand, leading her down the hallway. She followed without complaint, refusing to think beyond the now. They ended up in his bedroom, standing at the foot of his bed, not touching, just inches from each other.

Staring into his eyes, Sam saw the desire. She didn't know what love looked like. But desire she could recognize.

"You understand that once we take this step, I'm not looking back, right? I don't do things halfway. If I take you, I take all of you. I want you in my bed and in my life. I want to come home to you. I want your eyes to be the last thing I see before I close mine."

Sam couldn't look away, even though the panic was rising in her chest. "I'm not good at the relationship thing. I don't know how to do it. Haven't you figured that out by now?"

"I don't really give a shit about your past, Sam. I'm talking about you and me. Starting now. You don't have to be good at it. We'll go through it together. I screwed up with you once, and I don't intend to do it again."

"I—"

"If you can't do that, then we can't do this. Because I'm not doing the halfway thing, or the casual-sex thing. I'm not a casual person. Whatever I do, I do hard."

"Is that supposed to be a sexual euphemism?"

"You can take it any way you want. Do you want it hard?"

"I think I do," Sam said softly, finding it hard to believe these words were coming out of her mouth or that she was willing to take this step. Except she knew this was a runaway train she couldn't stop. And she was tired of fighting. She'd been fighting her whole life. "And soft and slow. And a lot of other ways, too."

"Good," Gage said, his voice a seductive growl. He reached for her then, grabbing the bottom of her thin tank and pulling it up over her head. He traced the line above her breasts, running his fingers over the top of her bra and touching her nipple, which reacted, even through the fabric of the bra.

"I need you now, Sam," he said. Then he tucked his fingers under the bra and pulled it over her head. She raised her arms and let him strip her of her clothing and all her pretenses.

He moved her to the bed, then pulled his own T-shirt over his head. They were both naked from the waist up, and Sam's breasts pushed against his chest as he rolled over the top of her and kissed her, exploring her mouth with his.

Explosions of electricity went off in her brain as he moved away from her mouth and down to her breast, suckling first her left breast, then her right.

Sam arched into him, and he quickly stripped off her capris and underwear. He ran his hand from the top of her neck down over her breast and farther down, first stopping at her navel, then moving between her legs and opening her up, exploring her with his fingers.

She gasped as he moved his fingers inside her, gently then a bit more insistently, and she felt herself grow slick with desire.

He brought her to the edge of orgasm, and she moaned as he pulled his fingers away, quickly stripping off his shorts and boxers and throwing them off the side of the bed.

"The first time you come with me, I want it to be when I'm inside you," he whispered in her ear as he entered her, his penis full and large, and she felt her inner walls close around him.

"Oh God," he moaned. "If you do that, I'm not going to be able to hold back."

"You deserve it," she said.

He began to move inside her with slow, rhythmic thrusts. He pulled her legs up around his back, opening her up wide, so he could get inside her deeper.

The world started to spin for Sam as she felt her muscles clench around his swollen manhood. She couldn't help a soft moan.

The harder his thrusts, the closer she came to the edge of orgasm, until he finally pushed into her so hard that she felt her entire body tremble and the little earthquakes between her legs became uncontrollable.

He sensed her climax and stilled deep within her until he, too, was shivering.

They stayed conjoined for what seemed like hours—or maybe only minutes—neither one speaking, just stroking each other's skin, bodies pressed together.

"This doesn't mean you get to take over my case," Sam whispered in his ear.

"I don't want your case. I only want you."

He grabbed her right hand and clasped it in his, then pulled it forward and spread it across the left side of his chest. "Can you feel that?"

"I can feel your heart."

"Yes, it's pretty strong. Sounds solid, huh?"

"Yes, Gage," she said sarcastically, "Your heart sounds very, very healthy. You must have been eating your Cheerios every morning. Is there a point here?"

"For once, Sam, just put it aside. Leave the defenses and sarcasm. Just listen." He pulled her head down to his chest, her ear resting just above his heart. She could hear the solid *thump-thump, thump-thump, thump-*

thump, soothing her in a way she couldn't explain. She did know it was comfortable there, in his arms, her head on his chest, listening to his heart.

She didn't want to move, to ruin the moment. God knows she had ruined plenty of moments in her past. But Gage had been different. She had wanted it to work. She had wanted to take the next step, and then he had her pulled from the case and destroyed everything she had worked so hard for.

Sam had believed then that leaving was the only answer—going back home, where she still felt she had something to prove. Of course, now she had something to prove in both places. And when she'd returned home teenagers had started dying. Maybe it was all somehow connected to her.

But in leaving Salt Lake City she had left behind a part of herself with Gage. Right now, for a moment, she felt just a little more whole.

"Can you hear it? I have a strong heart, but you nearly destroyed me when you left."

"No one could ever destroy you," she said softly. "You're the man of steel."

"No, I'm not," he said. His chiseled face and dark blue eyes—nearly the exact same color as her own—had drawn her to him before she had ever even heard his voice.

When he spoke, he was purposeful and determined and people listened. He never raised his voice. When he was angry, his lips tightened and his face darkened, his eyes turning an even deeper shade of blue.

Gage had a presence that stopped people short. He always seemed completely invulnerable.

Sam watched him as he let his defenses down. Now

they were naked together, before each other without pretenses.

"I ate myself alive when you left," he said. "But I didn't know how to fix it, because the truth is, you made a mistake. You were wrong. You shouldn't have done what you did."

"I know."

Later, they lay together in his bed, sheets on top of them, nothing between them. She'd craved this, Sam realized. She'd craved him.

Sam told him everything. Her mother's journal and sadness over her death. Sam's fear for Whit and Susanna. Distance from her father. And something she had never spoken about to anyone—Callie. Her voice in Sam's head, urging her on.

Throughout it all, Gage pulled her closer, if that was even possible, stroking her hair as she talked into his chest, feeling the warmth of her own exhalations.

"Sometimes I feel like I'm a little bit crazy," she said.

"Maybe you are, and maybe you aren't. Whatever the truth is, there is a reason for it."

"Callie didn't kill herself," Sam said, pulling away from him, looking into his eyes. "She was murdered. I can tell, when I go to a crime scene . . . . Okay, this sounds even crazier, but I really can tell if it's a murder, or a suicide. Each scene feels different. And all I remember about Callie's was the fear, desperation, and . . . She was killed, Gage. I have to trust in this. I have to find out what happened."

"Yes, you do," he said, stroking her arm. "And I'll be there to help you."

THIRTY-NINE

When Sam pulled into her driveway, weary of unanswered questions, she immediately spotted the tan car parked in front of her house—a car similar to both Paul's and the one that had run her off the road. Sam felt her mind flip. She *was* going crazy. Too many coincidences.

The hair on her arms bristled as the door opened, and she reached for her gun on her hip. But it wasn't Paul. Out stepped a tall, thin, elegant woman in trendy jeans and a red T-shirt covered by a lace vest. Her hair was shoulder length, elegantly styled with blond highlights running through a darker blond base.

She looked a lot like Susanna, only ten years younger, much more put together, and a lot less downtrodden.

Amy had returned home.

Or at least to her hometown.

As her long-lost sister walked toward her, Sam got out of her car. As soon as Amy was within ten feet, Sam spoke.

"How did you find me?" she said, without any other introduction.

Amy just shrugged. Sam had already figured out that Amy had to know someone on the force.

Of course she does, Sammy. And you know just who it is.

They were both cops. Odd, how that had happened.

"Why are you here?"

"You said I should come."

"And you said no."

"I changed my mind." Amy's voice had a Texas twang that was faint but spoke volumes about where she'd been for years.

"Why?" Sam asked.

"Because there are some things I need to tell you, especially now that Mom's gone. Some things we need to get straight."

"Well, then I guess you better come in."

Amy walked back to her car—obviously a generic rental vehicle that only vaguely resembled Paul's—and opened up the back door, pulling out a small overnight suitcase. She clearly didn't intend staying long.

Sam moved on ahead to her front door and went to put her key into it, only to find it ajar. Her heart raced—she never left her home unlocked—and her instincts immediately kicked in. She pulled the pink .38 Gage had given her out of her purse and let the bag fall to the ground. She also put her right arm back, palm out, a stop sign, warning her sister not to come forward.

Sam felt a presence behind her and turned quickly, to see Amy had her own .38 weapon drawn. Amy shook her head at Sam's gasp of surprise. *Call for backup,* she mouthed.

Sam grabbed her purse off the ground, stepped back outside the door, and pulled out her cell phone. She made a quick and quiet call to Dispatch, then tucked the phone in her pocket as she and Amy took protective stances on either side of the door.

Then Sam pushed through, Amy behind her.

Sam's town house had been completely ransacked.

Written on the living room wall in dripping red was one word: **VENGEANCE.**

"Guess you really pissed someone off," Amy said drolly as they watched the scurrying movements of the crime scene techs and officers. "Either that or you wanted to offer me one hell of a welcome home."

"Well, if I'd had any idea you were coming . . ."

Gage was shadowing them. He had shown up only seconds after the Smithland's deputies and Kanesville uniforms. He put his hand on Sam's arm.

"Are you really okay?" he asked her.

"Yeah, feeling a little violated, and not looking forward to painting, but other than that . . ."

He held her gaze for a minute and then seemed to accept her answer. He turned to survey the damage.

Chief Roberson stood by the vandalized wall, discussing the scene with two of the sheriff's deputies, including Lind Harris.

Lind wandered away from the chief, toward her and Gage. "Trouble just seems to follow you, doesn't it, Sam? About the only reason you always get yourself out of it is because you're a girl cop. Is that why you do it? Is this guy your newest victim?"

"You're a jackass," Gage said, his chin quivering as he pushed the words out between tight lips.

"Whoa, dude, I don't even know you, but if you are linked up with her I gotta warn you to look out. She's trouble. All of those girls are. Even the one who killed herself."

Sam was surprised to feel the motion of her arm, propelling her fist toward Lind's weak jaw. Even more surprised when pain burst into her fingers and up her arm as her fist connected with his face. There was a cracking noise as the blow whipped his head to the side and he stumbled back.

"You bitch!" he yelled, grabbing his face. The other deputy and Chief Roberson hurried in their direction while medical personnel stood and stared, not quite sure what to make of the scene. Amy tried to step forward, but D-Ray held her back.

"You incompetent asshole," Sam retorted, holding her sore hand but almost reveling in the feeling of its ache. "This is a crime scene. You know, those things you always fuck up because you have no idea what you're doing? You're a coward, Harris. Poking sticks at a grieving family. I remember you taunting me when we were in school."

She stopped, suddenly remembering that Paul had been Lind Harris's friend. Best friend, at least in junior high. Lind had become one of the "cling-ons" when they moved to high school. But she remembered him there in the background, with his ugly sneer and his trying to constantly steer Paul away from her and toward something else. Anything else.

Was Lind responsible for the dead rodents?

"I know why I hate you, Harris. But why do you hate me?"

He gave her a nasty look as he continued to hold his

jaw. "Because you're trash. Montgomery trash. Always have been. Just like your sister Callie used to be. She was a tease, you know. Always leading guys on, but never—" He stopped, looked around, and clamped his mouth shut.

Gage said through still-frozen lips, "Sounds personal, Harris. I think you need to get yourself out of here, now. Before I help you out. Headfirst." His fists were tight at his sides.

"What the hell?" Chief Roberson said to Sam. "You guys grew up together and you act like mortal enemies. You're cops. Kids in this town are dying. Harris, get out of here. I'll be calling your sergeant."

"And Montgomery . . ." She'd swiftly gone from "Sam" to "Montgomery," she noted as the chief turned to her. To her surprise, she saw compassion in his eyes, not the anger she expected. He waited until Harris was gone, fuming out the door, before he spoke.

"Sam, I don't like that kid. Never have. Sounds like he's been holding a grudge against you for a long time. I'll take care of this with his boss, but you'll probably get a suspension over the assault. Not much I can do about that." He paused, looked around, and blew out a heavy breath. "Now, all I have to say is you need to take care of yourself. Don't come back to work for a week. Then we'll talk."

The chief shook his head and walked away.

Inside, D-Ray and the chief spoke in low voices, discussing, she knew, the fact that she would now be removed from the case. She figured D-Ray would become the point man. It made sense, as she wouldn't be working the case any longer.

Sam and Amy sat on the back patio, drinking Diet Cokes.

Gage had left, taking evidence with him to the SLCPD crime lab, which had some newer equipment than Smithland County.

He'd taken a moment to squeeze Sam's arm, even though he knew others were watching. He had also leaned in quietly and asked her if she needed medical attention for her hand. She'd shaken her head no.

Now she nursed her sore knuckles, holding the cold can of Coke across them.

"Got anything stronger?" Amy asked as she sipped at her drink like a southern belle.

Sam studied her sister's face: she was still beautiful. Of all the Montgomery girls she looked the most like their mother. Sam had inherited her father's lean, angular body, face, and lines, but Amy was soft where women were supposed to be, curvy in all the right spots, and the lines in her face gave her character instead of making her look haggard and old, like Susanna. Amy's eyes were large and the same steel blue Ruthie's eyes had been, and her hair had the same consistency. Her lips were full and her nose small, and looking at her Sam got all warm inside. It was like seeing a replica of her mother, back when the world had been different.

Candy Land. Hot chocolate. Movie night.

But both Amy and her mother had left, in very different ways.

"What makes you think I drink? We were raised Mormon," Sam said, not betraying her inner thoughts.

"Gee, I thought we were Amish."

"Do Amish people drink?"

"Sam, I have no idea. But I know you left it all behind, too. I can see it in your face, and hear it in your voice."

"Dad told you."

"I haven't spoken with our father since the day I walked away from this hellhole."

"Then how did you know I was a cop?"

"I've kept track of you for years."

"If you tell me you have your ear to the ground, I might have to shoot you. I have a gun, you know," Sam said, thinking of Gage.

Amy cocked her head and gave Sam a quizzical look. "What's that supposed to mean?"

"Never mind. Kept track of me how?"

"I don't think you'd understand."

"Try me."

"I have a friend who keeps me updated, and this situation was getting too dangerous. I had to put aside my own fears and come."

"A friend?"

"A mutual friend."

"You know, you're starting to really piss me off, Amy. You disappear from our lives, we never hear from you, and then you come back and drop all these vague and mysterious things on me like 'I've kept track of you.' Like you even cared."

"She did care," D-Ray said quietly, and Sam jumped. She hadn't heard him come up behind her.

Sam turned to look at him. She'd known it was D-Ray. He and Amy had gone to school together. Sam had grown up knowing him as her older sister's friend. He'd always been there in Kanesville. He'd spent summers running through the backyards and wooded areas of Kanesville just like Sam did, with Amy and Callie and Paul . . .

"You've been spying on me?" Sam asked D-Ray, knowing her words were harsh, her tone angry and accusing, but unable—or unwilling—to control it.

"Oh yes, I asked to be assigned as your partner so I could ferret out information and send it to your sister," he said, sarcasm dripping off his tongue. "I haven't been spying on you. When Amy called and asked how you were, I told her."

"Why didn't you tell me you knew where Amy was? What the hell is going on here?"

Sam was angry and confused, unable to comprehend why her sister would disappear from her life and yet bother to keep track of her. And why her partner, D-Ray, wouldn't mention that he actually spoke to her sister.

"I couldn't come back, and I couldn't make sure you were okay, so I did the next best thing."

"Why couldn't you come back? I don't get this."

"Sam, let it be," D-Ray said, his eyes gentle and knowing. That made her even angrier. He knew something. Something she herself did not know.

Chief Roberson blundered out onto the patio right at that moment and collapsed into one of her patio chairs, the metal frame bouncing from his girth.

"Well, Montgomery. D-Ray is going to take over as lead detective, working with Flint, and Patterson will back them up."

Patterson, the one who spent most of his time as the D.A.R.E. cop, going around to schools and preaching the virtues of just saying no to drugs and alcohol.

He was also "a big weenie," according to D-Ray.

"Look, Chief, I know you think you have to take me off, but for all you know this could have nothing to do with the other thing at all. I've been questioning these kids, and maybe it pissed some of them off. Maybe it's someone I arrested in SLC."

"Come on, Sam," Roberson said, using her first name. Never a good sign. "I don't have a choice. I should have pulled you off when I read the report about the rat. Hell, you should have told me about it. You know that. I'm sorry."

He'd known. The whole time he'd known. This was a difficult man to outguess.

The chief hefted himself out of the chair and said, "Didn't help that you decided to assault a fellow officer, no matter how bad he was asking for it. Not sure how that one will turn out. And I'm afraid you're going to have to paint that wall. Nothing more we can do here."

He avoided looking at her, and Sam felt anger build in her. It was the "good old boy" system again. Let the guys do the work, because the woman couldn't handle it. She started to stand and follow the chief but felt Amy's hand on her shoulder. "It won't do any good, Sam. He has to do this. He *should* have done it the minute they found Whitney."

Sam shrugged her sister's hand off her shoulder and turned away, fighting off the salty ache of tears at the bases of her eyes. She would not give in to this.

"It's not over," Sam said, not looking back at her sister.

"No, it's not over. But if you don't stop now, you might die, too. I think this has more to do with us, with our history, than you realize. Than anyone realizes. We're both fighting the same demons, Sammy. Every time I arrest someone, I get a high. Score one for the good guys.

"We both live life on the edge. And all because Callie died when we were little. I needed to come back and face those demons—with you."

Sam caught D-Ray's gaze. She didn't know how to feel. He'd been feeding Amy information when Sam felt like she should have just returned and found out for herself.

"I don't owe you an apology," D-Ray said, in sync enough with Sam's thoughts that he knew what she would say. "She's my friend. She's your sister. When she called and asked me how you were, I told her. That's all."

"Stupid small-town cops," Sam muttered. "Why didn't you say something?"

"You never asked."

"And how the hell was I supposed to know my long-missing sister was checking up on me through my partner, her old school friend? I didn't even know you guys stayed in touch. And how did she even know we were partners? What about when I was in Salt Lake? What the hell?"

Sam felt the questions spinning in her head like orbs that were just out of reach. She closed her eyes and tipped her head back, fighting off the beginnings of a headache that threatened to turn into a roaring tormentor.

"He didn't tell you because I asked him not to," Amy said softly.

"Why?"

"Because then you would want to know where I

was, and why I left, and I couldn't tell you. I couldn't answer and I couldn't come back."

"Then why the hell are you here now?"

"I told you. Something told me you were in trouble. Deep trouble. I finally realized I had to come back and face the real demons—not the ones I see every day on the job. And I had to reconnect with you." She paused. "I want to show you something." She stood up and motioned Sam to follow her inside. In the living room she walked over to the purse she had put on Sam's coffee table a few hours before—after they had discovered the vandalism but realized no one was in the house waiting to cause any more, possibly lethal, damage.

She pulled out a thin, wildly patterned flat wallet. It was a snakeskin print—very popular—though the colors didn't resemble those of any snake Sam had ever seen.

Amy opened the wallet and took out a thin, ragged picture. She handed it to Sam. Sam looked, memories flooding her as she stared at the child she used to be, raggedy, motherless, poorly dressed. In the image she stood next to Amy, who had one hand on Sam's shoulder. They both frowned, no childhood joy in their faces, no excitement.

"I don't remember this picture."

"I know you don't. You were in a shell, trying to recover from the loss of your sister and, even worse, the loss of our mother. Dad took the picture. He posed us there, in front of the tree. Reminding us that this is what happened to bad girls. To girls who didn't do what they were taught."

"Oh, please. I don't remember anything about this. You've got to be kidding me."

"You don't know him, Sam. You don't know him like I do. He's different now, maybe. That's what I hear. But back then, he made sure we all lived by the Mormon law."

"So did everybody else's parents."

"Not like him. You don't understand. You weren't old enough to see what I saw. What he did."

"So he posed us in front of the tree. So what? So we look sad. So what? Why did you come home now, Amy?"

"I like to think I came home because of Callie. At least that's the thought that got me on the plane. She's still with us. And she's worried about you."

"You sound like a freaking nutcase," Sam said angrily, thrusting the picture back at her sister. "Carrying a grudge because of what happened to Callie. Carrying around this picture like it's your own personal cross to bear. That's just stupid. It happened. We were kids. And if you were worried about me, you should have stayed here. You should have taken care of me, instead of running out."

"I know. You're right. But he loved you. I thought you'd be okay. You were always his favorite."

Sam stood and watched a silent exchange between D-Ray and Amy. He shook his head roughly, but she backed up, her mouth a tight slit, and then turned to Sam.

"Sammy, it wasn't Callie. It wasn't Callie who was having sex. She was covering for me—for me and D-Ray. Dad saw us in the backyard, but he didn't know it was me."

"No, stop it."

"Callie stood up to him and said it was her. I tried to stop her, but she wouldn't listen."

"Stop—"

"And then she died. It was my fault."

Shock, then sudden and overwhelming compassion filled Sam's chest. Amy felt responsible for Callie's death. She'd been carrying that around with her—just like the picture—for all these years.

Sam didn't realize she was crying until she saw the moisture in D-Ray's own eyes. Sam could taste the salt as her tears reached her lips and she tried to wipe them away, but they wouldn't stop.

"Why? Why didn't you just tell me?" Sam asked D-Ray.

"I couldn't say anything, Sammy. Amy made me promise. We were both fourteen years old. I was just the town bastard that the Church and the people in it took pity on. If they knew about me and Amy, if they knew, they would have hurt her. They would have chased my mother out of town, and they would have destroyed us."

"So you let Callie take the fall?"

"I didn't know . . . ," Amy said, tearing up and wiping at her face with her hands. "I didn't know she'd kill herself over it. I didn't know it would be that bad."

Sam thought of her night run to the top of the road. Her realization about the scene of Callie's death. "Are you sure she killed herself?"

Amy paused. "What do you mean? Of course she did," she said, still wiping away the tears.

"But why would she kill herself if she hadn't done anything wrong?"

"Why does any teenager kill herself? Because it's the end of the world. Because things are never going to get better. When you are a teenager you can't reason beyond your emotions right then. Maybe she thought she would show him, or that she could stop it, and then it was too late. I don't know.

"But now you know why I had to leave and couldn't come back. Especially after Roger accused me of starting an affair with him. He kept trying to grab me, and I threatened to tell Susanna. And he said no one would believe me. It would destroy Susanna. I'd already killed one of my sisters. I wasn't about to do it to another one. And then he told her anyway. She suspected something, and he lied to her about me. I knew I could never come back here."

"But you did."

"Yes, I did. For you."

FORTY

Amy and D-Ray left after Sam convinced them that she needed time to digest all she had learned. Amy was staying in a hotel in Layton, and she and D-Ray had some catching up to do. Sam didn't want to know what all that might include.

She was at her limit. *No more emotion, please.* After they left, she went to her room to change into running clothes. She thought about calling Gage but decided she needed more time to think through the evening's events.

"No wonder we were the neighborhood basket cases," she muttered to herself as she tied up her running shoes and threw her fanny pack around her waist, snapping it securely in back.

A wave of heat seemed to roll over her as she passed the furnace room, and she stopped, wondering when she was going to remember to get someone in here to look at the air-conditioning. She would have plenty of time now, actually, since she intended to resign from the force. Enough time to get this place looking sharp and put it on the market and move away.

Maybe farther than Salt Lake City. Maybe another state?

You aren't leaving now, Sammy. You are too close.

"I can *leave,* if I want to leave," she said loudly. She could take care of herself.

The air conditioner chose that moment to make a sudden belching noise. Sam started. The noise didn't recur, and Sam stared at the door, transfixed. Several moments passed before she heard a scuffling noise. She jumped back. Something was inside. She pulled the gun out of her fanny pack. Aiming at the door, she reached for the knob. She took a stance and pulled the door open.

It was dark in the utility closet, but she could not see any human shapes.

She screamed as two little white mice ran across her feet.

Reaching in and flipping on the light switch, she saw nothing more. Rodents. A gift from Lind Harris, who had just been in her house?

Was he responsible for all of the incidents? Could he possibly have tried to run her off the road?

You should try harder to make friends, and not so many enemies, Sam.

It would sure help in narrowing down the suspect list.

Shaking her head, she looked around but couldn't see where the mice had gone. They would have to be found later.

Sam headed out for her run. It had been raining most of the day but was just letting up now. Sam inhaled deeply, enjoying the clean smell of freshly washed earth.

She was jogging through Kanesville at midnight. One of those stories you read in the newspaper and think, *How stupid was she? Why didn't she know better? She was a cop.*

She knew better. She also carried a gun that could do some serious damage to anyone who got too close— and she was a crack shot. She needed to do this. She needed to talk to Callie. Alone.

It was still hot, and Sam considered how far she could run. How far away she could get by morning. Maybe she would never stop. Running was in the family genes. It was what Amy did years before.

It was what her mother had done mentally, until she died.

It was what Sam's father had done every day as he pretended his wife was fine, just having a forgetful day. And it was what Callie had done. The ultimate getaway.

Callie had hung herself.

I thought we got this straight. I thought you understood.

Sam tried to ignore Callie's voice.

You felt it. I know you did. I took you back there, and you felt it. You felt everything that I felt, and now you are just back to the "she killed herself" theory? What the hell. I took you back.

Again, Sam remembered the sucker punch of the other night, the feeling of despair and fear, like she was somehow inside Callie's terrified head and swinging body.

I took you back.

Took her back to the scene of the accident and tried

to tell her it was a crime. Unless this voice was nothing but a little bit of bat-ass craziness that ran in the family.

Callie had died hanging from a tree. But was it death by her own hand?

And what about the other teenagers? The ones who had just barely died? Sam's niece, Whitney, who had narrowly escaped the same fate? What about the word "vengeance" written on Sam's wall in bloodred paint?

What difference did it make? It wasn't her case anymore.

The sudden sound of feet slapping the pavement and coming up quickly behind her made the hairs on her arms rise. She turned and ducked immediately into a protective stance, whipping out her gun before she could even distinguish the white figure headed toward her.

"Freeze!" she yelled. She would have laughed at her little pink gun standing out in the dim, if she weren't so focused on keeping herself alive.

"Hey, Sam," Paul Carson said as he stopped, eyeing the gun. "Sorry to scare you. I always run at night. It's too hot in the day and I have a hard time sleeping." He laughed. "Guess I'm not the only one."

Sam lowered the gun slowly. "You should know better than to run up behind a woman jogging at night."

"You should probably know better than to jog at night, being a woman alone and all."

"I have a gun, as you can see," she said, not appreciating his implication that she couldn't take care of herself. "I can use it better than anyone else on the Kanesville force."

"It's pink," he said with a half grin that reminded her of the teenage Paul.

"The color doesn't affect the way it works."

"Point taken. Well, since we're both out here, and we're both running, care if I join you?"

Sam remembered the car that had run her off the road: a car that looked just like Paul's. And just like the rental car her sister had arrived in from the airport. And probably at least fifty other cars in the small town of Kanesville.

"Ask and ye shall receive," she said.

"Huh?"

"You can take the girl out of the Mormon culture, but you can't take the Mormon culture out of the girl," she said wryly. "Fine, let's run. I have some questions for you."

She eyed him up and down and saw that he couldn't possibly have a weapon of any kind hidden in his running gear. He quickly met her cadence, setting a good rhythm as their feet and breath made the only noise in the still night.

"Why can't you sleep?" Sam asked him as they headed up 200 North.

"Because I killed my wife. I was responsible. Makes for some gnarly nightmares."

Sam felt herself reach for the gun again, resting her left hand on the zipper of her fanny pack. The hackles rose on her arms. Fear coursed up her spine.

She stopped and backed up. Pulled the gun out. Aimed it at him. He slowed and turned.

"What are you doing?" he asked.

"You just told me you killed your wife. You said you were responsible."

He just shook his head and laughed, but there was no humor in it. Sorrow emanated from his body, his shoulders slumped and his head low. "Put the gun away,

Sam. I didn't physically kill her. The day she died we were fighting. She'd found an old picture of me and you, together, standing in the lake, kissing, and she wanted to know who you were, and why I kept it.

"I should have just told her the truth. I kept it as a reminder of the man I could never be. The man I never was to you. But I was so damned ashamed I had sex with you and got you pregnant that I just told her it was an old picture and I didn't know why I still had it. Do you know where I kept it, Sam?"

She shook her head, never taking her eyes off his face, although he was looking anywhere but at her. Whenever their eyes would meet, he would wince and look away.

"Inside my Book of Mormon. The same one I took on my mission. And I took it out every night, and I was so disgusted with myself. I hated that you made me want you so much, and that I still wanted you, and that I did things to you that I never should have . . . ." He stopped talking, his hands on his hips, his breathing ragged, even though they hadn't jogged an inch for several minutes. "All I ever wanted was to be a good man. A faithful servant of God. A seminary teacher, and a missionary for my church, and I messed it all up. God punished you because of it. And I ran like a baby. Left you alone, went on my mission, and I've spent the rest of my life regretting it."

He paused, perhaps waiting for her to say something. She didn't.

"After she found the picture, she wouldn't let it go. She was angry. She was trying to find a scripture she wanted for her Sunday school lesson, and my book was closer than hers. She opened it up and the picture fell out. It might as well have been porn to her—you in that bathing suit top and the way I had my arms around you."

He shook his head and turned away from her, and Sam took it all in. She remembered the picture. Their old classmate Ricky had taken it. Summer of junior year, up at Pineview. She remembered the way Paul had made her feel. She remembered the look on his face just before he leaned in to kiss her. He tasted like lake water and chocolate.

Sam took her hand and moved it to her lips. It was hard to believe how much came back to you when you had a trigger. She remembered the picture. She had a copy of it tucked away somewhere.

"I don't know why she was so angry. It was obvious that the picture was from high school, wasn't it? I mean, she had to know it was from years before."

"It wasn't the picture, Sam. It was the way I reacted. I grabbed it from her like it *was* porn, like it was something that she shouldn't see. And I couldn't explain it. I'm sure she thought it was someone who meant something more to me than she did. Or . . . I don't know. But it hurt her. I hurt her, because I couldn't stand up like a man and tell her the truth. So she ran out. She was emotional, pregnant, irrational, and she took the baby and said she was going to her mother's to stay, because I obviously still had a thing for you. And I wasn't man enough to admit . . . I wasn't man enough to admit I was a stupid, faithless human being.

"I was ready to come clean, and tell her. But she left. And then she died. And our two-year-old died, and so did our baby, the one inside her. She was so upset, she was crying, and the police said she just crossed the centerline and that was it. That was my punishment. I've been living with it ever since.

"Then you came back to town, and I felt the same old desire again, and I have to wonder what else God will take from me if I give in to you? What else will I lose?"

"Give in to me?" Sam said, putting her arms down but not putting the gun back into the fanny pack. Instead of making her feel wanted, his long-term desire for her had begun to feel creepy. She had old memories and feelings but had moved on. Why hadn't he, especially when he wanted something so different from what she could offer? "I haven't once given you any indication that I want anything from you. Way back then, we were young and stupid and we went too far. I got pregnant, you ran away, and life went on. What kind of a God would kill a woman and two babies because human nature took over and you made a mistake? How can you possibly believe in this God?"

"Look up at the stars, Sam. How can you *not* believe in a God?"

Sam shook her head and put the gun in the fanny pack, zipping it back up. "How do you explain all the bad stuff, Paul?"

"I can't explain it. I have my moments. I wonder about it, too. But it has to be true. There has to be something."

"Or maybe there doesn't. And maybe we are all carrying around this guilt that is eating us alive. Or making us not eat. I think I've had enough of this guilt. I think it's time for me to move on. And for the record, Paul? You never were a bad man. We let our emotions go, we had sex, and then I got pregnant. It wasn't meant to be. We were too young to be married, and neither one of us was ready to be a parent. I, for one, am tired of atoning for the guilt. It's time to start living. I suggest you do the same."

"Sammy, you don't understand. I can't forget about you, but you're poison for me. You destroyed my life, and you didn't even know it."

"Oh, hell no. You are not turning this on me. You're the one who left. You went on a mission and I never heard from you again."

"You think I did that lightly? Just left without any thought for you? I went to your dad, and he told me I should go."

Sam felt a chill go up her spine. Her father had known about the baby?

"You talked to my dad, and he told you to just walk away?"

"It was the right thing, Sam. Your father is a wise man. I asked him about you and me, now, and he said it's still not right. Even though I'm alone, and you're alone, I still can't have you. Because I'm not supposed to. I'm not supposed to want you, but you tempt me. You're just like Callie. Like Eve tempted Adam, you have the—"

"What the hell? You talk to my father about me *now*? When? This is ridiculous. Get over it, Paul. I did. Did you just have a thing for the Montgomery girls, huh? Trash, I believe your friend Lind Harris called us."

He didn't speak, staring at her, his eyes almost invisible in the dark night.

"Tell me, Paul. Tell me the truth."

Sam's hand rested on her fanny pack, inches from the zipper.

"I don't know what you want me to say."

"How about a little honesty? How about some now? Just when have you been talking to my father?"

Paul was silent again, squirmy, almost like a grade-school child called into the principal's office. She stared him down hard.

"Fine. Since you want me to be honest, I will. Your father comes to clean the seminary building every week. It's one of his only outings. One of the ward ladies stays with your mother, and your dad comes to do service for the Lord. Is that what you want from me?"

"You lied to the police," Sam said, incredulous that he had kept this information from her. "Why would you do that?"

"Because if you knew I was talking to your father, you wouldn't come near me. I just wanted his blessing to finally be with you. I wanted him to approve. I guess I should have checked with you first, since you have all the answers. I have no idea what you expect of me, Sam."

"Maybe, just maybe, for once in your life, you should have been truthful. You've been lying to yourself and everyone around you for years. It's to the point where you don't even know a lie when you hear it. I'm scared to think you are teaching young kids about religion. Because you sure as hell don't seem to have a grasp on right and wrong."

"Callie, I—"

"My. Name. Is. Not. Callie." Sam knew she was flushing, though he probably wouldn't be able to see it in the dark. "And I am done with this. Get on with your life. Find a nice Mormon lady. Follow your dream. Leave me and my poisoned apple out of it."

"That's Disney, Sam. Snow White, not the Bible."

"It all means the same to me, Paul. It's all one big fairy tale. But there is no happily ever after. And you're no white knight. So please, leave me alone."

She turned and headed toward her familiar route, the cemetery, leaving him alone with his guilt, this strange obsession with the past and two Montgomery sisters, and maybe a little bit of enlightenment. She felt the constant ache in her gut ease up. She'd been hurting herself, guilty, just like him, for years. And why? Because they were human?

She turned a few times to see if he had followed her, but he hadn't. Slowly she began to feel the free flow of the night, and the air flowing through her hair. She relaxed as she ran, heading through the gates of the cemetery. She didn't feel safe with Paul; that was for sure. His clinging to the past was more than a little weird, but she couldn't see him running her off the road. He'd said he wanted her and knew he shouldn't want her. And he'd called her Callie. What if he was really crazy?

FORTY-ONE

Sam entered the cemetery at a near sprint, pondering her ghoulish thoughts.

She'd tried to call Gage but had got his voice mail.

She knew he would call her back. She also knew he would tell her not to run alone, in the dark, even though she'd been doing it for years.

But this was one trip she had to make. She was here to see old ghosts. Safe ghosts. Here to talk to Callie one last time, before she put it all behind her.

It was time to move on and away from Kanesville, at least physically. She could visit. Susanna would need her. Her father . . . well, it was time to say good-bye. For good.

A thin, eerie mist rose out from among the tombstones, twisting and swirling up and around the entire cemetery and shrouding it in a light white net of tulle. Just enough to make it hard to decipher whether a shadow was a moving, writhing demon or a still tree.

The temperature of the formerly hot night had dropped by at least fifteen degrees. Sam looked up at the sky. Fast-moving clouds obscured the moon.

She shivered as she surveyed the graveyard.

September fog was almost unheard of in Utah. Sure, nights might chill as fall wafted in, but it was rarely wet or cold or filled with the white mist that was so common in February.

And then there was the rain. Usually, the rains came in October.

Sam headed toward her familiar spot on the glistening, paved pathway—Callie's "resting" place, except she no longer really believed Callie was resting. They might have placed her body there, but her spirit, her power, her electricity, was still following around those whom she'd cared about—or wanted to see hurt.

Sam shivered as the temperature seemed to drop even more. She felt Callie's pain and fear. A charley horse in Sam's right calf nearly caused her to fall, and she knew she had to stop running. But the eerie fog, the tombstones, and Callie's voice in Sam's head had raised the hairs on her arm.

She stared out at the dark night, shadows dancing in and out of the tombstones as clouds covered and then moved away from the moon.

She couldn't see any living person walking among the monuments to the dead. But she felt a strong presence. It seemed as though someone was with her, walking next to her. Warning her.

Her cell phone rang inside her fanny pack. She jumped. She'd been staring so intently out at the landscape of gravestones that it caught her by surprise. She didn't recognize the number on her caller ID. She answered anyway. Even if just to feel a little less alone and scared.

"Someone is here. Someone is trying to get into my house," whispered an unfamiliar female voice.

"Who is this?"

"Bethany. I need help. You gave me your card. You said to call. Someone is trying to get in the door."

"Bethany, hang up now and dial nine-one-one. Do it."

"Okay," the girl whispered, and the line disconnected.

What if someone—the killer—got to Bethany before she made the call?

Because Sam had no doubt now, if she ever had. Someone had murdered Callie and the other three teenagers. That same person had tried to kill Whitney. And something told Sam that he would be here soon, waiting to kill her, too.

He. Because she was "just like Callie."

Sam quickly dialed 911, not leaving anything to chance. She told the dispatcher to get police on the way to Bethany's house, and fast. Sam was on foot, and they would reach Bethany long before she could even hope to.

But if the killer was at Bethany's house, why did Sam feel his presence here?

Because he gave up little pieces of himself with each murder, and they're here, with his victims. He was losing pieces of his soul, and he never even knew it.

Sam knew she should have seen this coming. She also knew she should run, but she wouldn't. He'd be on foot with no weapon but a rope or tie. She had a gun. The only question was, could she use it?

Her next call was to Gage. This time he answered.

"Where are you?" she asked, not bothering with a hello.

"Just headed to your house, actually. About a block away."

"I'm in the cemetery. Someone is trying to break into Bethany's house. I've sent the police. Make sure they follow through." She rattled off the address, which was only a block below Kanesville's cemetery.

"That's minutes from where you are!" Gage's voice sounded frantic. "What in the hell are you doing in the cemetery? Get out of there, now."

"I was saying good-bye to Callie." A shiver had crept into Sam's voice, and she couldn't control it. She felt like her legs were in cement, unable to move, to run. She had to face this, and whatever invisible force held her wasn't going to set her free.

"Sam, get the hell out of there. Run to the first house. I'm on my way."

"No. B-B-Bethany. M-m-make—"

"Goddammit, Sam, run!"

She shivered so violently she dropped the phone, and it landed on the hard cement. She reached down to pick it up, praying her body would obey her commands.

She could hear the sirens below the cemetery and prayed they weren't too late. Her phone rang again. Somehow, she raised her hand to answer.

"The police are here. They want me to open the door. Should I open it?"

The frightened girl's words snapped Sam out of her freeze. "Yes, look out the window. Make sure it's the police. And then open the door."

"I think this is nine-one-one calling me back," the girl said.

"Answer it."

Sam disconnected. Bethany was safe. Just one block away. Which meant the killer was on the loose.

Just one block away.

The phone rang again.

"He's going to come here. He'll be here. And I'll be waiting for him," she said into the phone, knowing it was Gage. And then she disconnected.

Through the eerie mist she could feel him.

It was almost over.

"Some cop you are, Sammy," she said, and she heard his voice repeating those same words, only in her head.

She should have known it was him. She had known, somewhere in the back of her mind.

Now he was coming to get her. She could stay alive. She was a good enough shot.

FORTY-TWO

She waited for him to walk out of the fog.

And while she waited, new memories flooded her mind. Things she'd hidden in the back of her mind. And then all the memories started coming back. Sudden, like a landslide. Things she had held inside for so long that they'd never seemed real. Memories that she'd thought belonged to the scary *Nightmare Theatre* shows she would watch with her mother.

Sam saw her father up on a ladder every July, picking the peaches and adding them to his bucket, careful not to push too hard on the ripe, juicy fruit, lest he leave a dent or bruise.

She saw him feeding chamomile tea to her mother, patiently wiping her mouth when the liquid dribbled down over her lips and chin.

She saw him holding a baby bird that had fallen out of its nest, shaking his head gently as she sobbed. "The momma bird won't take it back, Sammy. It fell out of the nest, and it's too little to fly. I know it's hard for you to understand, but the best thing for this bird is to put it out of its misery."

"No!" Sam screamed out into the thickening fog and darkness. A mother bird would never take back a baby that had fallen from the nest? Was this true? It didn't matter. They weren't birds. They were humans, evolved, advanced—and sadly brutal.

She saw him holding a rope and leading Callie to the tree.

And she remembered. D-Ray hadn't stayed. Amy hadn't stayed. But Sam had been hidden in the small cherry tree just to the right of the peach tree. In a familiar, comfortable groove between two large branches, where her small bottom fit perfectly and no one could see her. But she'd had a perfect view of the yard, peering out from among the leaves and large, ripe cherries.

Sam had seen the whole thing.

Now she saw him talking to Paul. Telling him to leave her alone to deal with a pregnancy on her own. And Sam saw him in the seminary building, helping clean it. She didn't need to be told this. It all fell into place now. Accessing the computer. Sending his message. Learning how to work a PowerPoint down at the senior center.

The flashes of memory were now painful, like lightning. Each jolt hit her as she saw the image of her father, coiling the rope around a crying Callie's neck, screaming at her to own up to her sins, hoisting her up into the tree. Hanging her. Killing her. Crying out for vengeance. It all sparked through Sam's mind, an electrical storm of memories.

He had killed Callie. He had murdered her, and Sam

had blocked it out, ignored it—until Amy came back. Until three teenagers died.

This wasn't some stupid kid game but a real, honest-to-God—ah, god—murderer. Serial murderer. Sam had never believed in recovered memories, but how could she have blocked this out? How could she have—

Because I didn't let you remember. You were too young. I had to wait until you were older. Until you were a match for him.

Callie. No. Now it all made sense. It hadn't been Callie speaking to her all these years but herself. Her own voice, her own memories, driving her to discover the truth.

Sam felt crazier than ever.

She heard a sudden sound behind her, like a foot breaking dried leaves, and whirled around, pulling her gun from the fanny pack faster than she thought possible.

She was pointing her weapon at the man who had given her life.

No one wanted to believe their father was a cold-blooded murderer. Even if they had seen the evidence firsthand.

"Sam, put the gun away. You don't want to hurt me." He stood with a rope in his hands. There were plenty of trees in the cemetery, one of them undoubtedly marked with her name. At least in his mind.

"But you want to hurt me, Dad. You've already tried. Running me off the road when I was jogging. That was you. In a car that could belong to anyone. You wanted me confused, looking everywhere but the place where I should have looked. *My own backyard!*"

Her father winced and Sam realized she was yelling. Something inside of her cringed. She'd only felt love and pity for her father for so many years. He'd seemed so gentle and loving. How had she missed all the clues? How could he be this monster?

"I'm doing the Lord's work, Sammy. That isn't always a pleasant thing to have to do. Sometimes, the Lord requires vengeance. I am that vengeance."

His voice was shaky, making her wonder if he was as terrified as she was—did he wonder if his favorite daughter would kill him? "Vengeance," written across her white wall, in bloodred paint. A warning. But he hadn't killed her. He'd tried to warn her off. Maybe Amy had been right. Maybe Sam was the favorite and her father had been trying to . . . to what? Save her from his wrath?

"You, Dad, are a killer." Sam didn't feel the calm her voice portrayed as she said those words. The gun wavered for a minute, but she kept it trained on his chest, her eyes hard and her soul weeping. "And I have an advantage the other kids didn't have. They didn't know it. They regarded you as a kindly old man, didn't they? Just the nice man who cleaned the seminary building. You weren't a threat, because they didn't know. But I do."

You have to shoot him, Sam.

"Put the gun down, Sam. You don't want to hurt me."

"You *tried* to kill me."

"It would have been out of mercy, Sam. Some sins can only be atoned for by the letting of blood. And if I'd really wanted you dead, I would have done it. I just wanted you back. Back to God's word. Back to me, to what you know is right."

"Sins? What sins? What did I do that made you want to murder me, Dad?"

"Having sexual relations outside of marriage is a grave sin, Sammy. I saw you leave that Gage's house late at night. I know you got pregnant in high school. I know because Paul came to me and confessed, and I told him to atone for it. To confess and go on a mission."

"You encouraged him to leave me alone. To deal with a baby on my own."

"Of course I did. God has a plan for our young people, and it is not fornicating like dogs. All young men should go on missions. Girls should not want to marry anyone but a returned missionary. I told him this again, too. I told him he had done the right thing. But you—how did you forget these lessons?"

"Maybe I didn't forget them. Maybe they were crap." Her father hadn't been ignoring her all those years. She hadn't slipped under the radar.

He moved toward her then, quicker than she would have believed, for he had moved slower and slower for so many years—all a charade.

"Don't fucking move. Don't take one more step."

"Then don't talk about the Lord's work as crap. That is blasphemy, Sam. The Gospel is all there is. It's all there's ever been."

"You're sick, Dad. You're sick, you made Mom sick, you made Amy sick, and *you hanged my sister from a tree!*"

"I did what I had to do. I had to teach you girls right from wrong. I caught her. I saw her fornicating."

"It wasn't Callie. It was Amy. And you never even knew. You killed an innocent child."

Her father's eyes furrowed, anger on his face. "What

are you talking about? What the hell do you mean it was Amy?"

"It was Amy. She was with D-Ray, and Callie stepped in to keep you from hurting her. She pretended it was her. And you killed her. You killed an innocent, sad, lonely teenage girl."

"You're lying. I never should have saved you. I should have done the same thing to you as I did to Callie. I should have known that you weren't worth saving the day you went to Salt Lake City and let those people murder the baby you made with Paul. God talks to me, and He told me to do what I did. But He didn't tell me about you. Why didn't He tell me about you?"

Sam winced as the truth of her actions, the guilt inside of her she had been trying to vomit up for so many years, came out. She hadn't lost her baby "spontaneously." She had gone to a clinic, all by herself, and paid $250 for a woman to scrape it out of her, to make it go away. Only it never went away. It built inside her until it practically ate her alive.

And her father had known. "So if you knew that, why didn't you kill me?"

"I thought there was hope for you. God told me He still knew you had a job to do here. He wasn't ready for you to leave yet. But He was wrong."

"I thought God didn't make mistakes."

Her father took another step toward her, confusion on his face. Then it cleared up.

"No, the truth was, I wasn't listening clearly, swayed by my own emotions. You were my youngest daughter. My baby. And I was weak. I didn't follow through with God's plans. That's probably why your mother had to die. He took her away from me because I wasn't faithful."

"Did it ever occur to you that maybe you weren't talking to God, that you were listening to your own sick mind?"

"That is not the way you talk to me, Samantha Montgomery. I am your father, your priesthood holder, and your patriarch, and God does not appreciate those who do not follow His teachings."

"Dad? You're sick, and Mom knew it. She tried to tell me before she died. That's why you killed her. And you did kill her, didn't you?"

"Ruthie was perfect the way she was. The other way, the questioning and the arguing and the stupid mindless games . . . That wasn't God's plan. She was meant to be the way she was. And then it changed. I had no choice.

"And you were getting too close to me. To my mission. God told me that you might stop me from doing it, and the Lord's work must always go on. Always."

Sam felt her head spin and whirl as she considered her father's words.

"Why did you kill them, Dad? Why did you try to kill your own niece?"

"Because I saw them. It was my job. I followed Whitney, and I saw what she and those other girls and boys were doing, and it was wrong. Sinful. Against God's plan."

"You tried to kill Bethany tonight, didn't you?"

"The gentile girl? Yes, she would have been next, but somehow the police were alerted. I had to leave. I've followed you quite a bit, so I knew there was a chance you'd be here. And if not, I'd be safe among God's spirits.

"And then I realized that it was all meant to be.

Maybe that girl has another purpose, a mission left to do. Maybe living here, she will join the Church, become a part of the Gospel."

Sam shivered as she watched him spin his deluded tale, a wisp of fog gathering around his face and shoulders, distorting his features. It thickened and roiled, and she stepped forward, as her father cocked his head at her. She took another step forward, wanting to reach out and touch the mist, to feel it.

"Callie?" she asked softly, her heart thumping inside her chest. She knew it was all in her mind, but suddenly she felt less alone.

"Callie's dead," her father said, his voice a gentle monotone.

He thinks he's vengeance. But you are. You will be my vengeance. You have to shoot him.

"Callie's here," Sam said, her ears filled with the pounding of her heart, a rush of blood making her feel light headed and dizzy. She didn't care if it was true or not; she wanted him scared. She wanted him confused, just like she had been all these years.

The fog thickened and swirled even more, and her father's laugh sent puffs of it away from his face, clearing the view for a minute so she could see him clearly: for the very first time.

And she saw it on his face, the religious insanity. The craziness that was her father. Lines and furrows gave his face character, made him look kindly, benevolent. Harmless. He was anything but. He was insane, and apparently, this type of psychosis was catching, for he had given it to her mother and maybe a little bit to her sister Susanna, who clung so tightly to her childhood faith while fighting the desire to keep her kids alive and well.

And maybe he had given a little bit of it to Sam, too.

A little bit crazy. Listening to a voice inside her head, a voice she believed belonged to her dead sister. Yet Callie had been dead so many years, how would Sam even remember her voice?

"You're a little bit crazy, Samantha Montgomery," Gage had whispered to her just nights before, after they finally made love and lay satiated and spent in his large bed.

A little bit crazy.

"Sam, put the gun down. You're fighting a battle you won't win. I've been given my job, and I'm following through on it. When the Lord speaks, you listen."

"You killed Callie."

"I helped Callie to understand the error of her ways."

"You *killed* your own daughter," Sam said, her voice louder but not nearly as loud as the roaring of anger in her head. "And three other kids. And you tried to kill your granddaughter."

He sighed impatiently and stepped forward. Sam automatically stepped back—though with his thin frame, stooped shoulders, and sparse gray hair her father hardly seemed menacing. He never had.

"Don't come closer," she said, warning him by waving the gun slightly. "I know you killed her. I was there. Somehow I pushed it all away, in the back of my mind, *but I saw you.*"

"I didn't kill her, Sam. God did. It was His plan."

"She loved you. You were our father. And you betrayed her."

His face hardened. "I love those who deserve my love. God's army is strong and mighty. The weak have no place there."

"You tried to kill me, too." Sam's heart sank as she said the words aloud. It made them real. They couldn't be taken back now or stored away in some unforgotten chest never to see the light of day. And yet that was what he had done with Callie and with her mother. Stored them away.

"I was just doing my job."

Sam looked down at her gun and realized she had lowered it as the shock waves hit her, as she pondered her father's words and actions. As she tried to digest the fact that this gentle man was nothing like he seemed. Not gentle. Oh no. He was Vengeance. Had sent her a very threatening note, painted on her wall in the color of blood. Her own father wanted her dead.

She raised the gun again, wishing it were steady, wishing she wasn't here, forced to make this decision.

"Sammy, put the gun down. It won't make things better at this point."

"And what will? Hanging me from a tree? Atoning with my spent blood? Did that spent blood get Callie into the Celestial Kingdom, Dad? Was it that important? Did it work? And what about Mom? You killed her, too. She tried to warn me, and you killed her? Where is she now?"

"You act like I'm some kind of animal, instead of a simple man doing the Lord's work. That tells me you just don't get it."

"That tells me you just don't get it, either, Dad. It's a little thing called murder. Maybe you've heard of it before?"

He took another step toward her. He'd bridged the gap from twelve feet to six feet, and she still hadn't fired. She knew she could shoot to kill. She never thought she would have to shoot her father.

"Don't! Don't move closer, or I will shoot you. This has become life or death. When you tried to run me off the road, you cemented our relationship. One of us is going to have to die, and it's *not going to be me.*"

Her father's voice was gentle when he spoke. "I would die for you, Sammy, if it would make a difference. I would gladly go in your place. But that's not the way it works. That's not the way God wants it."

He took another step.

"Don't move!" Sam screamed.

One more step.

Kill him, Sam. Stop him now, before anyone else dies. Before you die. Before I die again.

She fired, the roar of the .38 filling her ears. The acrid smell of gunpowder filled her nose, and she looked down at her hand, which didn't shake. Not even a little bit. It was a powerful gun, enough to stop someone cold. It had a pink handle. Innocuous, girlie, and yet it could do so much damage. Just like life. She squeezed her eyes shut as her father fell to the ground, only three feet from her, writhing in pain.

But her survival instincts were strong, and she only kept them closed for a moment. Because she had been taught how to shoot to kill. That was her job. It was her or him. And she wasn't about to die. She still had too many wrongs to right. Tears fought for release and poured down her cheeks as she watched him, moving, squirming, whimpering in pain. She fought back the instinct to go to him, to ease his pain.

Then his body stilled. Now he was nothing more than a resident of this burial ground. He belonged here.

She pulled her phone from her jacket pocket and dialed 911. It was after nine, so the emergency calls were all being routed from the Kanesville office to the Smithland County sheriff's dispatch center. The dispatcher who answered sounded busy and bored. Sam didn't care. "This is Detective Sam Montgomery. I'm in the Kanesville City Cemetery. I need a bus, and I need some officers. There's been a shooting."

"Are you hurt?" the female dispatcher immediately asked.

"No. But my father is. I believe he's dead."

"Who shot him?"

"I did," Sam said, and disconnected the phone. She stuck it back in her pocket and watched the blood seep from her father's chest and watched him gasp his last breaths.

I am no different than he is. I killed my own father.

You had to kill him, Sam. He would have killed you. He killed those three other kids. He would have kept going. You did the right thing. You are a savior.

"Fuck no!" she screamed at the top of her lungs. *I'm no one's savior. I'm just a cop. I'm not the same as him. I'm not a killer.*

The lights of a car pulling into the cemetery illuminated some of the gravestones, and she saw the blue and red flashes indicating it was a police car. But she had just called 911.

The white Jeep Cherokee pulled to a screeching stop, and Gage jumped out, gun drawn, scanning the area for her. When he saw her, he started running. Cautiously. Looking from side to side for danger, just liked he'd been trained. But fast.

When he got near her, he slowed, spying the body of her father on the ground.

"Oh, Sam," he said. Then he stepped in cautiously, checking for a pulse. He just shook his head, telling her what she already knew.

"It was him, Gage. It was my father. All this time. It started with Callie, and he drove my mother insane. Have there been others through the years? Every time a teenager died by hanging, was it him?"

Gage just shook his head and pulled her in close, holding her tightly. An investigation would be held. What secrets would come out she didn't know. It wouldn't be good. She realized she was shivering, and tears flowed down her face.

She'd never shot anyone before.

And the first time she did, it was her own father.

And the Montgomery girls were finally free.

FORTY-THREE

Later, much later, as Sam sobbed in Gage's arms, she struggled for understanding and acceptance.

"Why didn't I remember all this until now?" she asked him, between deep, shaky breaths.

"I can't tell you that. But you were so young. I remember waking up one night and finding out the sun was up. I wanted to go outside and play, but my dad wouldn't let me. I remember it as plain as day. Did it happen? No. But it doesn't make it less real."

"It's not exactly the same thing, Gage."

"No, but you were six. So little to see something so traumatic. How much do you remember about yourself at that age? Not much, is my guess. It wouldn't be that hard to forget this. Why would you want to remember it?"

Why would anyone want to?

Sam sighed. "I'm damaged. Damaged goods. Why would you want to be with me? Things aren't going to suddenly get easier. I have very little left. I'm a loner.

And I don't do relationships. I'm not that kind of girl."

Gage pulled her tighter, held her, and then pushed her away, so she was staring into his eyes, his hands on her shoulders. "Why do you think I got you that pink gun? What do you get a woman like you, to show her that you love her? Especially after you've hurt her. How do you make amends?"

Sam looked up at him as though he had touched her physically with his words. "Love?"

"Yes, Sam, love. I love you more than I've ever loved any other woman, and I wouldn't change anything about you. I love your body, and your hair, and your spirit, and the fact you struggle to eat and yet manage to make yourself stay well. I love that you can shoot a gun better than most men, and that you can take down a perp in two seconds flat, and that you can swear better than most guy cops. But I also know you're real, and vulnerable. And all woman."

"But I—"

"Just don't talk anymore. Instead, listen. Listen to what my heart is telling you. I missed you when you left Salt Lake City. It felt like you moved to Russia."

"But—"

"You just can't stop talking, can you?"

"Would you please let me say this?" she asked, her voice a whisper.

"Okay," he said, his voice a quiet rumble.

"I know."

"You know?"

"I know why you pulled me off the Clarkston case. I know you were worried about me. I don't know how to have anyone worry about me."

"Well, if you know that, then you also know I love you and I would do anything to keep you safe. And that's what I intend to do for the rest of my life."

He wrapped his arms around her, nearly suffocating her. She wanted to push him away, put up her defenses, but she also wanted to just let everything go. He traced the outline of her breasts and began stroking her nipple. Sam felt as though he were massaging her heart. Warmth flowed through her body, and a tingle made her shiver.

"I can feel your heart," he whispered.

You're safe. Safe.

Sam stared down at the body of her dead mother, saying her final good-byes. She carried Gage's voice around with her, saying those precious words. It would help her get through the day.

This was just for her. There would be no viewing. No traditional Mormon funeral. She'd arranged for a simple graveside service, attending by a nondenominational preacher.

Never again would Sam allow this religion to be a part of her life.

To Sam's surprise, or perhaps not, Susanna had argued against this. She had also argued they owed their father a funeral. Sam told her that one would be up to her.

The argument had been on the phone, since Susanna was still at the hospital with Whitney night and day. Physically, there was nothing she could do to change Sam's plans, because Susanna would not leave her daughter's side.

The mortician was hovering around behind Sam, muttering. He'd been very upset when she had insisted on redressing her mother. The body had been rigid and difficult to undress, and removing the temple clothing was a chore.

Sam had come prepared.

She had a pair of scissors, and she sliced it all up—the garments, the sash, the white dress—cutting it off and pulling it out from under the body of her dead mother.

Getting the beautiful floral purple dress—the one Sam's mother had never had the opportunity to wear—on the rigid body proved to be yet another challenge. While Sam was struggling with it, another pair of hands, a woman's hands, came into sight.

Sam turned to see her sister Amy standing beside her, tears pooling along her lower lids.

She'd finally come home. But Sam didn't think she would stay. This was no longer her home.

Her business here was finished.

They didn't talk. Just finished putting the dress on their mother. The strand of purple beads went on next.

Amy pulled a brush out of her purse and gently ran it through Ruthie Montgomery's hair. Then Amy pulled some lipstick out of her bag and put it on Ruthie's lips. Bright magenta, a "garish" color the girls' father had never allowed. After Amy was done, she dropped the tube into the casket.

Together, Amy and Sam held each other and cried, and then nodded to the funeral director to close the casket.

"What do we do now?" Amy whispered to Sam.

"We say good-bye to Mom and Callie. We forgive ourselves, and we start to live again."